THE BRIDGE AT VALENTINE

A Novel by
Renée Thompson

TRES PICOS PRESS
CALIFORNIA

Published by
Tres Picos Press
PO Box 932
Freedom, CA 95019
  www.trespicospress.com

The lyrics to "The World Has Need of Willing Men" by Will L. Thompson appear on page 70.

A portion of the poem "A Red, Red Rose" by Robert Burns, 1759-1796, appears on page 122.

Cover design by Alex Rose, www.predella.net

Library of Congress Control Number: 2010920026

ISBN-13: 978-0-9745309-2-5

For Steve Thompson

my partner and true love

"I only went out for a walk and finally concluded to stay out till sundown, for going out, I found, was really going in."
— *John Muir*

Chapter One

They called her July, though she was born two days after Christmas and her real name was Julia.

She clutched her horse's reins and trotted the sorrel in a tight circle near the barn door. Looking up, she hollered into its deep, dark cavern, "Let's go, Richard, Pa's waitin and so am I." She peered into the shadows, spied her brother in the back, a saddle in his arms. A shaft of light penetrated a hole in the roof, illuminating his slender shoulders and the slim, tight line that formed his mouth. He looked her way but didn't speak, just heaved the bulky mass onto his horse's back, straightened the blanket where it bunched up some, then dipped his chin to his chest and sighed. In the rise and fall of that one excruciating breath, July understood how much he hated to go, how all this time she'd tricked herself into believing he'd one day love the land as much as she did.

It pinched her heart to see him so, for how many times had she told herself he'd come around once he abandoned his warm, soft spot in the loft? Insisted he'd change his mind once he dampened the hem of his trousers in the dewy grass below Brundage, and felt the mountain's shadow against his sunburned skin?

No doubt her pa sensed Richard's reluctance and ignored it, for the man's expectations were high and his tolerance low. Among the Mormons of Idaho Territory, sons were called on to herd as many as a thousand sheep their first year out. If there weren't enough older boys to go around, younger ones were pressed into service, sometimes before their cheeks sprouted decent whiskers or their brains had fully settled in their heads.

At fifteen, Richard could have had the world had he grasped it, traipsed the hills to his heart's content. But July? Her pa wasn't one to send a girl to the mountains on her own. Though she was fourteen and her feet itched to tread the valleys and hills, July's place, save this one rare April in 1890, was to home.

Her pa had assigned Richard the task of tending one-third of the family's sheep, while Daniel, a thick-skinned herder from Arizona, and Pun, a Chinaman who'd shown up on their porch, scraping and bowing and begging for work some three years earlier, herded the rest, minus the old and infirm, and lambs lost to the winter past.

Heavy and wet and cold as Canada, that's how folks remembered it. Thousands of sheep and cattle drifted with the snowstorms all across the West that year, then froze in canyons or drowned in frigid water. Showers that began in the middle of February didn't let up until March, melting the snow and swelling the Weiser River. All across Idle Valley carcasses festered on hillsides. Ranchers, exhausted and broken by the expense of keeping up, left the creatures where they lay. Those not forced out altogether hung on. July's pa was one of them.

Isaac Caldwell was a man with close-set eyes and wavy brown hair, which he wore in a U dipped low on his forehead, a forehead his family employed as a guidepost. When it sprang up his eyes crinkled and his sons and daughters knew they'd pleased him; when it folded deep as a barrow pit, they understood their labors had achieved the opposite effect and his tongue lashed out in cruel reproach. "You got a lazy eye, Richard," he'd complain. "You got to set it on the hills and keep it there, watch the grass green up and the forbs pop out 'cause if you ain't watchin, how will you know when to turn the sheep from the sheds at the river?"

"You'll tell me, Pa, just like you done this year."

"Hell sakes, son, you got to learn it on your own, that's what I'm sayin."

July hated these sessions. Each time, their pa sat stern with his arms folded like he expected some grand response from Richard. When he didn't get it, he started in about the mysterious defect in

Richard's brain. "It's like you got somethin twisted in there," he'd go on, "like your head ain't screwed on right."

July gave Richard more credit although she'd never understood how he could dislike the outdoors when she loved it so. She jumped high as a spring lamb when her pa allowed her a sabbatical from school in Morning Tree to tend the herd with Richard. "Education is more than poetry and penmanship," her father told her. "It's trampin the hills and sniffin the air, cipherin how much rain the dark clouds carry and where they'll spill their moisture." But that wasn't the real reason he let her go; he thought her good for Richard, tolerating him and coaxing him from his melancholia where others could not. Her pa was a smart man, but had he been smarter still, he would have known she'd go to the hills with her brother if he had three heads and no brains at all, for she loved him that much, and the mountains too.

Isaac gripped Birdy's halter and led the sorrel toward the center of the yard. With his voice low he told July, "You take the lead, but let your brother think he's boss. Maybe it'll keep his mind on the sheep and away from home."

"I'll try," she promised, although they both knew Richard wasn't one to tell her what to do.

"And be careful, you hear? There's wolves and cougars out there, and any one of them will snatch your ankle and knock you down."

July leaned over and hugged her father's neck. "I'm stronger'n they are," she bragged. "Braver too."

"Just watch yourself, is all." He looked at her with earnest eyes, then grasped Birdy's cinch and tugged it hard.

Richard emerged from the shadows of the barn, his horse slowly clopping over to meet them. He'd already said his goodbyes to their ma, as had July. She saw him glance toward the house one last time. Their mother, Eliza, gazed from the kitchen window. She dabbed her eyes with a handkerchief, waved a reluctant farewell, dabbed a little more. Richard waved back, said goodbye to Tom Blakely, their father's foreman and somewhat standoffish nephew. To Raymond, their little brother, and to their older sister, Lilly, July shouted a cheerful farewell, her voice echoing her eagerness to go.

Anticipation pricked her skin as she led the way toward the great swell of land that lay between their pa's place and Brundage Mountain. She loped just ahead of the sheep while Richard trailed behind. Two pack mules jogged beside him, hauling everything they needed, for the Idaho mountains were too rugged to accommodate a sheep wagon. The creatures carried a tent, lantern, kerosene, a small Dutch oven, cornmeal for batter cakes, stewed plums, beans – everything July and Richard needed until Tom showed up six weeks later to drop off supplies for Pun at the lower camp, and Daniel's goods just beyond. By then Richard would have settled into a routine and Tom would tote July home.

Resplendent in overalls and work boots, a black bowler perched on her head, July sat tall in her saddle. Though she couldn't yet put her finger on what she'd one day become, she knew in her bones it was as big as the whole outdoors; that her heart understood its calling even if her mind hadn't yet formed its purpose.

She took in the sights and sounds of the countryside as she rode, let the shrill calls of the red-winged blackbirds sear her memory, for she wanted to recall every detail of her journey for all the days to come. She turned to gaze at the sweet faces of the ewes and lambs behind her. They were almost as noisy as the blackbirds, gossiping among themselves in a nervous vibrato, eager to sample the delicacies that awaited them in the hills. She knew these creatures as well as she knew the shearing grounds and lambing sheds near the river. Sometimes it seemed she'd spent half her life there comforting little Raymond who sobbed when bearded men with iron blades snipped off the lambs' tails then made quick work of the ram lambs' testicles, popping them between their fingers, biting off the tiny lumps, then spitting them into a bucket. "Don't cry, Raymond," she'd coo, patting his plump hand. "Those babies'll be fine, come morning." Now that he was eight, Raymond saved his crying for the lickings their pa gave him when he wandered to the creek without permission.

July looked from the sheep toward Richard, who seemed to be falling ever farther behind. He sat slumped in his saddle, his curly brown hair flopping over his forehead like a horse thief's. His face held a hangdog expression.

Thinking back on what her pa told her, she hollered, "Am I headed the right way?" though she knew full well she was.

He waved her off without looking up. "You're fine," he called. "Just keep goin where you're goin."

She could be heading to Timbuktu, for all he cared. She adjusted her frame and chewed her lip. An idea came to her.

"Betcha can't catch me!" she whooped, challenging him to pick up the pace. Either he didn't hear or was simply ignoring her. She waved in the direction of the bridge at Valentine, directing him to the structure with a broad motion of one hand. He raised an arm, indicating he understood and would meet her at its entrance.

Oh, she knew what he was up to. He had no intention of catching up. He didn't want her to see him, with his eyes red and rheumy and his cheeks smudged with tears. But once he'd wiped his nose with his shirtsleeve, once he'd persuaded himself the ache in his belly had more to do with their sister Lilly's cooking than the notion he was homesick, he'd come around, look to the dogs to do their part. For July knew in her heart Richard wasn't as off-kilter as their pa imagined.

Right about then, as July predicted, Richard hiccupped a command to the older dog. "Bring em in, Tick," he called, then to the younger one, "C'mon, Bug, a little closer now." A coded whistle set the border collies to work and they gathered the flock into a tight band until the sheep resembled a wooly white flag fluttering across the hillside.

July jabbed her heels into Birdy's flanks, so surprising the sorrel that it gave a little bounce and began to trot in earnest. For seven miles the horse kept just ahead of the flock, circling back only when July tugged on the reins. Richard and the dogs moved at a clip the sheep no doubt resented, but once they crossed the bridge they would travel in a more leisurely fashion, remaining at the lower elevations where they would graze on the small purple flowers of the shooting star and then slowly work their way up north.

July was already formulating the possibilities in her head, planning what she'd say to Tom to persuade him to let her stay with Richard the entire summer. "Remind Pa I'm his favorite," she'd tell him, although the action was bold and might earn a cuffing to her ears when she got home. Maybe she'd ask Tom to point out just how courageous she was; how *she'd* been the one to poke a stick up the pump when it ran so slow last November; how *she'd* been the one to yank a rattler from its faucet and fling it into the corral so Tom could shoot it and skin it and make himself a hatband.

She was still pondering the possibilities when Birdy's heavy feet padded past a stone shack surrounded by willows and a small stand of aspens. The house was constructed of white rock, held together with mud and clay, the windows framed in pink sandstone the owner hauled all the way from Oregon. There was a decrepit corral next to a roofless barn and a root cellar built into the side of a hill. The door to the cellar was gone, most likely removed from its hinges by a passerby – someone needing firewood to get an evening meal started.

Their pa once told of a family named Valentine who'd moved there in '73; a man whose wife went soft in the head after living only a handful of years in the Idaho Territory with but one husband, three children, and no neighbors to pass the lonely days. The woman came West with her man – a chicken farmer looking to make his fortune in land – trudging through the sagebrush flats of southern Idaho, worrying her husband would lay down his pack in the alkali dust and pronounce the place Home. When he selected 160 acres to homestead at the northern tip of Idle Valley she did a little dance until she understood she'd given up the comfort of a solid house in Pennsylvania for a shack made of stone in a community of gophers, chicken hawks, and rattlesnakes.

Over time, the story went, the woman's mind turned feeble then left her altogether. One day she picked up a gun and shot her husband in the head, then each of the children as they plucked carrots from the garden. The last bullet she saved for herself.

July always wondered about those children, why the first gunshot hadn't alerted them, made them take off for some hidden spot in the aspens. When she asked her pa about it he said it was Heavenly Father's mercy that kept them ignorant, and July wondered about that too. If God was merciful, why had He allowed that mother to go crazy and kill her children in the first place?

She looked back at the old house as she rode past, caught it beckoning with its evil eye. She tickled Birdy's flanks with her heel and the horse headed steadily forward, stopping abruptly when she reached the bridge. The creature never wanted to cross, and in fact refused to do so now. July hopped off and fetched a stick – not a big one with any real heft but a thin one with some bend to it. She shook it at Birdy, told her what was what. Birdy pawed the ground, snorting.

"What's the matter with you?" July scolded. "All we got to do is get to the other side."

When the horse still wouldn't budge, July gave Birdy's backside a smack then shoved the stick into the bib of her overalls for safekeeping. Birdy hopped onto the bridge and wriggled her mouth, the soft black hairs of her muzzle springing forward. She moved warily onward, pulling back every time July began to make a little progress.

"C'mon girl, we're almost there." July praised Birdy's efforts though the horse was stiff as a mule and twice as stubborn. Every so often July glanced at the river churning below, its aquamarine water spilling over stones and splashing against its banks. Three dead cows lay beneath the shade of a cottonwood, their ribs poking through shreds of decaying flesh. "Hooey," July said, fanning her nose. "I hope you don't stink like that when you die, Birdy."

The sorrel bobbed her head and whinnied just as the bridge moaned. July paused, listening hard. Hearing nothing more, she gave Birdy's reins a jerk. When they finally reached the end, Birdy pounced from the bridge, her hind legs kicking the air. Feeling the ground sure and sound beneath her hooves, Birdy walked over to July, nudged her pocket for a reward. July produced a slice of green apple from a square of newsprint. She fed it to the horse then tied her to a tree. She looked up to see Richard moving the sheep toward the bridge's entrance. He was coming quickly now so she pulled the stick from her overalls figuring she'd use it as a guide, a little something to encourage the sheep to veer left in the general direction of Brundage once they too leapt from the bridge. Standing near the bank, she waved her stick at Richard, indicating she was ready when he was.

He waved back. With Tick and Bug nipping at the flock's heels, the sheep gathered in a compact group, voicing in lusty blats their reluctance to cross the bridge. When one of the older ewes finally emerged as the group's leader and stepped forward, the others followed, adhering to the rule that what one sheep does, all will do. Richard raised a gloved hand and whooped, urging the animals along. Three dozen ewes clambered onto the bridge and lumbered across.

One by one, July ticked them on the shoulder as they hopped off. The ribbon of animals lining the expanse numbered sixty now, and as another dozen or so piled on, the bridge quivered and gave a terrible groan. With a queer rumbling in her ears, July looked across the river, saw Richard circle 'round and draw his horse to a halt. He'd heard it too, for he sat with his back erect and his eyes as wide as the Weiser.

Renée Thompson

Again the bridge groaned. All at once it tore from its bracing on Richard's end and collapsed, sending a ton of splintered wood and nearly a hundred sheep into the water. July flinched, then froze as a cable snapped. As if in slow motion, the heavy metal rope seemed to glide through the air in a wide, lazy S. It lashed the ground once before bouncing up and over, slashing July's chest with the single sharp wire protruding from its end. A haze of white light shot before her eyes, and all sound left her ears save the roar of the river.

Chapter Two

Richard's horse screamed and reared up. The sheep scattered wildly. Tick and Bug raced after them, barking and biting and charging the ground low, frantically working to restore order. Richard tugged on the reins and brought the bay around, straining to see through the brown pillows of dust roiling all around him. He coughed and covered his eyes, pulled back for a better view. His heart thundered as he stood in his stirrups, the veins pounding in his neck. And then the dirt pillow lifted and that's when he saw her, July on her back, legs spread wide, her little black bowler rolling on its rim toward the river.

Richard charged forward, halted. He saw no clear way across, as the water was clogged with debris and the bodies of his pa's sheep. He heeled the bay and rode upstream just beyond the wreckage, but the horse balked at entering the fray and would go nowhere near the river. Richard slid from his saddle and careened down the slope of the embankment, falling on his backside and skinning the palms of his hands. Sweat trickled down his face and his scalp itched wildly.

He tugged off his shoes and hurled them onto the rocks, then catapulted into the Weiser. The cold water punched his gut and bit his ears. He slipped into its hazy green depths, kicking hard as he shot to the surface. The current carried him until he was in the middle of the turmoil, dodging logs as they hurtled toward him; one caught him on the shoulder, skimmed the top of his head and sent him under the water. He sputtered up a second time and kicked harder still, losing his socks to the river. His shoulder throbbed as he bobbed across and when he struck the far bank and climbed out, his feet slipped against the rocks and he slammed to the ground, bruising his shins and knocking his chin against a boulder.

Tending his balance, he stood slowly and caught full sight of July. Her eyes were closed, her mouth slightly parted. Her overalls were sliced open. A gash began just below her collarbone and drifted down, raking diagonally between her breasts and ending at the curve of her left hip. The wound had the look of thick, floppy lips, and where it plummeted toward her belly, blood gathered in a pool.

Richard hobbled forward, touched his sister's face. It was cool where he expected warmth, and he snatched his hand away. His breathing quickened and he staggered back. Clutching his stomach, he vomited in the dirt, a small bit of sickness splashing onto his toes.

He'd killed July, sure as he'd plunged a knife into her heart and pushed it through. He'd let her take the lead while he cried into his shirt sleeve, let her cross the bridge while he lagged behind with the lambs. It should have been him on that riverbank with his chest split open. He turned to look at her when to his shock she softly moaned his name.

He stumbled forward, unable to believe, for a moment, she was alive. And then her foot twitched and his heart jumped and he instantly sprang to action. He tore off his trousers and fell to his knees, flung one leg over hers and gently lifted her up. He stuffed his pants beneath her back, pulled the legs up and over. He wrapped them around her torso and tied them in a knot. His shirt came next, and he bound her with that too. It was this last bit of tugging that finally brought her around. Her eyes fluttered and again she moaned.

"Keep still," he ordered. He frantically tested the knots, ensuring they would hold.

"My stomach," she groaned. She clutched her belly and pulled up her legs, twisting her torso as if to escape the pain. The movement brought a terrible cry, and Richard leaned over, planted his face in front of his sister's, and though he was dizzy with fear, he held her head in both hands and gave it a shake.

"Listen," he flared, "pay attention, hear?" She tossed her head from side to side and he twined his fingers through her hair, gripping it tight. "Cable tore you open, July. If you'd been standing any closer, it'd a cut you in two." He sat up and looked around, his weight full on her thighs. "We got to get you out of here."

At that, she opened her eyes and clutched his arm, begged him not to leave her.

"Hush now, I got to think." Standing, Richard strode toward the river's edge, no longer mindful of the rocks beneath his feet. He looked toward the shattered bridge, at the sheep floating in the water. More lambs than he could count lined the beach, their spindly legs broken. Several of them bleated pitifully and for a moment he thought his head would explode. Whatever composure he'd mustered left him now. He flogged his thigh with his hand and spun toward his sister. "What am I supposed to do, July? How do I fetch you home?"

She couldn't say, for she'd passed out again.

Richard glimpsed Birdy out of the corner of one eye. The sight of July's horse brought some hope to his heart. He ran toward the sorrel and struggled to untie her, railing against the knot when it refused to yield. When at last it came undone, Richard gripped Birdy's reins and skittered down the bank with the horse in tow, situating her near the water's edge. Scurrying back up again, he shook his sister, barked at her to sit up. He slid his arm under her neck. "I got to load you onto Birdy, get you across the river."

Her eyes had a faraway look and she stared somewhere beyond him. Her skin was blotchy with white patches and her lips were nearly purple. Richard knew it wasn't good, any of it. He looped one arm around her back and the other under her knees, grunting as he hoisted her from the ground. He'd taken no more than three steps when his legs sagged and July started to slide. Sucking hard at the air, he set her on her feet. "You got to help," he shrilled. "I can't do it alone." He held her steady, told her to count to ten, that he'd be back before she got to seven.

Something must have sunk in for she said "one" before she started to sway.

Richard raced toward Birdy. "Keep on goin," he called.

"Two…"

He jerked the reins and led the horse into the water, taking no guff at all. He told himself Tom would've done the same, just forged ahead like he'd planned it all along. He looked back at his sister. "That's the way, July. You're doin real good now."

"Three…" At this, her legs buckled like chokecherry whips and she went softly to the ground.

Richard moved fast. He dragged her over to Birdy, positioned himself to get some leverage and heaved her up and into the saddle. Once he'd fixed her there, fastened her in with the leather string she'd used to secure her bedroll, he steeled himself and crawled back into the frigid river. The water had cleared, but Richard gave Birdy no chance to hesitate, just tugged her reins and led her across. July slumped forward and Richard worried she might slip off and drown. But luck was with him and she stayed put. As soon as Birdy crossed the deep water and found her footing on the other side, Richard ran to his own horse and plucked a blanket from the bedroll. He wrapped it around July, hopping on behind her. Holding her tight, he took off for home.

He rode as fast as he dared, pleading with Heavenly Father not to take July. "But if You do see fit to claim her, Lord, please don't let her suffer." And when he finished that prayer he said another, this time referring to July as Julia in case God didn't know who he was talking about.

*   *   *

Eliza Caldwell felt a headache coming on. It seemed almost anything triggered the dull throbbing between her eyes these days, whether it was the sun shining hot on the back of her neck or clouds whipping in, bringing with them their ability to clog her head and muddy her thinking.

She'd tried all the remedies the Church allowed: lobelia enemas, packs and poultices; cayenne pepper mixed with cloves. In desperation she'd even tried a necklace of chicken feathers plucked in the light of a full moon. Liquor was prohibited by the Word of Wisdom, of course, so she couldn't numb the pain with whiskey, even if she'd a mind to, which she did not. She'd always lived a clean life and it was only in the last year she'd started drinking their Chinese sheep herder's special recipe, telling herself it wasn't strictly forbidden since it contained neither coffee nor the fixings found in black tea.

Pun's brew was magic. He concocted it from herbs and dried chrysanthemum, which he stored in a black pouch dangling from his neck. In winter months, when he worked at the lambing sheds near the ranch, he steeped the concoction in an iron kettle in Eliza's kitchen, sampling it now and then with a wooden spoon. When it began to reek, he pronounced it done, then served it up in a thin porcelain cup, claiming the drink removed toxins and kept the brain from binding. Pun shared the recipe with Eliza so that in the spring and summer and fall, when he was in the high country with the sheep, she could prepare it on her own. But she never achieved the desired results and eventually gave up trying. Why it never occurred to her that Pun held back an ingredient or two to preserve his position in the family is a mystery except to say Eliza was a woman of some naiveté. That Pun might gently manipulate the Caldwells in this way never crossed her mind.

Hunched in the garden, her head pounding with each thrust of her hoe, she attacked a dandelion sprouting wide as a fruit pie. She tried to ignore the driving pain behind her eyes just as she ignored her cracked and bleeding hands – hands damaged in the service to her family – for it wasn't her nature to complain. Rather, she prayed each morning for the strength to endure, to live as humbly and meekly as her Savior had, not because she viewed herself a martyr but because she desired eternal glory. Eliza wanted to prove to her Heavenly Father she was worthy of entry into the Celestial Kingdom, a heaven so beautiful, so glorious in the minds of Latter-day Saints, some claimed they'd kill themselves to get there if it weren't a sin to do so.

Eliza wished she'd pulled on a bonnet before leaving the house, for her skin was translucent as separated milk and sure to catch fire in the sun. She brushed back the tendrils feathering her forehead, but despite her best efforts a dozen curly hairs danced about her face like warriors on a prairie. She sometimes fought them with bacon grease, but not wishing to smell like a pig, even a cooked one, she often surrendered, letting them wreak havoc where they might. Today she'd plaited her hair in a single rope which she'd circled around her head like a cap. It did nothing to ward off the rays of the warm spring sun, however, and her neck burned hot to the touch.

She turned her attention to a clump of wilting rosemary, patting the dirt around it and lamenting its low sag to the ground. The little plant was said to prosper only in households where the mistress was master, which explained why it refused to thrive in Eliza's otherwise sprightly garden. She set the hoe aside and sat on a tree stump, letting the throbbing behind her eyes settle. She heard Isaac in the machine shed, pounding the life out of some sorry piece of metal. She'd not spoken more than twenty words to him since she'd learned of his intention to keep Tom home and send Richard to the hills in his stead.

She knew Isaac wanted to put some starch in their oldest boy; that he believed Richard spent too much time indoors, helping Eliza with chores. It wasn't Richard's kindness Isaac resented but the spirit in which it was offered, for Isaac also believed no man in control of his mental faculties would voluntarily perform women's work let alone recite poetry in the midst of carrying it out.

She looked toward the shed, wondering, for a moment, what her life would have been like had she not married Isaac, for she'd nearly taken the hand of a cowboy. Lucas Franzen was his name and she'd met him when she was fifteen, two years before she'd ever laid eyes on Isaac. But Lucas wasn't a Mormon and not likely to become one. She'd ignored his advances for nearly three months – though when she watched him from a distance, she thought his antics charming and lively and fun. In time he wore her down, persuaded her he was worth a smile and perhaps the quickest kiss. She knew by then he was a good man, but being a Gentile he'd never appreciate the notion of a Celestial Kingdom or what it meant to her. He'd never believe God would pick favorites, allow some folks into a special heaven reserved just for Mormons – and only the exceptional ones, at that – while shutting the others out. In the end, their differences outweighed their similarities and when he said goodbye, it was with warm, damp eyes. Eliza later heard he'd started his own cattle company and married a woman who could have passed for her twin, from the thick spirals of her lush brown hair to the dark circles beneath her eyes.

Isaac rarely dwelled on the Celestial Kingdom. Oh, he wanted in, but his challenges were many and she supposed he knew he might not make the grade. There was his temper, which ran hot as a woodstove, and his stubbornness too, which Eliza knew was some peculiar need to prove himself right on even the most wrong of occasions. And he was impulsive, once trading a team of horses for a piano that only Lilly played.

Lilly. She'd be lucky to get into the Independence Day parade, let alone heaven. And little Raymond? He'd only just been baptized so it was too soon to tell where he might go. But Tom – he was nearly without hope.

He'd come to them the same year Richard was born. His mother, Eliza's sister, died of fever a month after Tom turned ten and his father of snakebite some six weeks later. Despite Eliza's efforts to make Tom feel part of the family, to include him in morning prayers and assign him chores she'd one day assign Richard and the others, Tom held her at arm's length, declining to call her Ma. And not once had he called Isaac Pa.

Years ago, when he was but fourteen and they were headed for Sunday meeting, he catapulted from the wagon and confessed outright he'd been rolling cigarettes since he was twelve. "I don't care about no Celestial Kingdom," he informed them. "Perfection ain't my goal."

Isaac regarded him coolly. "What is, then?"

"I don't know, except it ain't herdin sheep, neither."

"Maybe you ought to get yourself a job with some ranching outfit," Isaac put in, "one that pays what you're worth, for any dimwit can see you're smart as a sheepdog." Tom knew sarcasm when he heard it; knew a threat too. He screwed up his mouth and puffed out his chest, but didn't say another word. Just walked the rest of the way home and hung out at the barn till he was half starved and had to drag himself in for supper.

Eliza worried Tom's attitude would rub off on July, for she was already more like him than anyone else in the family. Though July eagerly accommodated her pa where Tom antagonized him, Eliza saw in July the potential to veer left when the road clearly forked right. That her daughter would take to the hills so eagerly concerned Eliza, for it connoted a desire for a life July couldn't rightly claim. Her role as a Mormon wife was long predetermined, yet July's sprightly soul suggested she'd not automatically bow to her parents' will, or to God's either, and there she was much like Tom.

Richard, though? He had the makings of an angel and it seemed to Eliza he'd always walked in some heavenly haze – a misty shroud stirred up by God that served as his protector.

Thinking of her boy, she took up her hoe and gazed into the distance. There on the horizon a shimmering figure came into view. She squinted hard, for at age thirty-three she was more than a bit myopic. The vision, blurry and brown and hunched in a saddle, charged steadfastly toward her. Instantly she took its meaning and her heart picked up its pace: a son rushing the house so soon after he'd left it meant only one thing: someone was dead or about to be. She spun in the dirt and screamed.

Tom, who was mucking a ditch across the way, came running just as Isaac bolted from the shed. Raymond scurried from the barn where he'd been collecting bugs to put in a jar. Lilly, who was in the house washing mirrors, poked her head from an upstairs window. "What is it, Ma? What's happening?"

Eliza never took her eyes from Richard, just snatched her skirt in her fists and raced toward him. Isaac trotted after her, not immediately understanding, as she had, the terrible thing coming at them. He ran full tilt when he put it together, setting his feet hard in the dirt and seizing Birdy's halter as the horse scooted past.

The creature jerked to a stop.

"What done this?" Isaac cried, his eyes taking in the blood-soaked blanket and July's crumpled form. He yanked off the string where July was hitched and scooped her into his arms. Richard watched them go, his arms flopping to his sides and his head falling back in exhaustion.

Eliza ran ahead and burst through the door. She knocked everything from the kitchen table in a single swipe to clear a spot for July. As Isaac angled through the door, he hollered to Tom in a quavering voice to fetch Doctor Forbes, and when he stepped inside, he heaved July onto the table top, his fingers working fast, fumbling as he untied the first knot, stiff now with blood. July had a smell of rusty metal about her, and it grew stronger as Isaac peeled away Richard's shirt and trousers. He lifted her overalls where they'd been sliced, held his breath while his eyes took in the damage. He grimaced but held firm. Eliza turned away.

A moan started at the back of July's throat and fluttered past her lips. Her eyelashes quivered but she didn't come to.

"Pray the doctor can save her," Isaac said, shaking his head, "or we'll need an undertaker."

Chapter Three

Isaac's words shocked Eliza into action. She ran upstairs to fetch clean linens, grabbed all she could hold from a closet at the end of the hall then hurried down again. She propped a folded towel beneath July's feet, hoping any blood that had pooled there would flow like a creek and warm her child's heart. "I'll see to this," she told Isaac, nudging him aside. She turned to Lilly. "Rip those sheets into strips then set some water on to boil." She glanced at July, her eyes darting from her daughter's pale face to the slow rise and fall of her chest. She wrapped July as best she could but no matter what she or Doctor Forbes did to save her, the child was in God's hands now. Eliza prayed He'd treat her gently should July find her way to heaven.

Richard walked into the room, his footsteps heavy. He didn't look at his sister for he'd already committed her injury to memory. He sat at the far end of the table, his damp hair mashed against his forehead, his chest caked with blood.

Isaac pulled up a chair and sat next to him. "Tell me what happened," he told him. "Start at the beginning, and go slow."

Tears sprang to the boy's eyes and his body began to tremble. He glanced at his foot; it too was smudged with blood. It seemed there wasn't an inch of him that wasn't covered in red. "I didn't see it comin, is all."

Eliza glanced up, caught the hot look in Isaac's eyes. She knew that look, knew it was capable of bursting into flame; in turn, Isaac must have seen some fear in Richard's eyes. "Hell sakes," he snapped, "I ain't asking for a recitation, just the facts, is all." He leaned forward and glared at Richard, aiming to get them.

Richard wiped his palms against his thighs, scooted back and bit his lip. "I can't cipher it, Pa. I don't know what to tell you."

Oh, they were all listening now, Eliza and Lilly and Raymond, their eyes wide. The entire house was quiet. Isaac drew a breath and spoke evenly, working to check his temper. "You got to know what happened, you were there."

"I know," Richard said, nodding. "And yet it's like I wasn't."

Isaac looked at Eliza. "Can you make sense of this?"

Eliza told Lilly to come grasp July's bandage. She walked over to Richard, kneeled before him and rested her hand on his leg. "What will we tell Doctor Forbes when he comes?" she probed gently. "He'll want to know what happened so he can help July."

Richard furrowed his brow, taking a moment to recollect. Anyone could see he wasn't deliberately holding back but beset by a nervous memory. He started slowly, as his pa had directed, said July got to Valentine before him. He told the part about how it had taken a while to nudge the old ewes across the bridge. Eliza nodded. She glanced at Isaac as if to say, "See, he's all right now, just give him a minute and he'll come along."

"Next thing I knew there was an awful groan," Richard went on, "and the whole bridge went bustin into the river." He glanced at his lap, blinked and swallowed. "I don't know when the cable snapped, but when it did it went straight for July. I can see that part clear. It ripped her open clean as a panther's claw."

"Hold on," said Isaac. "You mean to tell me the bridge at Valentine went down?"

"Yes, sir."

"And a cable done that?" His eyes went wild as he gestured toward July.

Richard had seen that look many times, a look that sometimes led to a stinging slap. He leaned back, bracing himself.

"Son?"

"Yes!" Richard cried, flinching.

Isaac stood, slowly, the color draining from his face. Eliza reached out and grabbed his wrist. "What is it, Isaac? What's wrong?"

He snatched his arm away, sent her reeling to the floor; she landed hard on one elbow. "Silas Morrow sabotaged that bridge," he flared. "I know it sure as I know July's lying on that table."

Richard jumped from his chair and grasped his mother's arm.

Looking back at his pa, he said, "Silas Morrow weren't anywhere near the place. More likely a bolt come loose, or – "

"I say he done it," Isaac spewed. He was working up a lather now, for never was he one to stand on middle ground; he was either mild as a mountain lake or savage as a windstorm, gritty and dry and hot. "If he didn't do it hisself, he got one of his boys to fix it for him." He strode around the room, snorting and carrying on. "By gawd if he don't hate us, hate that we got a big band of sheep, hate that we're Mormons too. He'd do anything to get us off his range – don't matter we were here first. He's greedy, what he is, he's got to have it all."

Richard's face twisted in despair. "But it don't mean he did what you said."

"You don't know what you're talking about." Isaac lunged toward the door, thrust it open and burst outside. Eliza shot to her feet. She trailed after him into the yard.

"Where are you going?" she shrilled. "Don't do it, Isaac – don't go to Silas's place. Think of July."

"Who else would I be thinking of?" He hadn't slowed one lick. His boots hit the ground hard, kicking up dust around his heels.

So many times Eliza had bit her tongue. Now, she came out with it. "You're not thinking of July, you're thinking of the man that might have had me a long time ago. July's accident is just the excuse you've been waiting for – a chance to rake your plow across some cowboy's back." That stopped him cold but she wasn't done yet, for now that she'd opened the floodgates the water came spilling out. "You said you hoped we wouldn't have to call the undertaker," she went on. "But what if July dies while you're having it out with Silas Morrow?"

"Then I'll fetch her in a pine box and haul her to Morrow's place so he can see for hisself what he done."

"And if she lives, what'll you do then?"

"I'll take her anyway."

Eliza surged forward then, thwacked him on the chest with her open hands. "You'd risk July's life all over again? Just to get even with some cowboy you never met and a rancher you got no proof on?"

"I don't give a lick about a cowboy I never met. It's Silas Morrow what rankles me."

"And what if he did do it? You think he'll let you insult him and then bid you a fine farewell?"

The remark gave Isaac pause. He had plenty more to say about it and would have too, save the clapping of hooves careening up the path.

"It's Tom," Raymond cried from the porch. "He's got Doc Forbes with him." Raymond had come out to check on his ma and pa at Lilly's behest, for July had started to moan again.

Preston Forbes flew into the yard. He reined in his mount, and in one lithe motion flung his leg over the saddle and hopped to the ground, his feet skittering in the gravel. Tom never dismounted at all, just jerked on his reins and asked after the sheep.

"They're still up to Valentine," Isaac told him, hustling toward the porch. "Dogs too – fetch them back, will you, Tom?"

Tom took off while Preston grabbed a black satchel from his saddlebag and rushed toward the house.

"July's this a-way," Raymond said, pointing inside. He ushered Doctor Forbes through the foyer, past a tall wooden hat rack, a brass umbrella stand, then through a dim narrow corridor and into the kitchen.

"Thank heaven you're here," said Lilly when she saw him. "Ma and Pa have gone to pieces and my hand's about to fall off. I've been squeezing this bandage for I don't know how long now."

"Stay as you are a few minutes longer," Preston told her. "I'll relieve you soon as I can."

Lilly looked to Richard for help but he'd not moved from his spot in the corner. He simply stood, staring at the wall.

Isaac and Eliza burst into the room. If Preston realized they were arguing in the yard he made no comment but immediately began setting up, calling for a separate table on which to set his bag. He needed a kettle of boiling water too, something in which to sterilize his scissors and a needle. He looked around the kitchen, assessed its blue oilcloth walls, cast iron stove, and cabinets. There wasn't a crumb on the counter or a speck of dirt on the floor and never had he seen windows so shiny. If a germ ever grew here, Eliza Caldwell had killed it with a bucket of soapsuds.

He directed his next comment to Lilly. "I'll need a pitcher of cool water and some soap – you can set it on the cabinet there."

Lilly released July's makeshift bandage, grabbed a pitcher and filled it with water from the sink pump. Isaac stepped forward, his face stern, and shook Preston's hand. He wasn't sure what to call the man outside of Church, for inside their small circle at Morning

Tree the physician was Brother Forbes, and outside, Doctor. In the end, Isaac called him neither. "You made good time," he said, nodding toward Eliza. "We weren't sure what to do for July, aside from hangin on tight to her bandage."

"Who placed a pillow beneath her feet?" Preston wanted to know.

Eliza wrung her hands and dipped her eyes, preparing for a lecture. "I did," she said. It was Pun who'd taught her the trick when Raymond spliced his knee on a sheet of torn metal, and his little leg had gushed what seemed a pint of blood.

"Good thinking, Sister Caldwell – it likely slowed the bleeding."

He said nothing more, for he wasn't a man to fill time with small talk, as evidenced by his smooth and commanding manner. He cut quite a figure with his head of wavy brown hair and freshly trimmed mustache. And his chin was as competent as his reputation. "I'll need some help," he said, rolling up his sleeves. He washed his hands, pointed at Raymond. "You, my friend, can swat away flies – and you," he continued, indicating Richard with his formidable chin, "can light a lamp and hold it above my head while I sew."

Richard responded slowly, took up a lamp, and lit it. He stood behind the doctor and awaited additional orders.

"What about me?" Lilly asked.

Preston regarded her skeptically. "Are you prone to vapors?"

"I've never swooned a day in my life," she swore, although she'd actually fainted twice: the first time, at age eight, when she stubbed her toe on a fence post and drove a sliver up her nail, and the second when she pierced her ears with a needle from her mother's sewing basket. That time, she'd hit the floor hard as a ball-peen hammer.

Eliza was about to report Lilly's fib when she looked at Doctor Forbes, saw by the dip of his brow he'd already formed his own opinion. Instead of taking Lilly up on her offer to help, he turned to Isaac and asked if he was up to assisting.

"What do you need me to do?"

"Bring me a bottle of whiskey, for starters. I'll need to disinfect the wound."

"We hold no liquor in this house," Isaac told him. "I guess you ought to know that."

"Even the best of us ought to shelve a bottle of whiskey, Brother Caldwell. Why, who knows when an ax will fall on a man's finger or a knife pierce his thumb?" He bent low, peeled open July's eyelids and peered at her pupils. "Infections run rampant in the Territory – I'd venture to say they kill more inhabitants than snakebite." He stood up, gestured toward his satchel. "There's a tin of carbolic salve in my bag there. If you'll bring it to me, please?"

The salve was made of lard, white wax, balsam of fir and carbolic acid and was both soothing and healing. Isaac fetched the tin and then handed it to the doctor. Preston set it on the table, intending to treat July's wound as soon as he finished stitching her. Meantime, he asked Isaac to apply the chloroform when cued. Having departed so quickly with Tom, Preston had left without packing his inhaler. He resorted to the method practiced by his mentor, demonstrating how to fold a clean handkerchief into the shape of a cone, then pouring in a few drops while holding it loosely over July's nose. Preston handed Isaac the kerchief and medication. "And you, Sister Caldwell – if you'll help remove your daughter's clothes?"

Eliza stepped forward and glanced uncertainly around the room. "Shouldn't we ask the others to leave first?"

"Modesty has no place here, ma'am. Now we'll move quickly, please."

She too nodded, her fingers working nimbly as the doctor removed July's bandages then the bib of her overalls and her tattered chemise. Defying the doctor in this one instance, Eliza instructed Richard to divert his eyes before tugging off July's clothes and dropping them to the floor.

Richard held the lamp firm above the doctor's head and peered out the window toward the barn. His eyes scanned three bum lambs tottering in the corral, creatures refused by their mothers and ignored by others in the band. "The sheep," he said, looking at his pa. "There's some still alive, and I left them at Valentine."

"Tom's takin care of em. You take care of that lantern."

Richard remembered the lamb with the broken leg too. Thinking of that lamb now, and of July lying on the table, his face folded and his hands began to tremble. Preston looked at the boy, his face registering a certain understanding. Eliza could see the doctor had put a few things together, concluding without a single question that Richard had been through something nearly as awful as July. He didn't know the specifics of course, but when Richard's arm sagged and the lamp slumped low, Preston called for Lilly to take her brother's place.

Without a word, Richard handed the lantern over. He walked toward the door as though he would pluck the rifle from the hooks on the wall and take off after Tom. Oh, there were plenty of things he could do with that gun, but if Richard was brewing unsettling thoughts toward himself or any other, Eliza would simply circumvent them. "We'll need another kettle of water, dear," she sweetly told him. "Will you kindly get one started?" Richard paused at the door. Glancing at the full pot on the cook stove, then at his mother's anxious face, he took her meaning. Yes, he said quietly, he'd oblige. Eliza gave him a precious smile, the half moons beneath her eyes glistening like black plums.

Preston's gaze followed Richard. Hoping to ease the boy's burden, he said, "I give you credit for quick thinking, young man. Had you not wrapped the wound so tightly, July's blood would have spilled from her body entirely."

Despite the compliment, July's condition disturbed Preston deeply. Her hue, a peculiar lavender white, was that of a cadaver. The wound itself measured eighteen inches and ran half an inch deep. It resembled, rather eerily, the belly of a gutted deer. He guessed it would require some seventy stitches to close. He took a breath and exhaled. "Let's begin then, shall we?"

*   *   *

Seeing Doctor Forbes' handiwork, the speed and confidence with which he applied the stitches, put Eliza's mind to ease. He never even asked for help when he mopped July's blood, though when the child roused, blinking and sputtering and giving a good cry, he asked Isaac to reapply the chloroform. Preston leaned down, whispered into her ear, "Breathe deeply, now. Close your eyes and sleep." And with a smile he assured Isaac and Eliza their daughter couldn't feel a thing.

Raymond dutifully swatted flies. He dropped them into a jar while Lilly stood at the doctor's side, lamp in hand. That she made an impressive Statue of Liberty was not lost on her nor, she hoped, on Preston Forbes. She wondered if he'd seen her in last year's parade and, if so, what he thought. When he neglected to look around or even thank her after he finished with July, Lilly set the lamp on the cabinet and sighed.

Preston applied a bit of salve to the wound, then wiped his hands. "Dab some mutton tallow on her stitches after she's begun to heal," he told Eliza. "Lanolin will keep her skin supple and stop it from itching so." He left a bottle of Laudanum behind for July's pain, as well as an admonition to change her bandages three times a day. "I'll be back in two weeks to remove the stitches. Until then, keep her quiet and in bed."

"July in bed?" Lilly snorted. "Why, that's like telling a tick to stick to the weeds."

Eliza drew her lips tight. "Don't you have something to tend to? Ironing, perhaps?"

"No, Mama, I finished it yesterday."

"Then find something," Isaac snapped, and with that Lilly disappeared, red-faced, out the back door.

Chapter Four

July passed a fitful night, complaining loud and often of the burning in her belly. Eliza was up and down, checking on the child, feeling her face for fever. On the morning of the second day, Eliza pressed her cheek against July's and found it hot as a cookstove. Her stitches too, were oozing. Every few hours Eliza dabbed the wound with a damp cloth and changed the bandages as Doctor Forbes directed but still the injury flamed. When Eliza could no longer stave off the fear that July might die despite all Preston Forbes had done, she walked out to the machine shed and stood at its door, watching as Isaac sharpened his tools. She waited for him to look up. When he did she offered no smile, for now she had a new grievance against him. This business with Silas Morrow. Even so, she spoke quietly, knowing she'd get nowhere by calling up the voice of an old crone. "I was wondering if you'd fetch Pun from the hillsides," she said politely. "July's got an infection going and I was thinking maybe he'd fix her a poultice."

"Why can't you build her one?"

"I tried, but it's not working."

Isaac's mouth held firm. "I can't spare him, Eliza. I'm short as it is. If I pull Pun home I got no one to herd but Daniel. You know I got to have a herder for every band."

"Send Tom then – just until July's better. Or go on up yourself." She gathered her courage, told him since he was the one who loved sheep so – who stayed up all night fussing over them and worrying about the range – he ought to make this sacrifice for their daughter. But her challenge didn't set well, and Isaac's face grew dark.

"If I don't fuss over the sheep, who will? You got some other husband working to provide for you and your children?"

"They're your children too." She closed her eyes and took a breath. "Please, Isaac. I don't ask for much – please do this for me." He leaned into his knife, scraping it hard against its stone. Eliza set her mouth and turned to leave. Pausing, she said, "If you won't bring Pun home, will you at least call on Brother Kilker, ask him to come out and give July a blessing?" Isaac's scraping slowed and he looked up. Though he gazed somewhere beyond her, Eliza knew what he was thinking: He should have thought to call on the Elders himself; that he hadn't was but a small strike against him, but a strike nevertheless.

*   *   *

Eliza cooked a supper of chicken fixings rather than the common doings she normally prepared, seeing as how Isaac had killed a hen so she could make broth for July. She coaxed the child into swallowing a few sips of the warm, glossy liquid and gave her a dose of Laudanum to help her sleep. It wasn't until July drifted off that everyone finally sat down to eat.

Eliza was too exhausted to nibble more than a biscuit but Tom had no such trouble. He'd spent most of the previous afternoon and all that morning dealing with the aftermath of the accident and though he was tuckered he was hungry too. He hadn't eaten a bite since noon the day before. As was his habit, he sat at Isaac's side and bowed his head while Raymond offered the blessing. Raymond thanked the Lord for the boiled chicken and mashed potatoes and for sparing his sister July, and after he muttered a quick "Amen," Tom tucked into his plate with quiet determination, sucking gravy from his fingers and mopping his mustache with his thumb. When the meal was done he looked in on July, found her snoozing with her mouth open. He shut her door and retired to the porch for a smoke.

Looking across the way, he let his gaze settle on the creatures with the wide, white rumps, and pulled hard on his cigarette. He'd never developed the affinity for sheep that Isaac held, even though he too had spent several years as a herder in the high country. There was just no figuring the animals. One minute they grazed happily and the next they ran wild. It seemed the littlest things set them off

— a jacket slung across a fence post, say, or a shirttail flapping in the wind. There was so much variety in them it made Tom's head hurt. He preferred the predictable nature of working the ranch, of mending corrals and irrigating pastures, of coaxing alfalfa and hay meadows to life after an especially grueling winter.

Even so, he reckoned he'd never get away from sheep entirely. As the foreman of Isaac's ranch, his life would forever be entwined with four-legged creatures whose baaas rattled in his brain like mosquitoes at his ears. He could swat at them all he wanted but come February it would still be his job to help with lambing and in May he'd do his share of shearing. In fall he'd run the rams up to the high country to breed with the ewes and then trot them all home again, arriving just in time for Eliza's turkey dinner. In between though, he'd tend to the work *he* loved.

He rolled a second cigarette, balanced it on the sill of his lower lip. Now that he'd seen what July and Richard had been through over to Valentine, he was convinced herding wasn't for the boy either. The sight of all those sheep lining the riverbank, their limbs tangled in shapes he didn't know existed, made Tom sick. It would have killed Richard to lay eyes on them, although July might have handled it. Her constitution was stronger, and her head, harder. Richard would crumble seeing the sheep like that. One of them had landed so hard she'd bitten through her tongue. Another had smacked her head against a rock, splattering it like a melon. And there'd been a lamb with a broken leg crying for its mama. Tom had shot it at once.

No, he wanted no part of the sheep business. Didn't want to own or herd them, didn't care a lick about the money that could be made if he put together a band of his own. He preferred working the ranch and believed he could do a better job of it than Isaac, if given half a chance.

Isaac came through the screen door just as Tom was thinking badly of him. He sat in a chair of woven willows Pun had made him for his birthday. While the chair possessed an interesting weave, it had an odd tilt and hurt Isaac's back. He never told Pun, of course, though if he had, the man would have instantly set about making him a new one.

"What do you think?" he asked Tom.

"About what?"

"The bridge at Valentine. What do you reckon happened out there?"

Tom rubbed his rough-hewn hands. "Thing's so tore up I doubt an expert could figure it."

"Seems to me if I rode out there and looked at it myself I'd see the cable had been sawed."

"Don't know about that, but I will tell you no brown flood washed it out. Weiser was the highest I ever seen it in January but the water weren't anywhere near the top of that bridge yesterday."

Isaac pondered this. Tom wasn't well educated but he'd grown into a wise man. He might have grown into a genius had he stayed in school, but Isaac couldn't keep him there. No sooner had he hitched up the team, driven the boy three miles to Morning Tree and dropped him off than Tom scooted out the back door and headed for the river. It wasn't long before Isaac found him, building a city of mud and clay. He'd whipped the tar out of him, stropped him until his backside grew red as a tomato, but it fazed him no more than a willow branch dusting a rooftop, for Tom's will was strong as his hide.

"It would take an awful clever man to fix it so the bridge would collapse on a specific day," Tom went on. "If it was fixin to fall," he mused, "why didn't it do it when Pun and Daniel crossed the day before, or when Tinsley's sheep was on it, or Swanson's or Janks'?" The Tinsleys, Swansons and Janks were sheep families, too; good, practicing Mormons who'd moved to the area a handful of years after Isaac. But good or not, the country was becoming too tight to support them all. Between their flocks and his and the cattle owned by Silas Morrow and a handful of others across the Idle and Purdue valleys, there wasn't enough open range to go around. The increased competition for forage, along with droughts and blizzards, led to hostility among ranchers. Arguments broke out, and on one occasion a cattleman named Conrad Durty shot off a sheepman's ear over a grazing dispute. Doc Forbes had been the one to fix him up and had done a fine job of it too. But even if the doctor got the man to looking passable again there was nothing he could do about the fellow's mind, and in the end he flung himself down a well and drowned. Those were the kinds of things that happened when a man couldn't pay his debts, when he saw no way out save the sweet release of death.

"Morrow's been watchin us," Isaac said in that troubled tone he had. "Countin the sheep what crossed with Daniel and Pun, and figurin we got more – that we aimed to get them over before Tinsley and the others came on. They're slower to get movin and Morrow knows it. He knew from experience I'd get there first."

"I don't see how. It ain't like you move to no calendar."

The remark annoyed Isaac, surly as it was and incorrect too. He watched the hills like a hawk and could tell the first of April better than any calendar, for it was a time when the hills softened green as sage and the cinnamon teal filled his ponds, their red eyes gleaming. There were gray ducks too with their black rumps, and a gathering of speckle-bellies atop muskrat mounds where they settled in and built their nests.

But Isaac let the comment go. He figured Tom had already come to the conclusion he'd be sent to the hills and just wanted to get back at him. Insulting Isaac's internal clock was a good way to do it. And though it riled Isaac, he didn't speak to it, just moved the topic to where it had to go. "Eventually, I got to send Richard out again," he said, his words blunt. "You too, Tom."

"I knew you was gonna say that, but I don't see why you got to send Richard. You already got Daniel and Pun up there and in a day or two you'll have me too. Leave the boy home to grow up some."

"I'm bringin Pun in to tend July, which is why I'm sendin you. With you and Richard here at the ranch, I got no one to herd but Daniel."

Tom dropped his cigarette onto the porch, crushed it with his heel. "How long till I got to go?"

"Day or so – two at the most." When Tom offered no rebuttal, Isaac said, "Soon as July's better, Pun'll spell you and you can come home. Maybe by then Richard will be right again and I can send him up too."

Good gawd, Tom thought but didn't say. Musical chairs are more organized than Isaac Caldwell. Without a word he hoisted himself from his seat and walked toward the barn. All the next day he went about his chores with a cruel face, never uttering more than a handful of words from the time he got up till he went back to bed. And by morning of the third day he was gone.

That evening, when the house was still and the crickets were chirping their twilight songs, Brothers Kilker and Johnson arrived; solemn, straight-backed men in white shirts and black trousers, stiff hats perched upon their heads. Both wore beards and their dark eyes shone from sun-crisped faces. Holders of the Melchizedek priesthood

– men who possessed the power and authority to act in the name of God – they'd come to perform a laying-on-of-hands, a ceremony designed to cure any and all ailments from mumps to malaria.

They gathered in July's room, a small but cozy space with one window and two beds, the slightly larger one belonging to Lilly. An oil lamp glowed dimly from its night stand, illuminating a string of paper-doll cutouts tacked to the splintery wall.

The Elders squeezed in around July and waited while Isaac took his place at the head of her bed. Eliza stood in the doorway apart from the men, watching as Brother Kilker – the older of the two, with his creek-mud complexion and crooked nose – anointed July's scalp with oil. He placed his hand on her forehead. Isaac and Brother Johnson followed suit.

July's eyes twittered open, settled on her pa. "Am I dying?" she asked, though her voice was low and calm.

Isaac glanced at Eliza, who stepped forward and kneeled at July's side. "Of course you're not dying," she told her. "The Elders are here to give you a blessing."

"I feel like I'm dying." July clasped her mother's hand. She turned to her pa and took his too. He squeezed tight, told his girl she'd live as long as a ponderosa and grow twice as tall.

"Shall we commence?" put in Brother Kilker.

The men began murmuring, their voices filled with quiet authority, the words spilling from their mouths in fervent "thees" and "thous." Every so often Brother Kilker paused as if receiving divine inspiration. He sucked in the air and chewed at it, contemplating, Eliza supposed, what he'd do with the information.

She closed her eyes, said her own prayer, told the Lord July would make a fine mother if only He'd let her live so she might revel in His work – for releasing spirits from heaven was not only a Mormon's duty but obligation, and oh, how those spirits would rejoice to have July for their mother.

When the men uttered a collective amen, Eliza stood, blew out the lamp on July's nightstand and tucked the blanket beneath her daughter's chin. She led the men into the parlor and served them poverty cake and buttermilk. The cake was Richard's favorite, a concoction of thin cream, chopped raisins, sugar, flour, and spices. Sadly, Richard wasn't likely to get a piece, for he hadn't come in from the creek since the noon meal; he'd taken over where Tom had left off, diverting water into one channel, plugging it at another. Eliza chastised herself for failing to save him a slice before serving the men, for both of them held their plates out for a second helping before they'd finished their first.

"Your daughter's in a sorry state," Brother Kilker observed. He directed his remarks to Isaac. "I wish you'd called us sooner." Cake littered the shelf of his chest, though he'd opened his mouth wide to receive it.

"Indeed," groused Brother Johnson. "Why make it harder for the Lord to set July right by waiting two extra days?" He too slipped a bite of cake into his mouth, a mouth eclipsed by the thick white hairs of his mustache and beard.

Isaac hesitated only a moment before confessing he was a busy man and as such a forgetful one too. "It was Eliza who reminded me to fetch you," he told them. "Not for her, I'd still be sharpening some ax in the shed."

Eliza was so surprised to hear Isaac stumble forth with this small credit that her heart opened a crack and she forgot, for a while, her anger toward him. She glanced his way and smiled but her happiness faded when she looked at Brother Kilker. He'd fixed her with a hard, speculative stare. Though she didn't know him well, she lumped him with other men who had been driven from their homelands, hounded, hated, and scourged as furiously as the Chinese. By and by their own dispositions grew cruel as their tormentors' and in time they forgot altogether why they'd fled their persecutors in the first place. Now, it seemed, some lived merely to rule with rigid fists and harsh demands. She believed Brother Kilker was such a man and felt for the wives he secreted in his cabin at Labine, though plural marriage had been illegal for nearly a decade now. Eliza wondered what would become of those women, thinking it was a matter of time before all but his first wife would be forced underground.

How a man like Kilker could find his way into the Celestial Kingdom Eliza had no clue, but for whatever reason the Lord had called him into His fold. She accepted this because she had no choice and when she pulled herself up she told the men she was grateful they'd come, and she smiled when she said it. "It's a long ride from Morning Tree and a longer way home in the dark," she told them. "Isaac and I would be privileged if you'd stay the night.

You can sleep well into morning and when you get up I'll make you a breakfast of biscuits and eggs."

Brother Kilker drained his glass and smacked his lips. "Got a baptism up to Badger in the morning," he said, declining. And with that, Brother Johnson stood and set his plate on the table, even though he hadn't yet finished his cake.

Isaac walked the men to the porch and shook their hands. Brother Kilker climbed into his new buggy – a four-seater ordered from an upstart company in Boise – and settled onto its fine leather bench. Brother Johnson squeezed in next to him. Grabbing the reins, Brother Kilker told Isaac he expected to see him at priesthood meeting on Sunday.

Isaac nodded grimly. "Ain't missed one yet." He watched the men drive off then walked into the house. Eliza was sitting at the kitchen table. She had cleared away the dishes, covered the cake and put it in the pantry. She sat with her back toward him, rubbing her temples. The nubs of her spine formed a startling landscape beneath her dress and it was this testament to her vulnerability that touched him, made him regret he'd treated her poorly of late. He placed his hand on her shoulder and squeezed. "I'll brew you some of Pun's tea," he said, shuffling toward the cupboard. "Maybe it'll staunch your headache."

"You've got no notion where I keep the chrysanthemum or how to strain the leaves. I'm not even sure you know how to boil water."

He pulled out a chair and sat next to her. "Can't argue that." He smiled and patted her raw hands. How many times, he wondered, had she told him she'd grown up with a dirt floor and now that she had a wooden one she aimed to keep it clean? The scrubbing had all but ruined her sweet, soft skin yet she kept at it just like she kept at her faith. She obeyed all of God's commandments, save the notion of plural marriage. For as long as Isaac could remember, the prophets of the Church had encouraged it, arguing it was a great help to a woman to share the load with an entire household of women; that it gave them time to pursue other interests. But it seemed to Isaac that Eliza had no other interests. All she did was work. She buzzed around the house like it was a hive and her job to fill it with honey.

They all had their way of earning their spots in heaven, he supposed. Eliza planned to work her way there, and if God gave a man credit for being a good provider, Isaac supposed he'd get there one day too.

Eliza pursed her lips as though she had something to say but instead of speaking she set to plucking the dry, feathery skin around her fingers.

"What's eatin you, wife?" Isaac asked.

She tilted her head to one side. "I get the notion Brother Kilker doesn't like me, is all."

"He don't cotton to me either, but I don't let it bother me none."

"But the way he looks at me..." It took her a while to get it out. "If anything happens to July he'll blame me – because I'm the mother, you see? And he'll make certain everyone in Church blames me too."

"Hell sakes, Eliza. You ought not worry so what Kilker thinks. As for July, the only thing tougher is an uncooked turnip. She'll pull through – you'll see." He set his mouth and nodded, as though confirming his prediction.

Chapter Five

While Eliza struggled to embrace the Lord's contribution in Brother Kilker, she never questioned His gift of Pun. She knew Heavenly Father sent the cheerful man with the shiny black pigtail to tend to details she knew little of. When he peeked beneath July's bandage and saw the condition of the wound, he said, "Ho, dat bad sign," then immediately set to work crushing herbs with his wooden pestle, mixing them with the powdered root of the passionflower and other ingredients in his bag. He hummed while he worked, a tune that wandered high and low, as though uncertain where to settle.

Eliza hovered just around the corner, poking her head into the room three times before Pun asked, "Missus eager help?"

"Yes, Pun. What can I do?"

"Bring moldy bread, nice piece muslin."

Eliza scrunched her nose. "I don't see how –"

"Just do," he said, not hesitating to employ his father's tone, a tone he might have used on a child of his own, had he a wife and children.

Pun Loi arrived in America in 1870 at age twenty from the Pearl River delta region in Guangdong, China. Like other immigrants, he'd heard stories about the mountains of gold in America and had arrived a sojourner, a temporary resident intending to work for a short time before returning to his mother, Ai Feng, and his village in China, his suitcase filled with the money he'd earned from selling the brilliant dust.

Pun's first job was as a miner in the California foothills but having almost no success in the already played-out environment, he traversed the same harsh alkali flats the Valentines traveled before him, continuing up to Idaho Territory where he tried his luck in the mining districts of the Boise Basin. Things went only marginally better for him there. He scraped the old mining grounds for sparkling dregs and saved what little money he earned.

Just as it seemed his fingers held more dirt beneath their nails than Idaho held gold, he sat on a rock and contemplated his sorry suitcase and the hope it once held. If he was going home, he thought it better to leave with a damaged back than a broken spirit, and so the next morning he packed his bag and said his farewells. Not two hours after departing his lean-to, he was beaten and robbed of his money. It was a savage disappointment, for it meant starting anew with nothing but the coins clattering in his pocket.

This time he set his pick and ax aside to hitch himself to a yoke and work as a water boy. How many trips had he made to the cold spring at the bottom of the hill, filling his buckets with water then delivering them to his customers' barrels, all for a paltry fifty cents a week? He'd never once counted.

And when his back took on the hunch of an old man, he quit his water job and traveled as far north as he'd ever ventured, this time crossing the middle fork of the Weiser River, and into the mountains. Here he again worked the mines, quitting them forever and laying low when in the spring of '87 the situation in America turned ugly for the Chinese.

He had arrived a middle-aged man at Isaac Caldwell's door, his trousers in tatters, the emptiness of his soul echoing the rattle in his stomach. But along the way he'd tallied five hundred new lambs at the sheds by the river, so he offered his services as a sheepherder.

"Whoever heard of a Chinee sheepherder?" Isaac wanted to know.

"You take sheep to mountain," Pun argued. "Yes?"

Isaac nodded.

"Pun know mountain." He swung out his hand and made an arc over the north. "High and low, know all best places take sheep." When Isaac gave him a dubious look, Pun quickly added, "Nevah get lost." Since immigrating to the United States, his English had remained broken; this he attributed to the devil miners he'd worked with in Silver City, white men with bad teeth and foul-smelling breath who mangled the language far worse than the Chinese.

"Never lost? Not even once?"

Pun patted his temple with a slender finger. "Head smart. Remember."

Isaac noted the sallow color of the man's skin, the hunger in the eyes behind the round lids. It was difficult not to feel for him. There were those in Idle Valley who didn't like the Chinese any more than they liked Mormons and Negroes and Jews, not that he himself would know a Jew from a jumping jack.

"I'll pay one month's wages," Isaac offered. "We'll see how it goes."

That was three years ago and it had gone quite well indeed.

Pun shooed Eliza away with a wave of both hands. When she returned with the items he'd requested, he ripped the muslin into four sections, dipping them into an ointment made from crushed insects and herbs to which he'd added a scraping of mold. This he applied to July's stitches.

He looked into Eliza's worried face. "I make betta," he assured her. "You see."

Always, he hummed his song when he changed July's bandage and inspected her wound. When she complained of nausea, he filled her with warm broth and his special healing recipe, a brew he'd concocted from dried moss, willow bark, and the powered root of the marsh mallow, and which he served in Eliza's porcelain cups. On the morning of the sixth day, when she requested a biscuit to accompany her beverage, Pun nodded with satisfaction, told her she could have it if she could sit up to eat it.

"I can't sit up, it hurts too bad."

"Ho!" he squawked, carrying on so that July pretended not to hear the next time he told her what to do. It was a trick she'd learned from Richard.

Her brother came to see her late that afternoon, when the sun slanted through the window and warmed her sore stomach. He sat on the edge of her bed a while before speaking, his thick lashes fringing dark eyes, eyes that darted from July to his lap and back again. "It shoulda been me," he said at last. "I shoulda been the one cut that day."

"It ain't your fault, so don't be thinking it is."

Richard shook his head. "If I was doing my job like Pa wanted, I'd a been on the bridge before you – I'd be the one with my insides flayed, not you."

July told herself maybe she *should* be a little mad at him, maybe *he* should be the one laying there. But the truth was she thought her pa might be a tiny bit right about Richard. Maybe her brother's head sat upon his shoulders wobbly as a pumpkin's upon a scarecrow's, and one day the slightest bit of wind might bring the whole thing tumbling down.

She hated thinking unkindly of her brother and tucked the thought into a cranny at the back of her mind, choosing instead to praise him for all he'd done right. "Hadn't been for you, I wouldn't be here at all. I'm grateful, Richard."

"Pa thinks someone tinkered with the cable," he said, "maybe used a saw so the bridge would come down when we were on it." July gave him a look that told him she didn't believe it. "It's true," he went on. "Pa thinks Silas Morrow done it."

"That cattleman from Badger?"

"That's the one."

"What do you suppose Pa'll do about it?"

"Don't rightly know but reckon he'll do something. You know Pa."

She knew their pa all right, and it set her back to think on it. But when one day passed and then another and he still hadn't taken off for Badger, she guessed he'd found another way to settle his dispute.

And on the morning of the eighth day following her accident, July awoke at dawn to the sound of a mockingbird calling from the thicket behind the house. The bird's song was like Pun's, flitting high and low with nowhere to land. But unlike Pun, the mockingbird's story had nothing to do with its history; instead, its songs were a mixture of original and stolen phrases. When it ran out of pilfered melodies, it captured squeaky gates and barking dogs or the tinkling of a piano. July wished it had picked up "Beautiful Dreamer" somewhere, for that was her favorite song.

She rolled over and looked around the room, saw that Lilly was already up. July's sister had thrown her comforter over her slim little bed without bothering to tuck in the sheet or fluff the pillow. Their ma wouldn't like that, but Lilly wasn't apt to change. All she cared about was play-acting, whether it was on a wagon in the Independence Day parade or down by the sheds at the river. She'd once performed an entire scene from *Robber of the Rhine* for their pa's sheep. They made an exceptional audience, Lilly said, because even as they chewed, they watched with rapt attention.

July closed her eyes and lolled in the warmth of the sun. The aroma of something hot and greasy wafted from the kitchen and her mouth began to water. When Pun came in to see if she was awake, she opened her eyes and pleaded for real food, no more broth or biscuits dipped in tea, but bacon and eggs and flapjacks stacked as high as the ceiling.

"See how goes," Pun said. It was an expression he'd picked up from her father, but it almost always meant she'd get her way.

She smiled and slipped deeper under the covers. To her delight, Lilly walked in a short time later with a tray of home-cured ham and fried eggs, hotcakes and freshly churned butter. There was a tiny dish of blackberry syrup too. July sat up and received the tray with only the slightest twitch in her side. She complained not a lick and when Pun suggested she was well enough to assist him in the garden, she stuffed a hotcake into her mouth and threw back the covers.

"What're we plan-fing?" she garbled, her mouth filled with hot dough.

"Carrot and radish and rutabaga," he told her. "You hold seed, I hoe."

And so she hobbled outdoors in her nightgown and bare feet, her mother's knitted shawl slung around her shoulders. Lilly followed. "You'll catch your death if go outside without shoes," she told her.

"Raymond never wears shoes," July objected, "and he ain't ailin.'"

"Mama won't like it."

Pun gave Lilly a sharp look. "Keep mout shut, den."

"The two of you, I swear," huffed Lilly. She whirled toward the house and strode inside.

Pun scrunched his nose and shook his head. "Bitta heart," he said. And it was true. Lilly resented the time Pun lavished on July when he was home at the ranch, the hours he spent arranging plaits in her long brown hair. It irked her too that Pun called Richard into the house, hollering, "Come see, Richard! Jew-rye look just like Pun!," yet rarely did he call for Lilly. Yes, it was July and Richard that Pun favored. When Richard was cutting wood or milking cows or tending lambs abandoned by their mothers, he had to stay put and finish his chores. But if he was in the kitchen stoking a fire in the cookstove or stirring soup for their mother, he rushed to July's room the moment Pun called.

Richard loved being a guest at Pun's little parties. He sometimes tried on Pun's Chinese trousers and toggled vests. Reviewing his form in the mirror, he'd smile and say, "The Chinamen have all the best clothes. They're made for stooping and jumping and you can lie down and sleep in them if you've a mind to." And then he'd lament that he couldn't wear them too.

"No," Pun would agree. "Fadda not like dat."

And so the days passed, one folding into another, the morning opening in a sheen of rosy dew, the evening closing in a haze of dusty gold – what July called the Magic Hour. Leaves came to life on the cottonwoods and aspens, and cattails grew fuzzy new collars. And all the while, July grew ever stronger.

Chapter Six

Two weeks to the day after July's accident, Doctor Forbes arrived to remove her stitches. He expected to take a cursory look at the injury, report she was fairing rather poorly, and then inform the family they'd do well to keep the girl in bed another week or two. That she was up and about astonished him.

"My word," he said when he saw her. "To what do we owe your recovery? You look remarkable, July." He could hardly believe he was gazing at the same girl. A bit of color had returned to her cheeks, and though she wasn't yet as vibrant as a sunflower, she was clearly on her way.

"Not *what*," she beamed. "*Who*."

The compliment came as a delightful surprise and Preston felt his face flush. He'd done nothing spectacular at all really and, in fact, regretted having so few options available to guarantee the girl's good health. Other than asking the Lord under his breath for guidance when he sedated and stitched her, his actions were quite ordinary. Sheepishly, he said, "I can hardly take cred –"

July shuffled toward Pun, wrapped her arm around his shoulder. "He's the one who saved me."

Preston twisted in his chair to find a short Oriental fellow in traditional clothing standing in the corner. The man bowed but in Preston's confusion he did not acknowledge the courtesy. "I don't understand," he said, glancing at July. "This man is a doctor?"

"No, he's a sheepherder. But he's got a bag of bark and bugs that he mixed in a poultice – it healed my cut real good."

"What sort of bugs?"

"Beetles and crickets mostly, but I think there were some spiders in there too."

Preston was familiar with herbal remedies of course, but he'd never heard of spiders curing anything. He turned to Pun, suspicion clouding his face, and asked the man how he prepared his insects.

"Can't say," said Pun. "Family secret."

Eliza strode into the kitchen, her apron filled with a dozen brown eggs. "Why, hello Doctor Forbes," she said, her manner breezy and forthcoming. Isaac trailed behind her and offered the doctor a chipper hello. They were as cheerful as the April morning, and this Preston attributed to their daughter's recovery.

"I've come to remove July's stitches," he announced. "I honestly doubted they'd be ready but I see your herder here has conjured a miracle."

Isaac looked at Pun and beamed. "We had the Elders in too. They performed a blessing and Heavenly Father found it in His heart to spare our girl." He said nothing about Brother Kilker having chastised him for waiting two days to do it, however.

Preston clasped his hands. "If I could wash up?" Eliza set a bar of soap on the cabinet. She poured some hot water from the stove's reservoir into a porcelain basin. Preston scrubbed thoroughly, massaging the cuticle of each nail and the skin underneath. Pun left with Isaac to tend to Tom's chores while Eliza prepared July in her bedroom. Preston was deep in thought, astonished still at July's recovery, so he didn't notice Lilly until she stood on her toes, hands behind her back. She peered over his shoulder and chirped a cheerful hello.

He gave a start. "Lilly," he said, turning. "I didn't see you there." She said nothing more, just perched on her toes, smiling. He paused, his eyebrows furrowing almost imperceptibly, then turned toward the basin. He'd not missed her effort to impress him the evening of July's surgery, and apparently she hoped to try again now. He felt her eyes lingering on the back of his neck and turned again, briefly, to confirm his suspicion.

"How old do you think I am?" she asked. She inched closer and he caught a hint of lilac water in her hair. Scrubbing fervently now, he said, "Well, let's see…July's fourteen, Richard's fifteen, so you're what? Sixteen or so?"

She came down from her tiptoes with a thump. "I'll be seventeen this fall, but everyone says I could pass for twenty."

Once he thought on it, he said, "That you could. But why would you want to?"

"I'm going to be an actress in New York City," she said earnestly, "so it's important I project an air of maturity, don't you think?"

Preston swished his hands in the bowl and gave them a shake. He dried them on a towel. "I don't know about such things, but I think it's more a matter of acting mature than looking it." The remark seemed to have gone over her head, for she gave no sign it was geared toward her at all.

Eliza walked in, took one look at Lilly in her fancy dress and hair ribbons and asked why she was all dressed up. The girl's face folded, as if her mother had betrayed her. Eliza caught the look, and too late, took its meaning. Lilly had dressed for Preston Forbes. Eliza could think of no way to undo this small humiliation to her daughter and so she said nothing, just smoothed her apron and glanced at the floor. Lilly rolled her eyes and left the room in a hurry.

Eliza watched her go, then turned to Doctor Forbes. The moment was awkward yet he filled it graciously, pretending not to know what the girl was up to. "Lilly tells me she wants to be an actress in New York," he said casually.

Eliza sighed, for it seemed both her daughters were bent on living some other women's lives. "She's never even been to New York and doesn't know the first thing about it."

Preston nodded thoughtfully. "Perhaps she sees more promise in the city – Morning Tree's a small town with but a handful of Mormon families, and not many with sons her age – maybe she's looking to expand her world a bit." Though he tried to put a logical spin on Lilly's longings, Eliza only frowned. "I wouldn't worry about her," he went on. "All young women are subject to flights of fancy."

"I wasn't."

"No doubt you've always been a woman of practicality." He'd meant it as a compliment, but when her face fell he realized she'd taken it to mean she was ordinary. He immediately set about making amends. "I imagine July is just like you," he put in robustly, "a delightful girl and full of vigor. But it's her *practical* nature – her willingness to embrace all avenues of treatment, whether from a Chinaman or a practicing physician – that sets her apart from most young girls. It's a sign she's smart and sensible – no doubt she gets that from you."

Eliza beamed. "Why, thank you, Doctor Forbes."

"You're welcome," he said, though he hadn't meant a word of it. July Caldwell hadn't survived the accident because she was sensible; she survived because she was filled to the brim with spunk and vitality. And until that moment – until he formed that precise thought in his head – Preston Forbes had no inkling whatsoever those were exactly the qualities he was looking for in a wife.

He walked into July's room with a renewed sense of self, glanced at the furrow between her slim brows, and spoke as kindly as he'd spoken to anyone in his life. "I'll do my best not to hurt you," he promised. Something must have persuaded her that this was true, for she took a deep breath and slowly exhaled. Preston rested his hand on her shoulder, told her to close her eyes. He pulled a pair of scissors from his bag. "I won't do a thing without telling you what to expect first," he said. It was a custom almost unheard of in the medical community; most doctors preferred to snare a bit of skin and stitch it together, then yank the thread out later without so much as a how-do-you-do. But Preston found that his patients appreciated the chance to mentally prepare for the road ahead and often found the journey less daunting if they knew what was coming.

"This is the easy part," he assured her, resting the tip of the scissors at her collarbone and gently clipping the first stitch. He fixed his gaze on her warm brown eyes, and seeing no adverse reaction – no sign of pain or pinch of surprise – he moved down and across her breastbone. When he'd applied the stitches ten days ago there was no need to divert his eyes, for it had taken all his concentration to close the nearly mortal wound. Today, however, there was less to think about. There was no blood to conceal the milky whiteness of her skin, no pressure to speed things along before she drifted back to consciousness. And so he caught a glimpse, albeit unwilling, of the tender swellings that comprised her breasts, and of her nipples, pink and round. Although the room was cool, his forehead began to bead with perspiration. He swallowed and looked up. "Might I have a glass of water, please?"

"Certainly," Eliza said, turning quickly to fetch him a glass. If she noticed the tremble of his hand or the glossy sheen of his brow she gave no indication, and when she returned with a stout wooden cup he accepted it, closed his eyes, and drank the water down. He set the cup on the bureau, diverted his gaze to July's toes and asked how she was doing.

In a voice as small as a songbird's, she said she was all right. The uncertainty of her tone prompted him to tell her she was very brave, and he began working quickly, snipping each knot with renewed resolve. "Now comes the tricky part," he said after he'd clipped the last stitch. Unwrapping a pair of surgical tweezers from his kit, he held a small bit of gauze in his left hand, steadied his wrist against her throat.

"I won't lie to you, July," he said. "This is going to smart." And then he began to tug.

Her breathing quickened to accommodate the pain.

Preston hunkered down. With as much delicacy as he could muster, he urged the gray thread through her skin even as it protested its release. He dabbed at the bloody footprints the knots left behind, his fingers progressing down her body in a tug-and-blot motion as if he were performing a slow and rather tedious piano recital. It wasn't until he reached the halfway point that he looked up. Seeing a tear squeezing from July's eye, he hesitated, taking a moment to mask his distress. "Shall I stop? Do you need to rest?"

July bit her lip and shook her head.

He glanced at Eliza. She nodded, wanting him, no doubt, to be done with it. "Very well," he said. "We're almost finished, July. Hang on another minute."

When it was over, he slowly exhaled, letting go the breath he'd been storing in his chest. It occurred to him that no other girl July's age possessed one-tenth the courage she'd displayed: the few he'd treated on the workbench in his office had cried and carried on before he'd so much as touched the boils on their backsides, but July? She'd gripped her mother's hand and stared at the ceiling, letting him get on with his job. Yes, she'd summoned a tear or two, but nary a sound had escaped her lips, and his heart swelled with admiration.

He was about to tell her what he thought of her, for he wanted her to look at him the way she'd looked at Pun. Clearly, she thought the world of the smooth-cheeked herder with the mysterious brown eyes, and Preston wished to be equally admired. But when he licked his lips and formed the words, she sighed and rolled toward the wall. He stepped back and glanced at the door, relieved Eliza hadn't caught the flush on his cheek. He quietly packed the implements into his bag and snapped it shut, consoling himself by reasoning that the procedure had tired the girl and she needed rest. "Get some sleep," he said, "and ask your mother to let me know if you experience any problems at all."

Eliza saw Doctor Forbes to the door, stepping onto the porch with him as Isaac walked over to say his goodbyes. She thanked Preston for his good work, then left the men to talk while she checked on July.

"Can't thank you enough for tendin my girl," Isaac told him.

"She's doing remarkably well, considering. It was a terrible accident and she's lucky to be alive." When Isaac's face darkened at the reminder, Preston confessed he'd heard discussion in town – speculation, really – that the bridge had been tampered with. "I've not heard mention of any names, mind you, but some are saying it's the work of cattlemen."

Isaac's mouth puckered. "Silas Morrow, you mean."

"I didn't say that, nor have I heard it," Preston cautioned. "I'm only bringing it up in the event you'd like to discuss it with the sheriff."

"And tell him what? I got a hunch? He won't take the side of a sheepman."

"Well," said Preston, moving toward his horse and climbing on. "I've told you what I know, which isn't much. But if I were you I'd talk to him, register my complaint."

You ain't me, Isaac thought but didn't say. He tipped his hat and bade the man goodbye.

* * *

Whether Preston encouraged July or not, there was no problem in her mind that would warrant a trip to his office, for she would forever equate the pulsing ribbon of pain down the middle of her belly with his cold scissors and sweat-soaked hands. Where her torso had merely itched yesterday it now throbbed, and she couldn't imagine ever wanting to eat again. The smell of bread baking in the kitchen set her spit to bubbling and her ears to aching and before she knew it she was clutching her stomach and heaving over the side of the bed.

Lilly poked her head around the door. "Ma," she called, looking back over her shoulder. "July threw up again."

July lay back down, her belly burning and a sob building at the back of her throat. When her mother padded into the room, a bucket in one hand, a mop in the other, July let loose her tears.

"Why, July," Eliza scolded. "I'm surprised at you. You were strong as an ox when Doctor Forbes was plucking your stitches. Why are you crying now?"

"I'm sick of laying here while Raymond and the rest of them soak up the sunshine. I want to be outside too." She set herself to hiccupping and heaving again, this time throwing up on her comforter. What the blanket didn't catch, the floor did.

"My word," clucked Lilly. "How you carry on, July."

Eliza kneeled then, scooping up the watery puddle with a damp cloth. She asked Lilly to tote July's comforter to the back porch and soak it in water. Lilly groaned but did as she was told. She folded the four flaps of the blanket inward, wadded it into a bundle, then carried it from the room at arm's length. July said nothing, just let the tears trickle down the sides of her face and pool in her ears.

Isaac walked into the room, assessed his wife with stern eyes. She was perched at the edge of Lilly's bed, her head resting in her hands. "What's got into you?" he grunted, his good mood spoiled by Preston Forbes' rumors.

She looked up. "My head aches, is all."

He glanced toward July, found her gazing squarely at heaven, her cheeks pale and her eyes watery. Every so often she gave a quivery hiccup.

"Hell sakes," he said, speaking to Eliza. "We had two minutes' peace before Doc Forbes arrived, and now you're laggin on the bed and July's cryin in hers – even Richard's sulkin in the barn."

Eliza slowly stood, as if rising too quickly would stir the throbbing in her head. "Why is Richard sulking?"

"For all I know some skeeter bit his toe." Isaac set his mouth in that hard way he had. "Not only that, but Lilly's on the porch play-acting and I hardly seen Raymond since dinnertime yesterday. Where's he off to now?"

"He's down to the creek gigging frogs, and if you've a mind to whip him, let it go. I gave him permission." She sighed wearily. "If you got to strap someone, strap Lilly. I told her to set July's quilt in water and now you tell me she's play-acting."

"Dancin with a broom, to be exact."

July brought her head off the pillow, straining to look around. "Have you seen Pun anywhere, Pa? He told me ten minutes ago he'd bring me a cup of tea." Eliza asked July if she had a headache too.

July flopped back down on the pillow. "No, but my chest is on fire, my stomach's burning, and my backside is getting sore."

Eliza walked over to Isaac and put her hand on his arm. "We're not falling apart," she told him, scratching together a bit of compassion. "We're just going through a rough spot, is all."

"I'm just saying things would be a whole lot smoother if Silas Morrow hadn't set my family upside down."

Eliza dropped her hand from his arm. "I can't see where it's Silas Morrow's fault Lilly's play-acting on the porch and Richard's sulking in the barn."

Isaac hadn't much to say to that, although he managed just fine to call up that put-upon look Eliza knew so well, the stubborn pinch to his mouth that told her he'd made up his mind and would do whatever he pleased, regardless of what she thought. She clucked her tongue. "So that's it, Isaac? You're going to Silas Morrow's?"

He stuck out his chin, said, "I reckon I am."

"Then I may as well prepare myself for widowhood, for Morrow's men will surely shoot you once you accuse them of sabotage."

"They won't get no chance. I'm takin a gun."

"And July? Will you give her a gun, too?"

And just like that, he told Eliza he wasn't taking July. "Though I ought to. I'd like that man to see what he done, to go to bed every night for the rest of his life knowin he maimed my girl."

"Then you'll leave her home with me?"

"I said I would, didn't I?"

Eliza glanced at the ceiling, let go a great puff of air as if to say thank you, God, for giving this man a brain. She looked at her husband, saw that though he'd changed his mind he was still all business, so she asked when he was going. "Tomorrow," he said, and the news shocked her. She never expected he'd go it alone. "Won't you at least wait till Tom gets back, take him with you?"

Isaac thought a moment. While he was fired up to go now – right this minute, in fact – he saw some logic to his wife's thinking. It wasn't altogether smart to confront an enemy single-handed, although he and Tom hardly constituted a posse. "I'll wait," he agreed begrudgingly. He turned to walk from the room, pausing to look at July. "How long you plannin on warmin that mattress, young lady?"

She sat up, looked at her pa with moist eyes. "I don't know. Why?"

"I got milk to deliver in the morning. If you can find a way to shake them fits, I'll take you along." He cast his eyes at the window, looked speculatively toward the horizon. "I was thinkin we'd throw a line in the river on the way back, see if we can catch us a fish or two."

"She's in no shape to go fishing," Eliza objected. "She just threw up on her blanket."

"I'm feeling better now, honest I am." July sat up bravely to prove it. "Let me go, Ma. *Please*."

"Fresh air will do her good," Isaac suggested. And just like that, father and daughter got their way, and in the morning they were gone.

Chapter Seven

July hunkered down in the back of the buckboard, an old quilt serving as a pallet. She rolled onto her back and pulled a blanket up to her neck, drawing comfort from the bumpers Pun had built her. He'd fashioned plump little sausages from a tarp he'd stuffed with straw, situating them around her hips and shoulders so she wouldn't jostle in the wagon. Raymond hooted when he saw them, taunting her with the cruel songs of an eight-year-old, saying she looked like a baby in a cradle. She liked to sock him for it, but she wasn't yet moving as swift as she once had, and so she let it go.

It wasn't often she got the chance to travel with her pa. Ever since she could remember, she'd loved viewing the countryside, watching the slow, lazy escape of herons as they lifted from a pond, and taking in the sounds of meadowlarks, their throaty *chucks* exploding from cattails and bulrushes.

But the older she got the more she realized these weren't just jaunts her pa was taking, but tasks that ate up his day. The to-and-fro was hard on him; she saw in the crush of his forehead how much he worried about all the things that needed doing around the ranch while he was toting milk to Morning Tree. Although he was first and foremost a sheepman, he had drummed into all their heads it wasn't enough to simply run sheep – a man had to find a hundred other ways to make a dollar. Some grew extra hay and sold it to neighbors, some planted orchards and sold apples and plums and cherries. Isaac milked cows. He would have preferred to sell his cream directly to the creamery itself if for no other reason than they'd send a driver out to pick it up. But doing so required he pay the creamery a percentage of his profits – a luxury he couldn't afford – and so he performed this work while Tom dug ditches and ran the plow across the fields without him.

July shifted in her little bed and gazed at the clouds gathering in the bruise-colored sky. It smelled of faraway rain. If they were lucky it would stick to Brundage where the ground was hard and thirsty, maybe skip Idle Valley altogether where they'd already had more than their fair share of moisture.

The sway of the wagon made her sleepy and it wasn't long before she drifted off.

Isaac glanced back after a while, saw July's head swaying on its pillow and her mouth spilling drool. He picked his path carefully, not wanting to jostle her any more than he had to. It wasn't long before the road curved and the shrubs gave way, and he had a clear view of the Weiser. He spied Everett Lofgren on the river, a man slim as a stovepipe, balancing atop his ferry. Everett's business would pick up plenty now that the bridge to Valentine was down. It occurred to Isaac that the man had every reason to *want* to see the bridge go, but when the fellow waved and shouted a friendly hello, Isaac knew Everett hadn't the heart for sabotage. Isaac waved back but skipped the greeting, for he didn't want to wake July.

Come summertime, folks on horseback wouldn't have need of a ferry. They could cross the river where a sandbar had built up and a stand of willows sprouted. If the bridge wasn't repaired by fall – which it surely wouldn't be – Pun and the others could cross the sheep at a spot not far from town where the water was usually low. But if it rained and the river rose, they'd have to look for a slot twenty miles north, where Tom had likely crossed with the sheep some ten days earlier.

Isaac's thoughts turned to Tom then, how he was likely grumbling all the way to the hills. The world was strange that way. Here he had a nephew strong and sturdy as a Cotswold ram, a man who, had he any love for sheep at all, would have made a top-notch herder. And then he had July – a girl tough as a radish, but a girl nonetheless – who took to the mountains like a wasp to johnny cake, and who would go in a second if he asked her to. But he would not; he'd yet to reconcile why the Lord made a girl so clever when her place was in her pa's home till she left it for her husband's.

It seemed everyone in his family had some all-fired desire apart from his own. Oh, they worked hard, knew what it was to plant a garden and till the fields and cook from dawn until dusk, but they didn't seem to appreciate what it took, year in and year out, to provide for a family, ensure there were sheep to shear and lambs to sell and land on which to graze them. They couldn't see inside his head, couldn't know how he worried for their future, for it wasn't enough to call yourself a provider because there was mutton on the table and milk in a stoneware jug. A man had to do more, had to make something of the land he owned and scrounge up free range too, acreage unencumbered by browsers and squatters and whatever other baggage hurled itself upon the landscape. That was his job as head of the household, so why his family fought him so, Isaac had no clue.

As he contemplated all this, one of the wagon's wheels dipped into a rut and jarred July awake. She opened her eyes, rolled onto her side, and sat up on one elbow. "My bowler," she muttered, her voice husky with sleep. "I dreamed it was at the bottom of the Weiser." It upset her that she hadn't given the hat a moment's thought in the two weeks since her accident, for she loved her little bowler. To think it had been flopping around Valentine all this time, alone and ignored, grieved her severely. "What do you say we fetch it, Pa?"

Isaac snorted, told her it was ten miles in the other direction. When he didn't offer to search for it on some separate occasion, nor buy her a new one, she sighed and asked how much farther they had to go yet, for her backside had fallen asleep and her legs too.

"Got a customer right around the corner here," he said, pointing with his chin toward a ranch up the road, "and two more families in town. After that, we'll eat the dinner Ma packed and throw us a line in the river."

The deliveries didn't take more than an hour or so, and then they were on their way again, following the road along the water.

Just before they reached the turnoff for Everett Lofgren's ferry, Isaac guided the team past a cottonwood with a trunk as wide as a ponderosa's. He steered them onto a dirt path down a hill, brought the horses to a halt. July shook her legs awake then gingerly slid from her bed, wandering toward a scramble of silver sage. She stepped behind it and lifted her skirt, squatted, and trickled in the dirt. A dove cooed in the distance and she imagined Daniel, her father's sturdiest herder, taking a bead on the creature, shooting it as the little fellow poked around the ground looking for a pebble or kernel of loose corn. She hated knowing such a bird might die in the name of a grilled supper over an open fire but even as she disliked it, her mouth watered and she realized she was hungry.

Her pa had taken the quilt from the back of the wagon and spread it on the ground, anchoring one corner with the basket. July sat Indian style. Propping her hands on her knees, she surveyed its contents: there was cheese wrapped in muslin, two thick slices of bread tucked in a cloth napkin, a tin of dried apples, a jar of chokecherry jelly and a spoon to spread the jell. July and Lilly had picked the cherries last summer for their ma, who had stood over the steaming kettle of fruit, stirring the sugary mixture with a long wooden spoon until the juice thickened into sweet red jelly. Next to blackberry, it was July's favorite. She dabbed a little on a slice of bread and took a bite. Isaac did the same and they chewed in silence. Every so often he reached over and cut off a hunk of cheese, which he ate with a chip of dried apple.

July relished the quiet between them. Most times, a look was as good as a word anyway, and her pa didn't need to come right out and say what he was thinking. He could wriggle his forehead and July knew straight away where his thoughts had settled. Right now, for example, his face was smooth and his eyes droopy, and he was likely thinking on her ma's good cooking. He brushed the crumbs from his mouth, asked what she thought about heading over to a silky spot he'd spied at the river, maybe casting their lines in. She thought it a fine idea. After they'd packed up the basket and loaded the quilt into the wagon, they fetched their bamboo poles and walked down to the Weiser. July's nostrils filled with the scent of sage and the fine brown dust she kicked up along the way. A breeze blew from the south, pushing the clouds toward the mountains. The sun warmed her back and massaged her shoulders.

"Feels good to be out," she told her father. "I was getting antsy, cooped up in the house."

July's voice had such a serious quality to it, Isaac couldn't help but grin. He watched as she flicked her wrist and gave the line a snap. It sailed into the water, landing with a plop. Ripples floated along the surface and a series of small bubbles popped.

"There's a trick I used in the mountains," he told her, "where I'd let my mind go and all my troubles with it. You sit long enough, the bones just sort of leave your body – reckon that feels about as good as anything I've known."

Now it was July's turn to smile. She couldn't recollect where her pa had ever expressed real joy, let alone felt it. It did her heart good to believe his life wasn't all toil and trouble. "I'd like to get my bones like that," she told him, then set about practicing. She breathed in through her nose and out through her mouth, closed her eyes and concentrated. It was harder than she thought.

After they'd sat there a while and caught six fish between them, Isaac glanced over and saw July sagging on her little log seat. "We've had a good day," he told her, gathering the small string of trout. "What say we head home?"

She pushed herself off the log, then stood for a second while little white stars shot across her eyeballs. Isaac asked if she was all right. She said she'd got up too fast, is all. He reached out and she took his hand, slowly navigating the stones till her feet were right again. "Thanks for bringing me, Pa," she told him. He nodded, flopping the fish into a bucket in the back of the wagon. "Back in a minute," he said as he headed for the cottonwood with the mile-wide trunk. He loosened his belt along the way, his bladder as full as a milk sac.

July crawled onto the wagon, sat near its open end and lay back, her thin legs dangling over the edge. It felt good to have the pressure off her stomach; even though her stitches were gone now, the healing still tugged at her flesh. She closed her eyes and had just begun to doze off when a dog's shrill bark brought her around again. She sat up and peered over the edge of the wagon. A boy about her age rode toward her on a pretty little paint. He hadn't yet spotted her, for he was eyeing the dog, hollering at it to get on back to the road. The boy had hair the color of a rusty nail and a chin as square as a spice box. July didn't notice the others gathering on the road behind her, but Isaac did. There were two men hunched in a wagon, and two sitting sharp in their saddles. One looked darkly familiar.

Chapter Eight

Silas Morrow, like Isaac Caldwell, knew what it was to struggle. At age twenty he took a job as a cowpuncher, helped drive a herd of cattle from Texas to the territory of southwestern Idaho where there was a demand for beef in the mining district of Silver City. He saved his money, worked to better himself, got married. Eventually he settled on a ranch in the town of Badger, built a home, constructed a barn and a corral, and amassed a herd of cattle. As for actual numbers, Silas adhered to an unwritten rule that a cattleman never talked about the size of his herd. When asked how many cattle he owned, Silas was rumored to have said, "I leave those matters to the assessor, and he only comes around once a year."

By 1890, Silas was well established in the valley, with extensive spring, fall, and winter range that extended south into Oregon. But summer range – green feed found in mountain meadows and amidst the rocky atolls of the rugged terrain itself – was quickly becoming depleted, beaten down by Isaac Caldwell's sheep and the sheep of Isaac's cronies. Too, Caldwell's sheep were better at grazing the steep mountain slopes than were Silas's cattle, and were not, as a rule, affected by tall larkspur, a spindly plant that each year infected the mountainsides and killed a handful of his animals – factors which gave Caldwell an advantage.

Silas was a man who stuck to himself and the small circle of men who worked for him, keeping to the hills or his ranch or the far-flung valley of Perdue where he grazed his cattle in winter. On the few occasions that he drove to Morning Tree for supplies, he never tipped his hat to women or passed the time with the barber, since it was his wife, Lydia, who clipped his hair just above the collar. Even if he'd smiled some – which no one had seen him do – Morning Tree was not a town to embrace him. He was simply too aloof, too unknowable, and it made him an easy target for rumors.

He'd taken in an earful that day alone, some of it coming from a grocer pretending to be his friend. "They're saying a cattleman tripped up the bridge to Valentine," the man said as he loaded a sack of flour into Silas's wagon. "Saying he looked a lot like you, in fact."

Silas said nothing, just gave the man a sour look, mounted his horse and snapped the reins. Mads Larson, his foreman, rode alongside him while Slack Jaw and a fellow named Blink Neely sat in the wagon. Rory, his son, dawdled up the street with his dog, Dunkel. Silas called to the boy, told him it was time to get going. Silas didn't wait for his son to catch up, though, just set off without him and let him come along on his own. It wasn't long before Rory and Dunkel trailed after them. With Dunkel's squat figure, a body would've thought the dog slow going, but he could race fast as a coyote and burn up the grass with his legs.

Outside of town, not too far from Lofgren's ferry, the dog picked up the scent of a rabbit and tore off toward the river. Rory hollered at him and scowled as the dog zipped past a man standing next to a cottonwood, and then scampered for the fellow's wagon.

Rory looked over at his pa. He and the boys were slowing to have a word with the man. Rory didn't recognize the stranger but then he didn't get much of a look, either, for Dunkel was barking at something in the buckboard.

"Dunkel!" Rory cried, but the dog kept at it.

He trotted over to have a look. He thought maybe the stranger had a dog back there, although why the critter hadn't made itself known escaped him. Riding up loudly so as not to catch the creature unawares, Rory cleared his throat and waited for some reaction. Receiving none, he stepped forward and peered inside. All at once, a brown-haired girl poked her head up and glared at him.

"Dags," he cried, lurching back. "You liked to scare me to death."

"Your dog liked to eat my toes."

Rory called Dunkel off and for once the dog obeyed. He asked the girl what she was doing back there, anyway.

"Waiting on my pa."

"You look like you're hidin," he accused, and when she didn't say if she was or wasn't, he asked what her name was.

"Julia, but long as I can remember, my family has called me July."

"July? Why, that's a boy's name."

"Says who?"

He thought for a minute. "Well, August is a boy's name. Leastwise, I think it is." When he told her he reckoned he liked July better than Julia anyway, she said, "I reckon I do too." She smiled as though pleased he'd told her so, and when she looked up again she asked if his dog was fixing to bite her. He said he didn't think so, then asked if she wanted to hold him. She nodded, so he whistled and pointed toward July. "Load up," he commanded. Dunkel sprang up, situating himself between July's thighs, where the fold of her dress made a soft little nest.

Staring hard at July, Rory moved in closer. Never had he seen a girl so pretty, with her plaited hair and eyes the color of drugstore chocolates. Her eyebrows had the hue of sand but it seemed their tops had been painted with a brush dipped in gold, which gave them a peculiar glow. Her skin was smooth and her lips as ripe as berries, but her beauty was marred by the worried hunch of her shoulders. Whatever had caused her to lie back there in the buckboard must have weighed on her some, and though he didn't know her, he felt her pain and wished he could make it better.

He surveyed the bed she'd made for herself, the straw-filled bumpers, the pillow for her head. "You a invalid?" he asked, though it was forward and none of his business at all.

"No, just bunged up some."

He was about to inquire as to the nature of her injury when she asked his name.

"Rory," he said. "Rory Morrow." She sat up at that, asked if his pa's name was Silas. The question took him by surprise, and he told her it was. He looked over at his father. "You happen to know my pa?"

July turned to look behind her. Her gaze settled on the oldest man in the group. He had a barrel chest and a beard trimmed neat as a piecrust. Though his hair was gray at the temples, no horns sprouted from his head. He didn't look like a devil, but a man as mortal as her pa. The other fellow though, the slim one astride a tall horse, looked cruel as winter. July couldn't tell about the men in the wagon, for her eyes had shifted to her own pa now. He stood straight as a washboard, his arms dangling at his sides.

"That man up there your pa's talking to?" she said to Rory. "That's *my* pa, Isaac Caldwell."

*　　*　　*

Straight away Isaac recognized Silas Morrow coming toward him, though he hadn't seen him but once in over two years now. It was in Morning Tree when their paths last crossed, outside the general store. Isaac stood at the door, watching as Silas rode by on an eel-stripe buckskin, Mads Larson at his side. With his blue eyes icy, Mads threw Isaac a look of disdain while Silas pretended not to see him. But Isaac knew better, for he had noted Silas's stiffening spine and the way he defiantly drew up his chin when he rode past the store.

Isaac had spent the last two weeks itching to get at the man, and just like that, here he was, like some present the devil unwrapped and dropped in his lap. He quickly tucked in his shirt, tightened his belt and strode toward the road, his pulse hammering hard in his neck. He didn't think about his lack of a gun until after Silas had caught sight of him, but by then it was too late to turn around and fetch it. And so he stood at the edge of the road without it, waiting for Silas and his men to come upon him.

When they were within hearing distance, he shouted, "I got a ax to grind with you."

Silas pulled back on his reins. He regarded Isaac coolly and drew his mouth up tight, as though he'd known all along he'd eventually run into the man. "If anyone's got some complaining to do it's me, Caldwell," he hollered. "You got the best grazing on the whole damn range."

"First come, first served, that's the law of the land."

"To which you've got no title."

"Nor you," shouted Isaac.

Silas shifted, though his feet held firm in the stirrups. "Those animals of yours eat everything in sight and what they don't, your neighbors' do. There's no grass or browse tall enough for my cattle to get hold of, when your bands are done jerkin the hillsides."

"My sheep'll happily leave your grass alone if I can get them to the hills when I'm supposed to," Isaac countered, though it wasn't entirely true; a sheep's appetite was as hardy as a herder's and could do a fair amount of damage if not kept in check. He waited for the remark to sink in, adding, "But then, you seen fit to keep me from my job now, didn't you?"

"I never reckoned you were one to cotton to rumors, Caldwell."

"Ain't no rumor – you almost kilt my girl."

Silas glanced toward July, then back at Isaac. "I think the sun has touched you some," he said. "You best get on over to that cottonwood, lie awhile in the shade." Mads Larson chuckled at that, as did the men in the wagon.

"It ain't sun that's touched me, it's knowin you trashed the bridge at Valentine."

"Now hold on," Silas flared. "I never trashed that bridge or any other."

"Well, someone did. Sawed the cable, and when the thing come down a wire whipped around and caught my daughter unawares."

"I never harmed your girl, nor molested no bridge, either."

Isaac's gaze traveled to Mads. "Maybe you ought to ask Larson there what he knows about it."

Mads shot up from his saddle, jabbed a finger in Isaac's direction. "I had nothin to do with it. That bridge come down of its own accord."

"While my sheep was on it." Isaac turned to Silas. "My girl and boy were headed to Brundage, which happens to be on your map, as I recollect."

"Brundage is on every cattleman's map," Silas fumed. "It ain't no fault of mine if there's but a handful of ways to get there."

"Looks to me like some cowboy did you a favor Caldwell," Mads put in. "Now you got your girl at home to help you pat your butter." The insult was a reference to Isaac's milk cows, which cattlemen revered no more than sheep. "Anyway," Mads went on, "that daughter a yours looks sprightly enough to me. I don't see where the bridge goin down cost her anything at all."

"Cable cut her open collarbone to hipbone," Isaac said. "I'd say it cost her plenty." All at once his eyes went red-rimmed and watery and his lip began to quiver, though he fought it with all he had. "I blame you for that, Morrow. I won't stand for you tamperin with my family." He stepped forward like he aimed to prove it, his clenched fists his only weapons.

Mads whipped his horse around, drew his quirt and pointed it hard against Isaac's chest. "Hold up, Caldwell, or I'll make you wish you had."

*   *   *

Rory's eyes went wide. "Isaac Caldwell's your pa? Why didn't you say so?"

"I just did," July told him.

He glanced back, held his gaze on his father and the small group before his face folded in worry. July looked back too, saw that something in the men's demeanor had altered, grown stouter and meaner somehow. All at once the slim one stepped forward and jammed his quirt against her father's chest. "He's fixing to whip my pa," July cried. She shoved Dunkel from her lap and sprang from the wagon. When her feet hit the ground, a shock of pain rippled over her belly and stars shot across her eyes. The sky spun like a top, and she dropped to the ground.

Rory jumped down from his horse, and instantly scooped her up. He called for someone to help him, quick. No one heard him, though, for Isaac had made a move and Mads had brought his quirt down hard on the man's upraised arms.

"Pa!" Rory hollered again. He stumbled toward the men, July dangling in his arms like an injured colt. Mads Larson looked up just as he was about to strike Isaac a second time, but it was the vision of Rory toting July that brought him to a halt.

Chapter Nine

July was on the ground when she came to, her head in her pa's lap. She wiped her mouth and looked around. Silas and his men were gone now, and they'd taken Rory with them. She asked her pa what had gone on while she was out. "That lanky one whipped me with his quirt," he said, showing her his arms, ripe and red with welts. "Liked to hit me again when that Morrow boy came skittering up with you floppin in his arms. What possessed him to maul you, I got no idea – last thing you need is help from the likes of some hell forsaken Morrow."

July wasn't up to arguing, for her insides felt loose as custard. She put on a brave front, though, and climbed into the wagon, sitting alongside her pa. They hadn't gone far when the bread in her stomach began to tussle with the jam. She climbed into the back of the buckboard and lay down. Her breath caught when she bent to tug at the covers but she kept it to herself – there was only so much carrying on her pa would tolerate from his young ones.

The sky had gone pink and purple and a few stars had popped out by the time they spotted their house, rosy on the hillside. When Isaac pulled in front of the yard, everyone clamored outside to hear about their day – where they'd been, how many fish they'd caught, and how the deliveries had gone. Little Raymond wanted to know if July had fetched him a surprise – a brightly colored stone, or maybe a bird's nest with the eggs still in it – but Isaac, weary to his ankles, told his family not to pester them, as they'd had a trying day and needed to rest a while. All the Caldwell children, then, went to bed without the story they'd waited for. When the sun poked through their curtains just after daybreak, they gathered around their mother's griddle in the kitchen to hear their father's story. Isaac told it once, showed them the marks on his arms, where the welts had turned to bruises, and then repeated the tale when they insisted on hearing it again. Each time, the little group scooted in closer, their eyes stirring and glowing, hungry for details of Silas Morrow and his men.

"That Mads Larson is a bad seed," he told them. He looked at Pun. "Struck me as a vengeful foe, the kind of man who don't cotton to Mormons or the Chinee."

"Cowboy not scare Pun," he sniffed. "I know how pull trigger too."

"You ever shoot a man?"

"Not man, wolf. Same difference."

July tottered into the kitchen, her eyes puffy with sleep, her hair poking from the plaits she'd gone to bed with the night before. She'd been listening to the talk from the warmth of her bed, unwilling until now to put a penny in. "I'm with Pa," she said, sitting on a three-legged stool next to him. "That Mads Larson is cruel, and by the looks of him he doesn't get enough to eat. I reckon it makes him cranky."

"If he's skinny as all that, why didn't you whup him, Pa?" asked Raymond. He held his little fists in two tight balls, as though any minute now he'd hitch a horse, ride on out there, and clobber the man himself.

"Pa had no quirt," Richard put in like some wise old owl. "No gun either."

"Thank heaven for that," said Eliza. It was quiet a moment. "Why didn't you have your gun? I thought you took it with you."

"Did," said Isaac, looking a little sheepish. "All I could think of when I saw Silas comin was givin him a piece of my mind. Didn't remember the gun until I'd stomped on up to him, and by then it was too late to fetch it."

"Mads Larson could of shot you in the back!" Raymond cried. Again it was quiet while everyone thought on that.

After a while Richard leaned in, a worried look on his face. "What happens now, Pa? You think Mads will give you any more trouble?"

"I wouldn't put it past him."

July rolled a hotcake into a cigar and bit off its tip. "Pa told me on the way home he'd wring their necks if they mess with us again."

She looked at her father. "But you wouldn't hurt Rory, right? 'Cause he's the one that helped me."

"You stay clear of him."

"I'm just asking."

Isaac turned to Richard. "No, I wouldn't hurt anyone, lest he hurt me first."

The news calmed Richard and he sat back, his shoulders looser now. He rolled his own cigar, dipped it in sugar, then folded it in half and popped it into his mouth.

*   *   *

The days fell into a familiar rhythm then. Each morning and evening, July joined her father in the barn, milking five of his ten cows. The bounce in her step hadn't fully returned yet, although Doctor Forbes assured the family they'd see it by summer's end.

Gradually, as the color returned to July's cheeks and the meat to her bones, Eliza called on her to help with chores around the house. Once a week it was July's job to tote butter to the root cellar, where even toward the end of June the little lean-to was as cool as November. After her ma slapped the contents of the round-bellied butter churn onto the table, stirred the mixture with a paddle and scraped it into molds lining the counter, July gathered them on a tray, placed them on a shelf and covered the molds with cotton towels to keep the dust away.

Raymond had chores too. He was assigned the task of scrubbing the chimneys on the household lamps each Friday, and on Mondays Lilly did the laundry. Washing took the entire day, sometimes two in winter, when clothes hung crisp on the line until Tuesday or Wednesday morning. From sunup until suppertime, Lilly heated kettles of water, shaving lye soap into their roiling bubbles and sorting clothes into whites, coloreds, and work britches, and scrubbing the dirty spots hard. She had to rinse and hang those piles too, and when they dried, smooth them into place with an iron as heavy as a farrier's anvil. July sometimes suspected her sister wanted so desperately to move to New York City just so she could escape the dirty clothes piled on the back porch.

Not that July wasn't assigned chores she hated too. The mattresses were hers alone to freshen each spring and fall, and the task took the better part of a day. In years past, Richard had helped her haul the bulky rectangles onto the porch, but since he'd left for the high country Pun was now the one to lend a hand. By the time she was done yanking out the wool, carding it clean, and stuffing it in again, she would have happily slept in the barn on a blanket of straw.

There were seasonal jobs, too; planting a garden of cukes and carrots, of rutabagas and radishes, of peas and lettuce and legumes, all of which Pun used in his Chinese cooking. All summer long, it seemed Eliza leaned over pots of fragrant syrup as she stirred jellies and jams or arranged peaches in Mason jars for pies that coming winter. In the fall she stored in the root cellar fifteen-hundred pounds of potatoes and two dozen cabbages, their heads as big as pumpkins. When there was a bumper crop, she called on the men to tote spuds to the sheep, and the luckiest among them ate their fill and more.

The men had it hard, as well. Sometimes Isaac hired temporary help, when he could afford it, to get the work done. Toward summer's end they harvested alfalfa, stacking it with a pole derrick and Jackson fork, along with the natural hay that grew in the meadows. And when they weren't in the fields they were in the ditches constructing dams and diverting water to irrigate grains and gardens.

Isaac rarely stopped. Come early spring, the ewes dropped their lambs at the sheds near the Weiser River, where they remained, munching alfalfa, until the range greened up around the last of March. Most years the herders, ewes, and lambs had already started toward the hills by the first of April, where they lingered in meadows until May. Shearing crews from the Oregon, Utah and Idaho territories then trimmed the creatures' thick wooly blankets before herders ushered them to the high country. And there they stayed until October, when the ewe lambs were separated from the wethers, the old from the young, and all that would bring a profit were sold and shipped to Nebraska. Ewes were bred to rams with thick necks and fat noses, and a little before Christmastime everyone was home again.

With July feeling better and Pun's services no longer required at home, Isaac sent the Chinese herder back into the woods. For these last two months Daniel and Tom had worked alone. Before Tom left for the hills, Isaac promised he'd bring him back upon July's recovery, and he aimed to keep his word. Problem was, he'd have to send Richard up now, for Isaac still needed three men to herd sheep in the Idaho forest.

In his mind's eye, Isaac pictured Richard and Pun crossing the

Van Wyck stock driveway, heading toward the higher elevations. Pun would break toward the east, singing his Chinese songs, while Richard dipped west and cried among the trees. He could see his son now, slogging along, his nose running, his eyes dripping tears. He imagined the boy stopping at every ponderosa he passed, wrapping his arms around its trunk and sniffing its bark for the familiar scent of home. Some said ponderosas smelled of vanilla, others, of butterscotch; either way, Richard would think of his mother's cake and set to boo-hooing, and this worried Isaac. Richard would do all he could to protect the sheep, but he'd never hold a gun to a cattleman's head. It was this reluctance, Isaac feared, that might one day kill him.

Though Isaac hadn't heard a word from Silas Morrow's bunch, he knew in his bones he hadn't put the Mads Larson business behind him. Not long after Tom's return, he sent the foreman back to the woods, albeit briefly, under the guise of restocking the sheep camps. It was assurance he was after, and when Tom returned the following week with news that Morrow's men were on the far side of Brundage, a good distance yet from Richard and Daniel and Pun, Isaac slept with but one ear bent to the north instead of two.

In the days that followed he even allowed himself to contemplate attending not only the Independence Day celebration with Eliza and the children, but the get-together at the Grange Hall afterward. It was Doc Forbes who suggested it.

Isaac had run into Preston during one of his milk runs a week earlier. "Surely you can take one day off to join your family in town for a parade," Preston suggested, pointing out it was the celebration of the century. Isaac decided on the way home the doctor was right; they'd all earned a day off – he and Tom included – and if he could work out the details, they'd take it.

Lilly screeched when he told her the good news but her joy quickly turned to panic. Scurrying from one room to the next, she squealed she hadn't a costume for the parade or a dress for the dance afterward. July didn't care much for posing in a buckboard; it was the picnic she longed for – sampling her mother's first fried chicken of the year and dipping her tongue into a cold glass of lemonade. Raymond rejoiced too. But Richard and the others never got the good news, for they were committed to the mountaintop with nothing more than a jar of strawberry preserves to celebrate the season.

The next few afternoons blew past in a storm of activity while the women prepared for the trip to town. Lilly insisted on dressing up as something altogether different and far more dramatic this year, since she'd not been reelected to serve as the Statue of Liberty but would still be marching in the parade. Even though she'd never once cut a cow from a herd in her life, she decided to pose as the legendary markswoman, Annie Oakley.

Hunched over her mother's sewing machine, foot frantically working its pedal, Lilly constructed a skirt from the same bolt of calico Eliza had used to fashion curtains for the kitchen. Lilly wasn't the seamstress her mother was, but someday she'd head to town to assist Mrs. Abrams, as other girls in school had done. The woman owned a dress shop and would teach Lilly all she needed to know about stitching fancy skirts, and while Lilly's classmates would save their money to buy fabric for wedding dresses, Lilly would save hers for a train bound for New York City, as her goal was to perform on a stage with velvet curtains and gold braided sashes.

She snipped the thread from its spool, slipped on the skirt, and added a white blouse, scarlet bandana, and a loose leather belt. Posing in front of the mirror, she took one look at the girl staring back and wailed, "It doesn't work without boots, Ma!"

Eliza stood back, her head tilted in soft perusal, and in a tone far kinder than she usually employed with her oldest daughter, said, "Pa would love to buy you boots, Lilly, but we haven't got the money."

"Wait!" said Lilly, blinking. "Richard's got some I can use." With that, she whirled out the door, ran toward the barn, and inside, tore through a trunk pushed against the wall, through work shirts and overalls and gray felt coverlets, until she found what she was looking for. Plucking the boots from the bottom of the trunk, she kicked off her own shoes and stuffed her feet inside. The boots were easily two sizes too small, and when Eliza saw Lilly's feet jammed inside them, her toes bunched hard at the ends, she said, "You can't wear those. They'll hobble you like a horse." But Lilly being Lilly, she limped into the house and swore they fit just fine.

The next morning, the mockingbird sang before the rooster. Isaac was up at dawn, and as was his habit each July fourth, he shot his pearl-handled pistol into the air and whooped the cry of a soldier. Everyone hopped from their beds. The children especially were eager to see their chores done and the wagon headed for town.

July collected eggs from the hen house and fed the chickens. Raymond slopped the pigs. Lilly filled a basket with tin plates and cups and the silverware the family needed for their noontime picnic, while Eliza fried two chickens, built a pie, and baked two dozen biscuits. Tom and Isaac, meanwhile, milked the cows and readied the horses, and when that was done, went inside to change clothes for the celebration.

July sat at the edge of her bed in a pink cotton dress with a crisp underslip. She'd had no need to wear it, and hadn't tried it on since her birthday last December; it had grown tight across the chest and pinched a bit at her shoulders. The fabric groaned when she lifted her arms to plait her hair in the special way Pun had taught her. "Flench blaid," he'd called it. "Way dey do in Paris." She tied off the end with a matching ribbon and stood in front of the mirror to admire the result. She was pleased to find she'd grown nearly as tall as Richard.

By the time everyone climbed into the buckboard – Isaac and Eliza sitting in front, Raymond, Lilly, and July in back with the basket of chicken and pickles and baked goods between them – Tom had saddled his gelding, Brigham, and started out in front of them. The morning sun was warm on their faces as they drove into town, their moods as fine as the honeysuckle perfuming the air. Isaac gave the reins a snap, and to the surprise of the entire family, broke out in song.

> *Put your shoulder to the wheel, push along*
> *Do your duty with a heart full of song*
> *Let no one shirk, we all have work*
> *Put your shoulder to the wheel!*

It was his favorite, this hymn of toil and obligation, and everyone knew it well. They all joined in, stretching in their seats on the high notes, dipping on the low ones. Tom thrilled them all by singing the loudest.

"Why, Tom," enthused Eliza. "I never knew you could sing!"

The color in his cheeks rose, but the compliment didn't deter him. It occurred to July he was trying to out-do her pa, and when Isaac sang louder still, Tom followed suit. Her pa broke out laughing. Tom laughed too and it warmed everyone's heart to see that for one day, at least, they'd let their tribulations go.

How July loved her family. If Richard and Pun were there with them, the celebration would be very nearly perfect. She glanced toward the town of Morning Tree, the sheep grazing in open pastures on its outskirts, the poplars waving their welcome. She looked at the buildings, thought how pretty they were, gleaming on the horizon. Red, white and blue bunting hung from each rooftop and there was a banner erected at the town's entrance. She strained to read it but couldn't make it out until they were very nearly under it. "Congratulations, Idaho!" it proclaimed in gold cursive letters. "May 1890 be your best year yet."

And that, of course, was what July wished for them all.

Chapter Ten

Preston Forbes strolled the wooden sidewalk of Jefferson Street in his stand-up collar, polished shoes, and gray felt hat. He hitched his thumbs into his vest pockets and noted with satisfaction the progress the little town had made. He thought it a fine place to live and work and was pleased he'd made the decision to move to Morning Tree after laboring four long years as a physician's apprentice in San Francisco. The floors he'd swept, the books he'd devoured after the good doctor had gone to bed at night. Thinking back on it, he'd never stopped hungering for a practice of his own. It was the week after his twenty-second birthday that he finally packed a bag and fled for Idaho, unable to bear even one more day the shingle on the door that bore another man's name. And when he got his own shingle and his own door, when he rolled his name inside his mouth and let it go on the tip of his tongue, he smiled as he'd never smiled before.

Doctor Preston Forbes – what a ring it had to it!

His first winter was the hardest, and he spent a good deal of time playing catch-up. No doctor existed in Morning Tree and if folks weren't inclined to ride to Weiser, a distance of twenty miles or more, they weren't seen at all. The first month alone Preston delivered seven babies, treating many of them a few weeks later for various ills and wheezes. Soon enough he got to know their fathers too, and the sorry state of their fingers and toes. The men apparently made a habit of mashing them beneath some weighty chunk of hardware then letting the injury go until it was green with infection or black with gangrene. Although he only charged five dollars to amputate a toe, he was thinking of raising the price to ten, since he now had three years' experience and no competition.

Yes, Morning Tree was the place for him. It boasted a hotel and barbershop, a bank and general store. Though he wouldn't dream of stepping foot inside the saloon, he rather enjoyed the clatter of its piano as it wafted into his open window on a calm summer evening.

Owing to Preston's encouragement, a drugstore had recently been added to the town's landscape. The establishment abutted his office and featured myriad bottles of ornate design, as well as show globes filled with brightly colored liquids. In addition to prescribed medicines, the place sold shaving mugs and brushes, oils and paints and glassware. And there was a soda fountain that featured six flavors of ice cream, including fruit salad, his favorite.

As he strolled the wooden sidewalk, it began to fill with people from all across Idle Valley. The streets, too, filled. Horses and wagons and children clamored for their spots in the parade. How many teams of oxen would Preston count that day, their yokes decorated with American flags? How many women in purple sashes toting signs proclaiming "Mercy" and "Goodness" and "Love"? He paused, hands poised in his pockets, to grin at the wee ones scampering for penny candies tossed by the sheriff and mayor.

It was shaping up to be a fine day and he looked forward to the celebrations. A picnic on the knoll would follow the parade. Come evening, fireworks on the plaza would illuminate the dark Idaho sky so it sparkled like a rock candy necklace. Absentmindedly, he twisted the hairs of his mustache as he thought about the dance at the Grange Hall scheduled for later that night. He pictured a young woman in a pretty dress, calling July Caldwell specifically to mind. That she had captivated him was still something of a surprise, for while he was eleven years older, he was apparently none the wiser. His heart beat like a schoolboy's at the thought of her, and when all at once she appeared at the end of the walkway with her youngest brother in tow, he quickly pivoted and gazed the other way, wishing to appear nonchalant, as he was worried someone might guess the inner workings of his mind.

Moving on, he plied the crowd with polite hellos, shaking hands with all the men he knew and some he didn't. He tipped his hat to the women and tousled the feathery blonde hair of the boys.

When Emeline Houston rode past on a hay wagon driven by her banker father, Solomon, she sat up brightly and called Preston's name, addressing him as Doctor Forbes. She was perched on a throne of baled hay, holding a Bible in her left hand and a torch in her right.

"You make a fine symbol of justice!" he called out to her. Her sweet smile told him she was pleased and he thought the city council had done right to choose Emeline over Lilly Caldwell, who last year held the torch a bit too high.

His opinion was reinforced when Lilly suddenly sprang behind him, hooting, "Bet you can't guess who I am."

He halted, turned and smiled. "Hello Lilly."

She gave a dramatic little spin, nodding expectantly.

He eyed the outfit. "Calamity Jane?" he ventured.

"She's an old woman by now."

"Annie Oakley, then."

"That's it!" She gave a little jump and clapped her hands. Stepping forward, she looped her arm through his. "I've got to find my place in the parade," she told him, turning serious now, "so I can only visit a minute." Preston complimented her costume and she chatted demurely about its details, how it was just a little something she'd thrown together at the last minute. She emphasized how effortless it all was with a seemingly careless but altogether studied wave of her hand. Preston immediately saw through the charade – the careful tilt of her head and methodical swish of her hips – recognizing it as dress rehearsal for the New York stage.

As quickly as she'd transformed from country girl to socialite, she was back again. "Golly, I've got to go!" She hopped from the sidewalk into the street, hollering, "Be sure to watch for me, will you, Preston?" And with that, she scurried into the crowd. He watched her weave between crisscrossing wagons, her petticoats flying, and wondered about the strange little limp she seemed to have acquired since he'd last seen her. He considered asking her about it later at the Grange Hall, then thought better of it. She had her sights set on him, despite his giving her no encouragement whatsoever, and he'd do nothing to lead her on. He considered skipping the dance altogether when he turned to find July and her little brother very nearly upon him. Just like that, he changed his mind, for July was pretty as a fresh-picked rose. If she was planning to attend, he'd certainly be there too. "Well," he said, his face flushing, "isn't this a nice surprise."

"I got a penny to spend on a popcorn ball," announced Raymond. He unfurled his hand, revealing a single coin. "Pa give it to me."

"Aren't you the lucky one?" Preston said. He stepped back, putting some space between them. He assessed July with what he hoped was an air of casual observation. Since he'd seen her last, it seemed she'd filled out considerably; her cheeks were nicely padded, and the angles of her shoulders had softened some. "And what about you, young lady?" he asked. "Will you be buying a popcorn ball, too?" He instantly regretted the question and its tone, for in trying to deflect his interest in July, he'd made her seem a child no older than her brother.

She met his eyes briefly, glanced across the street. "I might buy a lemonade. I see they've got a washtub over there with some ice in it. We hardly ever get ice to home." She kept her gaze fixed on that spot in the distance as though reluctant to look his way.

"I was thinking the same thing myself," he said cheerfully, hoping to make amends. Damn these Caldwell women, he thought – first Eliza and now July. What was it about them that made him mangle his words so? Made him come out with precisely that which would offend them? Deep inside he knew it was him trying too hard; him wanting to please July or her mother so she'd put in a good word for Morning Tree's doctor.

He exhaled exuberantly. "Mind if I join you?"

"I don't mind," she said, but her hesitance told him she was uneasy. She'd likely caught him casting sheep's eyes at her while he was removing her stitches that day at the house. And though she was too polite to refuse his request, she made it plain she was wary of him, scowling at his gaze, which she surely took for admiration. She had no interest in holding herself up as a hero to Preston Forbes, he saw plain as the frown on her face.

"Hurry up, July," whined Raymond. He tugged on her fingers, urging her across the dirt road toward the candy stand.

"You don't even want that popcorn ball," she chided. "You want the flag inside the package."

"I'm gonna wave it during the parade," he told her. "Gonna holler Lilly's name too."

July turned to Doctor Forbes. "We got to go," she said before sailing off in the other direction.

"Give your folks my regards," he called after her. He waved goodbye, his hand lingering in the air, but she never looked back or otherwise indicated she'd heard. He stood there, feeling more awkward and alone than he had in a long time. Slowly he brought his hand down and stuck it in his pocket.

It wasn't until Solomon Houston, the corpulent banker with the blue, bulging vein splitting his forehead, clapped him on the back and offered to buy him a glass of lemonade that Preston smiled again.

* * *

After the parade, everyone rested on a blanket on the grass and recounted the parts they liked best.

"I liked the treats," said Raymond. A dab of sticky red sugar clung to the top of his lip. July said she thought he didn't care about the candy, that it was the flag he wanted, and he told her it was, before he knew a popcorn ball tasted so fine. He turned to their pa. "Can I have another?"

"No," said Isaac. "You'll get gut-wallered as it is."

July asked her ma what she liked best. Eliza said the Relief Society wagon and the women in their sashes. "Maybe next year I'll inquire about walking in the parade too," she told them. She held a parasol, which she tilted against the sun.

"What would your sash say, Mama?" Lilly wanted to know.

"BEST COOK THIS SIDE OF UTAH." Oh, how this surprised them, for their mother was never one to brag.

"Maybe I'll walk alongside you," Isaac chuckled, "only my sash'll say BEST PROVIDER TO THE BEST COOK THIS SIDE OF UTAH."

"Well, I want in on this one," Tom weighed in. "I'll march too, and my sash'll read BEST FORMAN TO THE BEST PROVIDER TO THE BEST COOK THIS SIDE OF UTAH."

Lilly sat up. "Well, I –"

"Never mind," said Eliza. They all laughed, and then it grew quiet as they again settled on the blanket. July asked Tom what he liked best about the parade. He said he couldn't pick a favorite, but when she pressed him, he said if he had to choose, he supposed it was the fellow on the bicycle decorated with streamers. "Although it was really those dogs in his basket that I liked best."

July said she liked the horses with the plumed head ornaments, then informed her family she might ride in the parade next year too.

"Birdy will never go for that," Lilly scoffed.

"She will if I coax her with a green apple," July put in, although she recalled past dress-up failures with animals and promptly kept quiet. At Easter one time, July dressed Tick and Bug in old bonnets of her mother's. Bug ran off, darting across the yard like a black and white bullet, and didn't come home for two days. When she finally trotted in, tongue hanging, the bonnet drooping around her neck, Isaac scolded, "Bug liked to strangle herself with that thing." But then he rounded the corner, chuckling to himself.

"You should try out for the Statue of Liberty," Lilly said as she kicked off her boots. She rubbed the blisters sprouting at her heels and big toes. "Even you could beat out Emeline Houston – why, she's quiet as a mouse, and far as I can see, looks like one too." Lilly scrunched her nose, held her hands floppy to her breasts and made little chewing sounds with her teeth stuck out.

Raymond snickered but the remark didn't sit well with July. "Don't make fun of Emeline. She's the nicest girl in school."

"All right, then," Lilly amended, rolling her eyes, "she's a *nice* mouse." She looked up, caught sight of Preston Forbes at the top of the knoll and announced, "There's Doctor Forbes – he's going to dance with me tonight whether he wants to or not." And with that she was off, barefoot and fresh-faced, her sprightly gait giving no indication she'd just marched a quarter mile in boots two sizes too small.

Raymond jumped up and ran the other way, eager to meet up with friends he hadn't seen since school let out in May. Isaac called after him to be back by noon. He turned to Eliza and said he thought he'd catch up with the doings at the auction.

"Bring me a surprise," she told him, smiling.

To July's delight, he said he just might do that. "I think I'll head out, too," she told her mother, "go over to Van Dyke's and sip a strawberry spinner – Pa gave me a nickel."

"You'll stay right here and take your rest," said Eliza, patting the blanket, "and that's *all* you'll do."

"Oh, Ma, I'm fit as a fiddle – Doctor Forbes said so himself."

"I don't care what he said, you're peeked as pie dough. You'll sit here with me until your color comes back."

July flopped back onto the blanket. "But I *do* feel fine," she complained. "Only time my scar pinches is when I'm digging carrots and such."

"Or carding mattresses," Eliza pointed out.

"Or milking cows," Tom put in.

"You're just saying that 'cause you like to milk cows," July countered. "Next to digging ditches it's your favorite thing to do." Tom would gladly milk a thousand cows if it kept him snuggled in some cool, dark cranny on the ranch. As it was, he'd offered well in advance to head home just before sunset to tend to the animals, which meant the family could stay in Morning Tree all night if they wanted to.

If there was one thing July aimed to do it was have fun. She'd spent far too many weeks cooped up as an invalid. Besides, she couldn't remember a time when her father had let them all stay for the dance before; in the past they'd always been among the first to leave, but having Tom at the ranch freed up her pa, and whenever Tom got the chance to take time for himself, he didn't hesitate to grab it. Once when Isaac insisted it was Tom's turn to stay behind and kick up his heels, Tom's face grew so long and his disposition so sour, everyone in the family understood there was nothing so entertaining to him as a quiet evening at home.

It wasn't long after Lilly and Raymond returned that Isaac wandered over, his arms filled with six ceramic chamber pots. "Made us a nice trade," he said proudly. He stacked the portable toilets at the edge of the blanket. "Four milk cans for six pots – now we got one for each room in the house."

"No one can say we haven't got a pot to pee in now." Lilly grinned broadly.

"Lilly, please," Eliza admonished, though anyone could see she was holding back a smile, "we're just about to eat here." With that, the family bowed their heads while Isaac said the blessing. He thanked Heavenly Father for the food and the fine day, for the sweet songs of birds and the feel of sunshine on their faces. Just before closing he asked the Lord to keep Richard and Daniel and Pun safe from harm. "Don't let the wolves get em, nor cattlemen, either," he put in, and when he was done, the family chorused a vibrant "Amen."

Eliza cracked open the picnic basket and passed around the food. Tom heaped his plate with drumsticks and biscuits and chokecherry jelly, swearing he'd never tasted fried chicken so good.

"M-m-m," agreed Raymond, licking his lips. He sat with his head thrown back, draining the last of the juice from the pickle jar. He let go with a burp as lusty as a bullfrog's.

"For pity sake, Raymond, where are your manners?" asked Eliza.

"In the pig pen, Mama." He giggled, and all but Eliza laughed.

July lay flat on her back, letting her ankles flop loosely. "I'm full as a tick," she said, patting her stomach, though she couldn't roust a burp as healthy as Raymond's.

"Got some color in your cheeks, too," said Tom. He looked across at Eliza.

"Oh, aren't you the sly one," Eliza told him. "Don't worry, Tom. You can go on home without us. I'll keep July right here with me and you can spend the whole night on the ranch by your lonesome."

"I *am* feeling better, Ma," July reminded her mother.

"I heard you the first time, dear."

"You'll let me go to the dance, then?"

"You don't know how to dance," scoffed Raymond. He crammed his entire fist into the jar and rimmed the bottom with one finger, scraping up the last of the spices. Plucking out a bit of red pepper, he poked it into his mouth.

"Not everyone who goes to a dance knows *how* to dance," Lilly put in. "Some go to visit old friends, some to meet new ones." She nodded toward the crest of the knoll. "Like that boy over there. He's been staring at July since he and his mama sat down to dinner. I'll wager he'll be sharing a plank with her before the night's over." She grinned knowingly, although what she knew July couldn't say.

All eyes turned toward the top of the hill.

The boy sat with his knees up, his forearms propped against them, chewing a blade of grass. He must have seen the Caldwells glance his way, for all at once he dropped his gaze and self-consciously plucked at the blanket. The woman sitting with him was talking to Solomon Houston's wife, a stout woman with a set of fleshy chins and a nose as pink as a piglet's. The two shared a laugh and then Mrs. Houston leaned forward to grasp the woman's hand and give it a squeeze.

Isaac sat up for a better look, peering hard into the distance. "July, you recognize that boy?"

When she had him in her sights, she said, "Looks like Rory Morrow."

Everyone perked up at that. Tom hopped to his haunches and Eliza to her knees. She stretched her neck and said, "You don't suppose Silas Morrow is here too, do you?"

"Don't see him," said Isaac, his tone wary. He looked this way and that, but sensing nothing out of the ordinary, settled back down on the blanket.

"Well, what are they doing here?"

"Celebratin, I suppose."

"Don't they have a celebration of their own to attend?"

"What are they gonna celebrate in Badger, Mama?" asked Lilly. "They've only got one store and a school as small as a bed mite."

"I don't like that they're here," Eliza clucked. "Anything to do with Silas Morrow makes me skittish."

Isaac picked a thumbnail. "Don't know why you're gettin so riled, Eliza. Not so long ago you was the one defending him."

"What's that supposed to mean?"

"Means you got a soft spot for cowboys."

They all caught that one, even if no one had the nerve to speak on it. July itched to know what it meant, for every now and then her pa got fired up about something in their ma's past and set to stewing on it. Anyone could see he hadn't let it go, nor had her ma, for Eliza sat still as a heron. "I don't know what business his wife's got in Morning Tree, is all," she told him, her chin pointed sharp at her husband.

"Maybe Silas is looking to take out a loan," Isaac told her, "and he sent his wife to butter up the banker."

"Does he expect he'll get a loan on a holiday?"

"Hell sakes, Eliza, how do I know?"

It was quiet a moment, but instead of changing the subject, or at least letting it go, July asked why Mr. Morrow hadn't come too. It was Tom who posed an answer, said he was likely up to Brundage with his men. He asked Isaac if he thought Silas left Mads in charge of the ranch. Isaac shook his head, said Mads was too hot headed. "Though I doubt Morrow's got the sense God gave him to put someone cooler in charge. Be just like him to turn a devil like that loose on his family."

July jabbed her tongue at her back tooth, chewed on a piece of chicken she pulled out there. "If Rory stays for the dance, I'll just ask him where his pa is."

"You'll do no such thing," Isaac scolded. "We ain't befriendin no Morrows, nor cowboys, neither." July made no comment and therefore no promise, for something in her head told her Rory wasn't a cowboy. And while he wasn't a friend yet either, he would be, and soon.

Chapter Eleven

The dance didn't start until after the fireworks, when the night lit up like woods afire. Blue streaks scooted across the sky while orange sparks spit like flames under timber. Pinpricks of light fell like stars and disappeared into the creamy white band they called the Milky Way. And the noise! Ground-rattling explosions followed by shrill, spinning whistles. Girls screamed and covered their ears while boys ducked at each throttling volley. Men whooped and women cheered, and when it was all over everyone lingered a while, the smell of gunpowder sharp in their noses.

They marveled at the meaning of it all – freedom and liberty and a place to call their own. Idaho was named the nation's forty-third state just one day earlier, and as such, the residents of Idle Valley vowed to stand as one, even if only for a single night in the summer of 1890.

There'd been plenty to fight about. Cattlemen still clashed with sheepmen, and contempt for Mormons – Chinese, too – was as strong as ever. Some said Latter-day Saints were disdained because they were a blasphemous lot, their religion based on superstition and voodoo shenanigans. That Mormon men took up to twenty or thirty wives whenever they had a mind to set folks' teeth on edge. Others argued it wasn't plural marriage that threatened the good citizens of the nation but the Mormons' influence on government – there was just too much of it, for Church members were a tight-knit group and had all but filled the entire state of Utah with their own. The Gentiles of Idaho, though, weren't about to bow to a Mormon government. They clamped down on the Saints, as some other states had done, disenfranchising Church members by stripping them of their right to vote or hold office or serve on a jury, all in the name of righting the wrong that was polygamy. Anyone with a brain could work out for themselves what it was really about: squashing the Mormons' power and taking away their ability to fill City Hall with the friends and relatives of their beloved prophets.

But on that Friday evening in early July, a brief spirit of cooperation enveloped the little town of Morning Tree, for if townsfolk couldn't embrace one another, at least they could ignore those that rankled them most. They wandered with willing hearts into Roberts Hall where men settled themselves on inverted washtubs with their fiddles in their laps while their wives juiced lemons for lemonade. Tables were covered with blue-checkered cloths and lined with pies of all variety – raisin and apricot and sweet and sour huckleberry – and there were green apple dumplings by the dozens. Before everything had been arranged, before the women gave the signal to start, the men stomped their feet and struck their strings and called for the dancing to begin.

The night was a memory maker, some would later say, a time when women had no patience for the gossip and petty cruelty of small town life. Lydia Morrow proved it true enough when she approached Eliza Caldwell and offered her hand. That Eliza took to Lydia gave her pause, for while she would have taken Silas's wife for an angry and resentful woman, the crinkles at the corners of her eyes spoke more to her compassion than any ill will she might have harbored against the wife of her husband's enemy.

Eliza could see how the woman, with her easy attitude, fit in anywhere. Why, she hadn't even held a parasol to shade her face from the sun, so sturdy was her construction. Eliza doubted the cattleman's wife had ever excused herself from a gathering with a headache to spend the evening hunkered beneath the covers, sipping Chinamen's tea. No, Lydia Morrow wasn't one to get headaches. If anything, she gave them, and that was the difference between them.

"I see your daughter's feeling better," Lydia said, smiling.

"She is, thank you," said Eliza. She looked toward the pies and let her gaze linger there, though she wasn't the least bit hungry. She turned to Lydia. "Your son helped my Julia after she fainted not so long ago and I really ought to thank him for it. Maybe you'll do it for me?"

"I will, but there's no need." Lydia's smile slipped slightly. "He was raised to do right," she added, "just in case you're wondering."

"I'm not wondering, not one bit," Eliza said a little too quickly. Truth was, she found Lydia's comment disconcerting. Instead of getting deeper into a conversation she couldn't comfortably get out of, however, she excused herself and quietly walked away.

July sat on a hay bale, the dry grass piercing her backside, while she nibbled the edges of a cinnamon dumpling. Though she didn't know Rory well – he went to a different school, a white clapboard building clear up to Badger – she'd had her eye on him since Lilly pointed him out at the picnic. July caught him watching her as she perused the pies. Each time she broke off a sample and popped it into her mouth, she casually looked up as if she hadn't a care in the world, spotted him inching closer. When she finally sat down with her selection – smoothed her dress over her knees and waited for him to saunter over with his hello – she began to wonder if he'd changed his mind, for it took him a long time to venture forth with his greeting. She'd almost finished eating before he shuffled her way at last, hands in his pockets, a smile on his lips.

"Hullo July, remember me?"

She licked a dab of filling from her fingers. "Of course I do," she said, striving for nonchalance. She didn't want him to think her too eager, for she'd hardly sorted out the peculiar feeling in her chest. Never before had she cared whether a boy looked directly at her or far above her head, but now it mattered. She wanted him to see her. She wanted to see him too. She shifted on her bale to get a better look, as she hadn't perused him as particularly as she might have that day she passed out at the river. His hair stuck up here and there as though he'd been wrestling with friends, and his face, warmed by the sun, was the color of a bruised peach. A dozen freckles dotted his cheeks. Now that he stood before her she thought he carried himself with an assurance most boys lacked.

"You got some color to your cheeks now," he told her. "You recovered from your spell?"

July felt his gaze lingering at the lacy bib of her dress, curious about the scar beneath it. She guessed Rory's pa had filled him in on the details, and she brought her fingers to her collarbone and touched the place where the pink snake began. "Doctor Forbes says I'll be good as new by the time we're back in school." She looked across the way, found Preston chatting with Emeline Houston, the banker's daughter. Emeline caught July's gaze and waved, then said something to Preston. They both chuckled and a moment later Emeline pranced over and kneeled at July's side. She gripped July's arm. "I'm so happy you're up and about. We all wanted to come see you after your accident but Miss McBride said it wasn't proper. Now that it's summer, though, she can't stop us – not me, at least!" Miss McBride, their teacher, was a commanding woman with more rules than students. She'd listed fifteen transgressions and their accompanying punishments in a stiff white line on the chalkboard, reminding each child what he'd suffer for straying from the rules. Talking with your mouth full at lunchtime earned a teaspoon of chili powder on the tip of the tongue, whereas speaking without being called on landed you in the corner. Forgetting your homework was the worst – five hard raps to the knuckles.

"Why wasn't it proper?" July wanted to know.

Emeline's eyes slipped toward Rory, then back again. She hesitated as she wasn't one to repeat a rumor. Instead of saying what she'd heard about Silas Morrow's men, how they might have had something to do with July's accident, Emeline she said she didn't know what, specifically, was on Miss McBride's mind that day. "Maybe she thought we'd ask a bunch of hair-brained questions," she suggested, though Rory, for one, saw through Emeline's charade.

"My pa had nothing to do with July's accident," he put in. He looked at Emeline with earnest eyes and her cheeks flushed red as a rooster's comb.

"I didn't mean to imply –"

"But that other man might of," said July. Rory asked what other man, and she told him the gangly one, with a face as sharp as barbed wire.

"Mads?" Rory thought on this a minute and July could tell he was weighing the possibilities. "Well, I dunno. He's got a dark side, but there's a bright one too. He saved my life once."

"Mads Larson saved your life?" Emeline sat up at this, for clearly the gossip-mongers hadn't churned up this part of the story, though she seemed well-versed in the names of Silas's men.

"This is my friend, Emeline Houston," July told him. "We're in school together at Morning Tree." To some other boy she might have added, "Whatever you got to say to me, you can say to her too," but something held her back. She thought maybe one day she'd like to share a secret with Rory Morrow, a secret she told no one but the great night sky and its stars. She hoped he might save his story about Mads Larson just for her, but then he asked Emeline if she'd like to hear it. Emeline said she would, and scooted forward so as not to miss a word.

He sat on the bale next to July, asked Emeline if she was sure she could handle it.

"I think so. Yes."

"All right then. When I was ten, I took off in a rowboat on a pond alongside our house. I'd been told to stay out of the boat and stick to the dock 'cause I couldn't swim, but I'd dug a bunch of worms from Ma's garden and had my fishin pole and it seemed that boat was just callin my name, waitin for me to climb in. Naturally, I did."

The sight of Emeline clinging to Rory's words like a vine to a fencepost rankled July, and she jumped in at the break. "Is this a long story or a short one, 'cause I ain't got all night."

Rory smiled. "Ain't too long," he said.

"All right. You can tell it."

Emeline sat on the floor, cross-legged, and settled in. "Yes, Rory. Tell us what happened."

"Well, I cast my line out, and dags if I didn't get a bite hardly before I knew it. Turned out it was a clump of pond grass but I didn't know that at the time, so I'm tuggin on it, and to get a little leverage I stand up in the boat. Long about then Mads spots me, hollers at me to get down before I fall on my face. Well, looking up at him like that got me off balance, which got the boat to heavin, and sure as the world –"

"You fell in!"

"I fell in."

"But you couldn't swim."

"That's right, and though Mads wasn't the best swimmer in the world, he come to my rescue, charged that pond like a bull at a wrangler, then jumped into the water. I was kickin and splashin and carryin on, 'cause I was drownin, see?" Here, he paused, the natural tint of his face deepening, so that anyone could see the memory haunted him. Heaving a sigh, he picked up where he left off. "Mads snatched my collar and yanked it hard, hollered at me to calm down. He wrapped one arm around my neck and kicked back to shore, me sputterin all the while. When we got back, we lay in the dirt, our chests heavin, thinking on what might have been, which was me floating at the bottom of that pond. I'll tell you one thing, I ain't been near it since. Ain't been in a rowboat either."

"Your pa whip you for that?" July wanted to know. "My pa would've whipped me purple."

Rory nodded. "He come runnin to see what all the commotion was, and when Mads told him I fell into the pond, yeah, he licked me. Like to have stripped the hide off my backside with a razor strap, but it sunk in I'd done wrong 'cause I never took that boat out again. Not that I'd want to, trust me."

Emeline's eyes grew wide, for her own pa had never raised his hand to her, nor uttered a harsh word in her presence. "Your pa whipped you after you almost drowned?"

"How else you impress a ten-year-old to stay away from the water?"

"Maybe you just teach him to swim."

"Well, no one ever taught me, and I ain't got no interest to learn."

July could see by the gleam in Emeline's eyes that she just might offer to teach him, but then Mrs. Houston called from the far side of the room. Emeline's face folded, and she hesitated before waving at her mother. "I've got to go," she said. Standing, she kissed July on the cheek, told Rory she enjoyed making his acquaintance, then dashed off to join her mother.

After she'd gone, Rory turned to July. "Emeline enjoyed making my acquaintance."

"Don't get all puffed up. Our teacher makes us say that."

"Well, look at you," he said, sitting back. "I think you might be jealous."

"I ain't jealous. Emeline's my best friend, practically, and anyway, what have I got to be jealous of?"

"Nothin, I guess." It seemed there wasn't much left to say, and then Rory spoke, his tone serious now. "You might like to know I rode out to Valentine to have a look at that bridge – it seems to me the river washed it out."

"'Cause that's what your pa told you." July guessed Rory would support his father, just as she'd support her own, even though she would never believe her own pa capable of such a deed. Tom, though? He sometimes got that faraway look she'd seen in Mads' eyes, although she'd never known him to kick a chicken or pull a pig's ear out of spite.

"My pa never told me nothin," Rory objected. "I figured it out on my own."

Whatever Silas Morrow said or didn't say, July knew she wouldn't hold it against Rory. She could see in his expression the same sincerity that molded Richard's face, and so she listened when something inside told her to believe him. "When you were up to Valentine did you happen to see my hat? It's black and shaped like a bowl and it's got a ribbon wrapped around the crown."

Rory screwed up his face, trying to remember. "Don't recollect I saw any hat at all."

"I was wearing it the day the bridge broke down. When it fell off, Richard didn't think to grab it."

"Richard?"

"My brother. Ma actually bought the hat for him but Pa said bowlers were for barbers and such. Pa made such a fuss about it, Ma gave it to me."

"Why?" Rory snorted. "You gonna be a barber when you grow up?"

"I got no interest in cutting hair." When she said nothing more, he added, "How about you and me ride out to look for it? I bet we can find it, if we try."

"We can't do that," said July. "If Pa found out I was poking around Valentine, he'd take the hide off my backside like your pa took yours. Anyway, aren't we supposed to be enemies?"

"I don't care one way or another if you come from a sheep family. To my way of thinkin, sheep's got as much right to graze the open range as cattle do."

This response surprised July, and made her think Rory Morrow was nothing like his father. Which got her wondering. "I'm curious why you and your ma are here today without your pa," she said.

"Pa ain't social, it's Ma that likes to dance."

"It set my own ma back some to see you here today," she confessed. "She gets nervous real easy, probably because she ain't been around Gentiles much. She don't know what to say to them."

Rory glanced toward Eliza Caldwell. "She don't look nervous now."

July looked across the dance floor to find her mother do-si-doing around Lilly and two of her friends from Sunday meeting. Eliza pranced across the dance floor, her back arched fine as a pony's. She clutched a handful of skirt in her slim white hands and smiled as she dipped behind Solomon Houston. Mrs. Houston glided toward the other side and took her place next to Lydia Morrow. Rory's mother was high-stepping it with a heavy-set man whose belly strained his vest. July didn't know the man's name, but she recognized him from her father's milk run. She recollected he bought more top-milk than the Tinsleys and Janks combined, and reckoned he drank it all himself. Doctor Forbes, deep in conversation with the mayor, stood near the door. He fingered his mustache and nodded his head, and all at once he clapped the mayor on the shoulder, then doubled over in laughter. He was a smooth apple, that one. July looked around and when she saw Lilly heading his way she smiled a secret smile, for it meant Preston's watery gaze would now alight upon her sister's face and leave July's alone.

Her pa sat on a hay bale, his elbow propped against a table featuring a dozen different pies. His legs were crossed at the knees, one foot tapping absently in time to the music while he watched her. July could see the little wheel in his brain turning, spinning ideas and worries, both real and imagined. On the way home in the wagon he'd want to know about her conversation with Rory. And except for the part about deciding right then and there to meet Rory at Valentine, July intended to tell her pa the truth. "He told me the river knocked that bridge out, just like his pa said, and that his ma came to Morning Tree to dance." The light would fade from Isaac's eyes when he learned the news was as bland as that, and then he'd bellow and blow and holler his curse words, for if he couldn't blame Silas Morrow for knocking out the bridge at Valentine, he'd blame him for something else.

July turned to Rory. "How you planning to slip away from your house?"

"As it happens, I just got over the grippe. I'd still be at Brundage with Mads and Slack and Blake Neely if I hadn't got sick. Mads sent me home with a fever, which didn't set well with Ma. I guess she thought he should've pulled a doctor outta his hat or seen me home himself, but I'll tell you what – I can feign a fever as good as the next fellow. When I get home I'll tell Ma the cold air at the fireworks must of set me back some. That'll keep me on the ranch a few more days and we can slip off to Valentine on Sunday, when everyone else is to church. What do you think of that idea?"

"You sure came up with it easy."

"I got good reason."

July stared at him bold as a jaybird, for his smile told her she was his inspiration. "You mean me?"

"I do."

She sat up proud and strong. "All right, then. I'll do the same as you – say I'm sick and can't get out of bed. I think my ma will go for it."

"Let's shake on it," he said, offering the pinkie of his right hand.

She glanced quickly at her pa. He must have grown tired of peering so long in her direction because he'd wandered off to talk to the man in the too-tight vest. Seeing she was safe from her father's gaze, she locked her little finger around Rory's and gave it a squeeze.

"I won't let you down," he promised. And just like that, July had herself a secret.

* * *

"I seen you talking to the Morrow boy at the dance tonight," her pa told her in the wagon on the way home. "How many times I got to tell you to stay clear of him? You're the daughter of a sheepman and it won't do to have you mixin with no cattlemen."

"He's a nice boy, Pa," Lilly said in July's defense. "Emeline Houston told me so herself."

"Even so," said Eliza, "there's no point in pursuing his friendship. He's a Gentile and a cowboy – what good could come of it?" No one in the family caught the look she gave Isaac, save Isaac himself.

"She's not marrying him, Ma," Lilly put in. "What's the harm in visiting?"

July grunted. "I'm sitting right here and you're all talking around me like I'm some sort of haunt in a dead man's wagon."

"You're not a haunt in a dead man's wagon," reproached Isaac, "you're a daughter in *my* wagon, and you best not forget it."

"I won't forget it," July told him, but the moment the words left her lips, she let his warning go.

Chapter Twelve

July didn't say much on the way home, practicing as she was for her stomachache. She began complaining of a knot in her gut and an ax in her head late Saturday afternoon. Just before supper she headed for bed. Once she'd sunk beneath the covers, she used her tiny voice to persuade Eliza she was miserable as a bird fallen from its nest. "But if I feel better in the morning, I'll go to church with you and Pa," she told her, leaning weakly on one elbow.

"Posh," said Eliza, "you won't be going to church in the morning. You're running to the privy every ten minutes as it is, July. How do you expect to get through Sunday meeting?" She pressed a warm palm against July's cool forehead and turned to peer at Isaac in the kitchen. "I can't cipher it," she called out to him. "She's got no fever at all."

Isaac sat on a stool, sucking a chicken neck. It was the last piece in Friday's picnic basket, and if he didn't eat it, Tom would. "Jasper Janks tells me the grippe's going around," he said, licking his fingers. "Why don't you make her a cup of Pun's recipe? Might settle her stomach, some."

Eliza set about filling the iron teapot with water from the pump. July heard her mother in the kitchen, popping lids from the metal tins in the cupboard. A moment later, a spoon tinkled against a porcelain cup. "Works better when Pun puts it together," Eliza said as she shuffled into the room. She handed July the fragrant liquid and nodded as the child touched her tongue to the cup's hot rim and gingerly sipped its contents.

When Isaac got up from his stool to wash his hands, July made a show of setting her tea on the nightstand, flinging back the covers, and running to the privy in the back yard. She sat on the hard wooden seat in the dark, listening to the call of a great horned howl, while counting to one hundred. Once she'd gone back into the house, she clutched her stomach, repeating the process twice more before crawling into bed for the last time that evening. She feigned a lively burp, closed her eyes and smiled smugly under the covers, thinking her acting far superior to Lilly's. And when she rolled over and began to drift off in earnest, she was already dreaming about the little black bowler and how good it would look, propped decidedly on her head.

* * *

The fat brown rooster crowed just as the sun showed its face on the hillside. July awoke, warm and rested and more than a little famished since she'd barely eaten a morsel since dinnertime the day before. But it wasn't until she rubbed the sleep from her eyes that she remembered she was pretending to be a sick little bird, unable to chirp for her breakfast. She sat up and gazed over at Lilly, took in the arch of her sister's back, the rise and fall of her slender shoulders beneath the blanket. How many times, July wondered, had she awakened in the middle of the night, startled by a thump on the rooftop or the call of coyotes down by the corral, only to look over at Lilly and draw comfort from her sleeping form, her gentle wheezing and reassuring presence? July lay back and closed her eyes, not wanting to dwell too long on the deception she'd planned, for thinking on it would only make her stomach ache for real.

The family began to stir at last and it wasn't long before Eliza rustled into the room to feel July's forehead. July moved just enough to let her mother know she was alive, and with that small bit of encouragement, Eliza tucked the blanket into the mattress and kissed her cheek. As soon as everyone had piled out the door and clicked it softly behind them, July bounded from bed, peeked out her bedroom window and watched the bobbing, springy gait of the wagon as it disappeared with her family.

Scurrying to the front door, she opened it a crack and peered at Tom, keeping an eye on him until he hoisted himself onto his horse and trotted toward the creek. He'd spend all day at the water's edge, tinkering with his dikes and dams, repairing damage done by beavers and working through dinner. He wouldn't look up until his stomach rumbled near suppertime and then he'd wander back to the ranch. By then, July's ma and pa would be home from Morning Tree. Her father would find the note she'd left him on her slate, the one with the shaky handwriting she'd practiced until it looked just right.

> *Dear Pa,*
> *I got lonesome and it seemed Birdy did too. I took us for*
> *a ride. Maybe the fresh air will do my stomach good.*
> *Love, July*

Her pa would never guess she'd trotted off to Valentine not twenty minutes after he'd left for church, nor would he imagine she'd spent an hour with Rory Morrow. July worked out in her mind just how it would go upon her return that night, how she'd wobble in, complaining of dizziness and dehydration, berating herself for having believed she was fit to ride when her head felt thick as ram's wool. They'd drink it in too, for she'd never given them reason not to – not counting the time she and Richard pulled the mean trick of catching chickens and letting them go in Jim Goodnight's house. Afraid of a licking, she and Richard denied knowing anything about chickens roosting in his loft, their droppings gathering soggy as mud pies and stinking clear to heaven. It was the only time July had lied to her parents, but then she'd never wanted anything so badly until she'd lost her bowler, and then met Rory Morrow.

All the way to Valentine she congratulated herself on her cleverness. She even made up a tune concerning just how smart she was and hummed it to the trees. The morning sun felt fine on her face, and for the first time since the accident her scar wasn't tugging at her skin and making it itch. She breathed the goodness in, tipped her chin to the sky and had a chat with Heavenly Father. "Can't You persuade Pa I'm a better herder than Richard, Lord?" she asked, thinking if it were up to God, He'd never tell her it wasn't right for a girl to head to the hills on her own. But the Lord had given her pa the authority to keep her to home if he wanted to, and it had taken all her power – and most of her ma's too – to persuade Isaac to let her go along with Richard that day of the accident. But now? Her pa would just as soon nail the soles of her shoes to the porch steps than let her herd sheep to Brundage. "Hell sakes, July," he'd say. "Silas Morrow's men liked to kill you once. You aim to let them succeed?"

She thought on this another mile or two and was beginning to feel a bit down when she spotted Rory in the distance. Her heart lifted high as the treetops to see him trotting toward her on his Indian pony, his hat slung back on his head. When he stood in his stirrups and waved, she nudged Birdy, hurrying her along, and when the two horses met, they greeted by bumping noses.

"I was worried you couldn't get away," Rory told her, turning his horse to ride alongside her.

"I feigned a sickness to get out of Church – the rest of them went on without me."

"How'd you do it?"

"High-tailed it to the privy four times last night – just sat out there and twiddled my thumbs and counted to one hundred."

"Dags!" snorted Rory. "That's a good one, July. I never thought of that."

She liked the way he said her name – 'Joo-lye,' with just the slightest twang to it. "How'd you get away?" she asked.

"Got up early and did my chores, though I left the stall-mucking to Pa. Reckon I'll pay for it when I get home."

"I don't want you to take a licking on account of me."

"Pa doesn't lick me much anymore – I've grown too old and tall. He'll just holler some at Ma for letting me go."

"I don't want your ma to take a licking, either."

"She can hit hard as him, I guess."

July grinned despite herself, then nodded toward the big bundle of gear in his saddlebags. "You spending the night or what?"

Rory twisted in his saddle to inspect the baggage in the back. "That's my tripod," he told her, indicating with his chin the three wooden legs he'd gathered in a bundle. "It's a gizmo that steadies cameras so photographs come out clear." He nodded toward a leather satchel lashed to his horse's opposite hip. "That there's my camera."

"You lugged a camera out here?"

"Got it from a catalog," he said. "Cost me fourteen dollars. I'll take your picture, if you like."

"What would I do with it? Hang it on the wall and admire my freckles?"

"You'd give it to me, and I'd put it in my picture book."

She hardly knew what to make of that – or of him. Here he was, a boy with a camera, a tripod, and his very own picture book. "What you need with all that stuff, anyway?"

"I got no intention to herd cattle all my life," he said, his voice stern now. "Ain't takin over my pa's ranch, either. I'll leave it to Ma if it comes to that – she's the one with the head for ciphering and bill-tracking, anyway."

"If you're not gonna herd cattle, what're you gonna do?"

"Work as a photographer, open my own shop in Morning Tree." He told her he'd seen a whole slew of photographs tacked to the wall of the general store taken by a Montana man name of L.A. Huffman. Told her too how the pictures had captured his attention and held it, like some sort of mysterious and marvelous glue. There were photos of roundup outfits and sheepherders, of buffalo hunters carving skins and tongues. But there was one photo in particular – a picture of a young warrior the Cheyenne called Snake Whistle – that captured his attention. What a grand figure that Indian made, with his deerskin moccasins and furry bracelets wrapped snug around his ankles. The red man's hair fell halfway down his back, and on his head he wore a dress of sprightly feathers. Clearly he'd been posed, Rory said smartly, for surely no Indian thought to sit in a chair so just his profile showed. It was this notion that had so infatuated him, that put him to a mind he too would pose people someday, in their homes and on the prairies.

"Seems to me the only thing that Huffman fellow got wrong is that he photographed a lot more men than women – as for me, I plan to fix it so it's the other way around, for there's plenty of men want portraits of their wives and children – why, I even met a man once who asked me to take a picture of his dog, and hoo! That critter was the rangiest thing I've seen." They both laughed, and then Rory's gaze lit on July's face and settled there. "But a girl as pretty as you – I could take a thousand pictures and never quite catch the light in your eyes – the gold behind the brown."

Rory's admiration warmed July's blood and set her face on fire. "I guess I don't mind if you take my picture," she told him, although she felt shy about it.

He looked around. "Where you want to pose?"

"What's wrong with where I am?"

"Sun's not right," he said. "How about over there?" He pointed to a clump of willows behind the old Valentine place.

"We can't go there – that shack is haunted."

Rory said it wasn't haunted, but inhabited by the tender spirits of children. Still she balked, and so Rory suggested a spot near the trees beyond the house, and July agreed to try it. They walked down to the creek, now empty of its water, and Rory suggested she sit on a rock, one knee propped up, casual-like, her hands resting in her lap. "Smile when I count to three," he instructed. "Everyone always looks like they're fixin to die in these things. When I get my own shop, I aim to change that too."

"How you going to do that when no one wants their bad teeth showing?"

"The hounds with rotten teeth can frown," he said. "But pups like you, they got to smile." The shutter clicked, and Rory captured for time and all eternity the sweet look of consternation on July's face. In later years, when he turned the photograph over in his ink-stained hands, he referred to it, if only in his mind, as his portrait of July.

Hopping from the rock, July raced to the camera and peeked inside the box. "Where is it?" she said. "Can I see it now?"

"Got to develop it first." Rory released the camera from its base and hefted it to July while he folded the tripod. "Once I do that," he said, swapping the tripod for the camera, "we'll have to come up with a new plan so I can show it to you."

Anticipation died in July's face. "I don't know as I can arrange it. It took a lot to get here today."

"I know how you feel," Rory said, nodding. "Lying makes me queasy too, though I done it today so I could see you, and if I have to, I'll do it again."

Her heart beat faster then, and she confessed she would too.

Rory suggested they venture down to the fallen bridge to try and find her bowler. July again hesitated, saying now that they'd come all this way, she wasn't sure she could do it. Rory understood why she'd be a little frightened, said he'd be right there with her, holding her hand if she wanted him to, sticking with her all the way. She shook her head, said it was more than that – not just the bridge and its tattered remnants, although that was bad enough, but the skins and bones of the ewes and lambs strewn upon the rocks. "I hadn't thought much about them until just this minute, but I heard Tom tell Pa it was an awful sight, and I don't know that I want to see it."

He thought on this, chewing his lip while glancing at the water, as though appraising it. It seemed then he was wrestling with his own reluctance, but when he again looked at July, he sat up a little, said, "I'll go down to the river myself – leave you here, if you want. I won't be gone but a minute."

July imagined that while he was trying to be brave, he was scared he might fall in. She couldn't guess how that might happen, unless he hurled himself from the shore, but his fears were his, as hers were hers, so she suggested a compromise. "How about we go together? Watch out for one another?"

Rory said he liked that idea, and so they rode their horses toward the lowest spot on the river, where the bottom reached up and showed its rocky belly. July scanned the shore for old bleached bones, and once or twice sucked in her breath when they came upon a skeleton. Each time, Rory reached over and took her hand, told her not to look. And when they'd ridden past the offending corpse, its bones stripped but still ridden with flies, he said she could look again.

The hat was nowhere in sight. They'd almost given up when Rory spotted it at the base of a tree, lodged in a nubby crevice. He hopped off and plucked it out, then slapped it against one thigh to dust it off. He handed it to July, and she tapped it onto her head. "How do I look?"

Rory laughed. "Your pa ought to have let your brother keep it."

"I don't care what you say," she said, smiling. "It makes me feel good inside."

She and Rory picked their way across the sandbar then, July leading the way. The river ran slow and easy on both sides of them, but even so Rory breathed a sigh of relief when they clambered up the bank. Their task accomplished, Rory wasn't yet ready to let July go, and when he glanced over to the house where the Valentine woman killed herself, he suggested they look inside.

"Go on, if you want to," July said. "I'll wait here, by the road."

He hopped off his horse and went in, poking his head out the door a few minutes later. "Come on in," he hollered. "It's right cozy in here." She set her mouth and shook her head. "Well, then," he said, striding toward her, "I'll just come and fetch you."

"Got to catch me first." She pulled back on Birdy's reins, but she wasn't quite quick enough, and Rory grabbed them before she could get away. "I won't let anything hurt you," he said, offering his hand. "Come on now." She studied his face, drew comfort in its kindness, and took his hand before hopping down from her horse.

She walked into the little stone house, inhaling its earthy aroma. Rory batted the dead crickets and beetles trapped in cobwebs hanging low from the ceiling while July stood in the shadowy coolness. Her eyes took in the room's contents, the double bed perched on a fine wooden frame, three smaller beds in the corner. A broom with beaten-down bristles leaned against a wood stove, and a braided carpet, covered in dust, lay rumpled on the floor.

Standing there, looking around, July didn't see the woman's apparition, nor did she catch the scent of blood. July felt no fear at all, only sadness – for poor Mrs. Valentine had spent so many lonely hours sweeping a dirt floor that would never shine like the one she'd had in Pennsylvania.

Looking out the window, her gaze settled on the remnants of an ancient garden so overcome with weeds that even a potato would find it rough going. "Who do you reckon found the family?" she asked, turning now to Rory.

"I heard pa tell of it once. Said a drifter come through, hoping for a handout. He took one look around, figured for himself what happened, then took to Morning Tree to fetch help – they didn't have no sheriff then. Couple of folks came out and gave the Valentines a proper burial, but wasn't long before coyotes dug them up and drug them off. Reckon their bones are scattered clear to California by now – poor folks."

He walked over to the cupboard and plucked a tin from the shelf. "Look at this," he said. Popping its lid, he sniffed its contents and lifted his brows in recognition. "Cinnamon." He smiled and gave July a sniff. When she nodded, he looked around and said, "I like this place, July. I can see myself living here. Can't you?"

"With your folks, you mean?"

"No," he said. "With you."

July scoffed. "Pa would skin me alive if I was to move here with you."

"I don't mean now, just…someday."

She looked into his soft, crumpled face, saw that she'd hurt him. "If you want the truth, I can see myself doing lots of things someday," she told him. It didn't seem to comfort him though, and with her heart beating quick as a mourning dove's, she took his hands in hers and leaned in, intending to kiss him on the cheek. She hesitated, never having kissed a boy before, and when she did, he pulled her in and pressed his mouth against hers. His breath was warm and sweet as anise, his lips as soft as sponge cake.

They stayed that way a long time, hands and lips touching. And when Rory pulled away, July didn't blush or say one word of foolishness, but touched his cheek and smiled.

He grasped her hand and kissed it. "Don't tease me now, July, but I think I love you."

"You haven't known me but a month or two."

"Pa only knowed Ma six weeks when he married her."

"Do they get on all right?"

"Not very," he allowed, chuckling, "but we would. I feel it in my bones."

She smiled, saying, "I think I feel it too."

Chapter Thirteen

She thought about him all the way home, agonized over when and where she'd see him again. Oh, why couldn't she be sixteen, like Lilly? Why couldn't her pa accept that a girl of nearly fifteen knew her own mind? Knew what she wanted and respect her some, no matter that the boy she loved was a Gentile and the son of a cowboy? She sagged in the saddle, dreading how much her pa would fight her once he learned of this thing with Rory. He'd forbid her to see him again, going so far as whipping her until she couldn't sit down, as he'd once whipped Tom and Raymond.

When she got back to the ranch, she put Birdy up in the barn and stuffed her hat behind the trunk filled with tablecloths, family trinkets, and Richard's old clothes and boots. She met no one's eyes as she passed through the kitchen, murmuring only that she'd been out, pressed the day too hard, and made herself sick again. There was no need to feign illness now, for the ache in her bones was as real as any fever.

She refused a cup of Pun's tea when her mother offered it, rolled to her side, and quietly drew the blanket over her head. And when the door clicked shut, July let go, releasing all she held inside for Rory and the crazy woman at Valentine, and for the lies she'd told her ma and pa.

She lay in bed the next morning long after the rooster crowed, listening to the sounds of her family going about their day; her mother's kettle whistling in the kitchen; the clanging of hammer against metal as her father repaired a wagon wheel in the front yard. And from somewhere off to the back, July heard Lilly singing a song about old Kentucky, infusing it with extra feeling and pronouncing each word with care. July supposed Lilly wasn't so bad – she was just ornery because she was growing up and itching to get out on her own. For the first time, July felt a sister to Lilly's feelings.

She rolled onto her stomach and found Raymond peeking at her from the door. He was leaning against the frame, one dirty foot propped against his scrawny little leg. "Hi July," he said, his bug of a nose dotted with a dozen amber freckles. "You got to run to the privy now?"

"No, I'm done with that," she said. She threw her legs over the side of the bed and pushed herself up. "You know if Ma saved me a biscuit?"

"She saved you three," he said. "I wanted to give one to my grasshoppers, but she said they don't eat crumbs, they eats crops, and we don't have none to spare."

"You ought to catch yourself a ladybug, instead."

"Where would I find one?"

"Out to the garden, on a sunflower."

"All right," he said, and just like that he was out the door, his heels pounding across the dirt outside. July dipped to watch him out the window. In the distance she saw Doctor Forbes coming up the road toward the house. Her father must have seen him too, for he called out a greeting and asked the man to come inside and rest.

"Believe I will do just that," Preston called back. "I've got news of Silas Morrow's boy and thought you'd like to hear it, seeing as how you've got an interest in that clan."

July gripped the windowsill and sucked in her breath. *Go on*, she willed him, *go on*, but whatever it was Doctor Forbes had to say was interrupted by the cheery hello of her mother. July stepped to the other side of the window, angling for a better view. She saw nothing but the doctor sitting casually astride his horse, heard nothing except muffled laughter. Her heart pounded, for she couldn't imagine he'd heard of her visit with Rory yesterday, for Rory would have gone to the grave with their secret. She would too, and very nearly wished she had. When she could stand it no longer, she ripped off her nightdress and threw on a shirt and pair of Richard's old overalls. There wasn't time to plait her hair, so she ran her fingers through the tangles and let it go at that.

She was standing at the window in the kitchen when her mother and the men walked in. She took a bite of her biscuit and looked at them blandly, as if settling her stomach was all she cared about.

"Why, July, you're up," chirped Eliza.

"Hello Mama." July kissed her mother on the cheek. Eliza gave her a squeeze, asked if she was feeling better. "A little," she said. She looked at Doctor Forbes and offered a polite hello.

"Hello July," he said. "I'm sorry you've been under the weather."

"I suppose we shouldn't have let her out in the cold on the Fourth of July," Eliza put in, "but it hardly seemed fair to send her home when everyone else was having fun."

"She looks none the worse for it," Preston said. He walked over to July and pressed two fingers against her throat. "Although your pulse is racing – maybe you should sit a minute and catch your breath."

July stepped away, shrugging him off as delicately as possible. "I'm fine," she told him, walking over to the table. Her pa patted the chair next to him, and she sat down.

"Tell what you know, man," said Isaac, slapping the empty seat on the other side.

"Just came from Morrow's place," Preston said, settling in. "Seems a badger startled the boy's pony – horse's feet skittered so, it stumbled and fell backward, landing on its rump. Tottered sideways somehow, and crashed to the ground with Rory's arm beneath it." He shook his head. "Worst break I've seen in ages."

"Glory," said Eliza, forgetting for a moment her fear of Morrow's men. "What all did you do for him?"

"Set his arm, but I'll tell you, it was a challenge. I'm not sure it will ever be the same." Preston crossed his legs and leaned forward in his chair, his voice animated where earlier it was serious. "Most interesting part, though, is that he was out taking photographs when it happened."

July kept her gaze in her lap and held her breath, not daring to meet her pa's eyes. But when Preston made no mention of Valentine, or of Rory meeting a girl at the bridge, she realized Rory had kept their secret. She slowly began to breathe again.

"Photographs?" said Isaac. He rolled the word around his mouth, tasting its meaning. "What of?"

"Scenery and such. Apparently it's a calling – he insists he'll hang his shingle in Morning Tree one day, refer to himself a photographer." Here, Preston chuckled. "Could be something to it – he seems to see things in a way that I, for one, do not. For example, while I was working on his arm I suggested he tell me about this hobby of his – to distract him from his pain, you see. 'How do you select your subjects?' I asked, so he tells me it's all about composition –"

"Composition?" Isaac interrupted, drawing back. "What in hell is that?"

"That's what I wanted to know," confided Preston, "so I asked. Boy says, 'Take a dry leaf and hold it between your fingers. Study its shape and form, the veins running through it like arteries. Then place it in your true love's hand and take a picture of it. That's composition."

"Why, that's lovely," said Eliza. Anyone could see she was taken with the notion, if not the boy, himself. Isaac bristled, reminding her that even though a man's words were as pretty as a picture, it was the stuff inside that counted.

"I know," she said, tilting her chin. "It's just difficult to imagine he's as hard as his pa, is all. Seems the boy's got a soft side too."

"That's what I've been trying to tell you," said July. "Emeline and Lilly – we've all seen it. He's nothing like his pa, and doesn't want to be, either."

All eyes turned toward her, her own pa's dark as the forest.

Preston seemed to realize he was in the middle of something he didn't wish to be part of, though he hadn't yet put together July's relationship with Rory. He pulled himself up and changed the subject. "Whether the boy's hard or soft I can't say, but I'm sure he suffered a great deal before I got there. Unfortunately, I was delivering a baby out to Brother Kilker's place and couldn't get to Morrow's any sooner than I did. Shame too, because Kilker's *other* wife – the one he keeps in the pantry – could've easily managed without me."

Preston's eyes drifted July's way. She didn't look at him, but at her father. "I just wish you'd hear Rory out, is all. He doesn't believe his pa would try to hurt me any more than I believe you'd try to hurt him." But then, as if her words didn't ring true, even to her own ears, she said, "Right, pa? You'd never hurt Rory?"

Isaac's eyes narrowed and his mouth grew tight. "What do you care whether I hurt him or not?"

"I like him and want you to treat him fair."

"Well, you can quit likin him, and I mean right now." Almost imperceptibly, Isaac raised his brow and studied July. He said nothing, but his stern eyes held hers, as though awaiting the lie that hid behind them. With pursed lips, he turned to Preston. "Why wasn't that boy up in the mountains, herding cattle with Morrow's crew?"

Preston too glanced at July, then back at Isaac. July guessed he'd likely say if he knew. "I don't know," he told them. "I didn't see his father at all, and it was his mother who sent word to fetch me. She's the one who paid me too – ten dollars, though I should have charged her twelve."

"Why, you only charged us five for stitching up July," said Eliza, "and not a dime for the chloroform. We didn't pay you near enough, Doctor Forbes."

Preston dismissed her with a courteous wave. "I should have done it for free, seeing as how July makes a glowing advertisement for my work." His smile wobbled some, as though it couldn't be contained for the joy it held.

Isaac and Eliza must have caught some longing for July in that smile, for they shared a look that told her they were of a mind to arrange a match between her and Doctor Forbes. And now that he'd planted the seed in their heads it was sure to sprout quick as a dandelion. Once it began to grow she wouldn't hear the end of it, though for all she cared that sprout could shoot up to the Celestial Kingdom if it had a mind to. She'd marry Preston Forbes the day the devil danced on the moon.

Chapter Fourteen

Had Richard known about July's attraction to Rory, he might have warned his sister against running off to meet a boy by the bridge, for he understood well what it was to displease their father. "You ought not lie to him," he would have warned her. "He'll find out what you're up to and knock you flat."

"Who's gonna tell him?" she'd want to know. He could see her now, her hands on her hips and her mouth stretched hard. Well, it wouldn't be him, that's for sure. He was locked up in the mountains, without a body to keep him company nor a hearth to keep him warm.

There were some, like Daniel and Pun – and July too – who loved the hills; who made companions of the chipmunks and marmots, and even the trees. July was one to give them names, like Lightning Jack, a lodgepole pine with its bark seared black, and Short Stuff, for the stubby little fellow that greeted them at the base of Brundage. But Richard had never made friends with the trees. It was as though the tangle of pines surrounding his camp knew he wasn't a herder or a woodsman, and held it against him, somehow. As he crouched at his morning fire and nibbled his home-cured ham, he stared at the dark mouth of the forest and weighed its disapproval. Each day it seemed the trees resented him more, and it wouldn't surprise him to awaken one morning to find their prickly tentacles wrapped around his neck.

It wasn't until the sun finally filtered through the dense boughs that he relaxed enough to sip his tea, a beverage made from the root bark of a spiny plant that reminded him of home. The place he longed to be.

On Sunday afternoons, when chores at last gave way to thoughts of the Sabbath, he was permitted to sit with his books, reading the poems of Robert Burns. "My Luve is Like a Red, Red Rose," was among his favorites. He liked Longfellow too, as did his mother. Before he'd left for the mountains she'd often asked him to recite "Hiawatha's Childhood," which he'd done with pleasure.

While he sat and drank his tea, he glanced up from time to time to check the sheep. He loved the way they paused from their chewing to watch him, their caps of curly wool propped just so on their heads, their ears sticking out at the sides. He loved their smooth white faces, and their eyes, trusting and sad. Most, though, he was enamored with their mouths, which he found so strangely human. He didn't love them like his pa did, but he didn't harbor Tom's bitter attitude, either. He'd never thought them stupid, but simply cautious, for they moved readily from a dark area to a light one, and from a confined space to one wide open. And always, they scurried toward food. That struck Richard as smart.

He drained his cup and tidied up, pushed the sheep off the bedground with the dogs' help. He grazed them slowly toward water, which he reached around noon. While the flock rested, he lay on a mossy mattress on the ground, a log as his pillow, and read for a few hours until it was time to get the sheep going again. Other days, he simply sat atop a hill on his horse and let the creatures spread far and wide – up to two or three miles if the browse was good. If he wanted the sheep to turn, he'd send Tick around to do the job. At the end of the day, after the flock had grazed back to camp and the dogs had organized them for the evening, he'd prepare a supper of fried fish if he'd caught a trout in one of the streams, or a dozen or so frogs' legs, though they hopped so in the pan it unnerved him some to cook them. Just before dark, he checked the mules and then the sheep, taking one last walk-around as the animals, ever watchful for predators and vigilant against danger, slowly began to lie down.

Such was Richard's life at the top of the mountain, where his cohorts consisted of sheep and dogs and all the cruel creatures in between. He figured out in a hurry there was a big difference between lonely and boring and there were times when sheep herding was as fretful as July's accident at Valentine. Bobcats, coyotes, and cougars were a constant threat, as were eagles and bears and wolves.

Wolves were the worst, though, because they killed not only for hunger, but sport. They'd hit the camp twice now.

His pa had warned him to keep a sharp listen for their howls but that first moonless night, after the campfire had burned to embers, Richard heard nothing but stampeding hooves as he stumbled from his cot. Frightened sheep run wildly but silently, never uttering a sound, and in the dark they scrambled everywhere. Tick and Bug were trained to protect them, to nip each outlying individual until it headed toward the center, so that its vulnerable throat wasn't accessible to the predator.

Richard hadn't been able to see well enough to draw a proper bead on the intruders, so he aimed at their eyes, glowing red in the dark. By the time he fired off one hesitant shot and then another, wolves had killed seven of his father's ewes. The second time the wolves came to call Richard got to his feet in a hurry. Aided by the light of the moon, he fired a volley of shots toward the tree line. At least one bullet met its mark, and he knew he'd nicked one of the silver-haired demons when its pained cry pierced the night. Yet on neither occasion was he prepared for what he found. While he'd thought the scene of his sister at Valentine a horrible thing to behold, it didn't compare with the trauma these wolves inflicted.

Carnage. That was the word for it.

Sometimes wolves just tore up the sheep then took off without eating much of anything. Other times they ate the liver, kidneys, and heart, leaving the lungs and stomach untouched. But no matter whether they ate or not, they always left a sight that wrenched Richard's soul. "The best way to describe it," he told July when he saw her again that fall, "is to imagine a shotgun blast blowing out their insides – leastwise, that's how it looked to me."

While the nights were often fearsome, Richard still found the days harder to get through, even though he knew Pun and Daniel would one day surprise him, show up with their own bands of over one thousand sheep apiece. On that day, he and the men would sit a spell and catch up on their doings while the animals lolled in the grass, the late-afternoon sky a purplish-gray, the clouds hanging low and powdery in the distance. He'd listen to the men talk, embracing the sound of their voices but not saying much himself, thanking the Lord for providing the company he craved.

Yes, Pun and Daniel would arrive soon, and when they did the three men would gather up the lambs, urge them gently from their mothers' teats, then trail the youngsters away in preparation for Tom's arrival. For in September Tom would bring up the rams for fall breeding, and the ewes had to be ready to receive them.

And there they'd all remain until October first, when they'd head downhill toward the Van Wyck stock driveway, thirty-six hundred sheep between them, and then at long last make the broad turn toward home. By the first of November the sheep would graze on hay meadows near the ranch until Thanksgiving when Isaac would start his supplemental feedings of alfalfa. In between, wether lambs fattened on mountain grasses would be sold and shipped to market, along with the toothless old ewes known as gummers.

None of this would come soon enough to suit Richard, but until Tom finally showed up at camp he knew he was on his own.

One morning, when the sun gleamed hot and the sheep grazed on the low-lying shrubs winding down from the mountain, a single rider on horseback appeared in the distance. Richard looked up, alerted by hooves drumming the dry ground. When the fellow got closer, Richard saw by the man's hat and big blue bandana that he was a cowboy.

The hairs on the back of Richard's neck stood up, and he ambled toward his horse where he'd stored his Winchester in its scabbard. He figured it smart to behave as though he were heading for a leisurely smoke or maybe a slug of chaw, neither of which were on his actual menu. He moved deliberately, just as his pa had taught him, and recalled his father's admonition all those months ago in Morning Tree. "Never pull your gun unless you aim to use it," Isaac had told him, his hand firm on Richard's shoulder. "A cowboy's motto is shoot first, ask questions later, and if he thinks you're fixin to tie into him, he'll plug you before you can blink." Richard believed it, having read as many dime novels as poetry books.

Using his horse as a shield, he peered over the saddle and called "Hello!" as the cowboy charged up and then braked hard. That the rider so rudely entered Richard's camp, dusting up his belongings, was another indication he meant no good.

"You Richard Caldwell?" asked the man. He was a stringy sort about Tom's age with pale blue eyes. He wore pointed boots and a long-sleeved shirt that hadn't seen a washtub since Easter.

"Who wants to know?"

"I do."

"Then I'm him," said Richard, his voice uncharacteristically stout. He was glad he had his horse between them so the cowboy couldn't see his knees knocking.

"I got a message for your pa." The man's mare was restless and kept slinging her head. Richard said nothing, just wrapped his fingers around the butt of his rifle. The cowboy watched him do it, but made no move to shift his reins so his hands were closer to his gun. "Your pa's men crossed the deadline," he said, referring to the imaginary boundary Silas Morrow established to keep Isaac's sheep off his range. "Morrow's got his cattle up to the north end of Brundage and we seen some of your woolies there." He spat on the ground and a little of the dribble stuck to his chin. He wiped it with the back of his hand. "Thanks to you and yours, the place is plumb sheeped out."

A queasy feeling crept up from Richard's stomach. This was Mads Larson, the cowboy his pa warned him about, the one with the heat under his blood. "I haven't been anywhere near the north side," Richard argued. "I been on the south all along."

"No, but that other lamb licker has, the one named Daniel. Your Chinee herder too."

"Maybe it was Tinsley's or Swanson's sheep," Richard put in. "Coulda been the Janks', for all we know."

"Weren't them," said Mads. "It were your pa's men, and if they don't steer clear of our ground, they'll regret it."

Richard stepped out from behind his horse's thick neck. "Is that Mr. Morrow's message or your own?"

"One and the same. Just make sure your pa gets it." He smirked, taunting Richard's bravado.

"I'll see he gets it, all right, soon as I get home."

With that, Mads' expression grew tight. "Don't dally, boy," he told him, his blue eyes cold. He whipped his mare around, heeled her hard, and took off.

Richard didn't know what to make of Mads Larson. How dangerous could he be if he upped and warned a fellow before he whooped him? Yet the man was all business, Richard was sure of that. He may well have had something to do with July's accident too, and if he did, how far would he go to finish the job?

For years now Richard had heard stories about desperate cowboys, and not just yarns but real events. The way he saw it, romantic writers of the western novel got it all wrong. Why, any sheepman would tell you there were plenty of cowboys cruel as Plains Indians, and though he'd never known a cowboy to lift a man's scalp, his activities sometimes demonstrated the mob spirit in one of its most cowardly forms. Some of their tortures were too gruesome to conjure as Richard lay on his cot, alone, in the dark, but come they did, and all the worst ones too. Stories of cattlemen clubbing sheep and setting herders' dogs afire. Masked men rim-rocking unsuspecting animals or gathering them in some corner and shooting them in the head. He'd even read of cowboys slicing off herders' ears, tossing them to the coyotes. If violence flared, a lone herder like Richard didn't stand a chance.

He hardly slept that night, worrying about the possibilities. With every crack of a branch beneath his settling horse's feet, Richard craned his neck, held his breath, and peered into the shadows. The flame of his campfire flickered and the wood spit and all around him it seemed the trees were closing in. He lay still and watchful for hours, until his eyes burned with the need to sleep.

And so it went the second evening, and the third, as well. When he awoke the morning of the fourth day with his ears intact, he began to rest easier. Even the trees seemed to have receded some. But it was the sight of Daniel and Pun coming over the brow of a rising hill with the sheep in tow that made him whoop for joy and run to greet them.

"Ho!" hollered Pun, his short arm painting a broad swoop across the sky. "Hope you got plenty tea for Daniel and me!"

"I got enough to take a bath in," Richard hooted. "I got apricot turnovers too. How's that for a greeting?"

Daniel looked at Pun. "I got my mouth set on peach," he groused. But when he settled his wide frame on the log beside the fire and slipped the tender crust into his mouth, the hairs of his mustache twitched and his eyes twinkled, and for the first time in a long while, all was right with the world. At least until Tom arrived a week later and Richard told him about the Mads Larson incident.

Daniel and Pun had heard the story twice now but when Richard told it to Tom, they leaned in and nodded as if the information were coming to them new.

"What did Larson say he'd do if we beat him up here next year?" Tom wanted to know.

"He didn't say anything about next year," Richard told him. "Just said mainly that me and Daniel and Pun would regret it if we dallied on the mountain. He was talking *this* year, Tom."

Daniel shifted uneasily on his bench. "Any fool can see we'll be heading home soon as we get them ewes bred. Can't he wait another week or two before he goes off half-cocked?"

Tom stared into the fire and made no reply. Instead, it was Richard who spoke. "Now that we've come down off the mountain he might not go shooting his guns, but he's got to know we'll be back again next spring, right, Tom? I mean, where else we got to go?"

"Nowhere," said Tom, "and yes, he knows that as well as we do." He shook his head. "He'll find all a you, bring some wranglers with him to shoot up your camps, maybe Isaac's sheep too."

"Would Morrow let him, you think?"

"I don't know. Whole thing's got so tangled, I don't know what Morrow's got in him and what he ain't. But now that Mads Larson has come around and made his threats, we got to take him serious." Tom thought back on his discussion with Isaac all those months ago; how he'd given his uncle so little credit. Now he reckoned he should have given him more.

"I hear Mads comes from Wyoming," put in Daniel. He glanced across the fire. "That's just the kind of shenanigans they pull over there, so Tom's right – we got to keep an eye on him."

Pun frowned. He was remembering the time he'd been robbed all those years ago, how lucky he'd been to escape with his life. He'd not fought the stinking devils back then, for white men in that part of Idaho sometimes lynched Chinamen just for the sport of it. But now? Pun had nothing more to lose, for if they robbed Isaac of his livelihood they robbed Pun too, and there was no reason not to fight them. His only fear was dying in America. He wanted to die in China, or at the very least, have his body sent to his homeland if his heart quit beating in Idaho. "If die here, send home," he said sternly, nodding toward the Far East.

"Doubt you'll die, Pun," Tom told him, "but if I was you I'd hang on tight to my pigtail."

Daniel puffed his barrel chest and issued a loud complaint. "This land is Isaac's as much as it is Morrow's. Hell, it's Tinsley's and Janks' too. Why, the range is free for anyone to use. Morrow don't hold no claim at all."

And so the argument went, into October and beyond, the men endlessly alternating between fear and indignation. When Tom and the rest of them got back to the ranch the first week of November, Isaac dropped his head into his hands when he learned what had happened. He told Tom he needed him more than ever now, that come spring Tom would have to help Richard herd the sheep back up the hills toward Morrow's so-called deadline. Stay there until they knew what Mads was planning. "If you quit me over it, Tom, so be it. But I won't send Richard up there alone. I shouldn't ought to done it this year."

Five months earlier Tom would have dreaded hearing the news, but now that Mads had stepped forward with a threat, Tom had a hard time turning it from his mind. He supposed he'd head up to the hills with Richard all right, for once Morrow figured out he and the others were on their way north, Morrow were sure to sic his men on the boy. They'd be quick as coyotes too, snarling and spitting and biting at Richard's heels. Let them try to bite Tom's heels, though, and he'd set Mads Larson and his boys straight where Isaac had not.

None of this was spoken within earshot of July, but she learned about it one day when she joined Richard in the hayloft after dinner. "It's worrisome," he told her. "Morrow's men could show up to the mountains next April or May and pick us off one by one, anytime they want to. And if Mads gets hold a Pun, who knows what he'll do?"

July's brow bunched with worry. "Pa's not sending you back, is he?"

"He's got to. Daniel and Pun can't fight no war on their own."

"I hate that they're fighting at all. Why can't Pa and the rest of them get along?"

"Cause they're cattlemen and we're sheepmen, July. We all want the same thing."

July looked over at her brother. "There's something I got to tell you, Richard." He stuck his lip out and nodded, waiting to hear it.

"Remember I told you Silas Morrow had a son – a boy your age named Rory?"

"Sure – he was the one that fetched you when you fainted. You said you met his ma at the picnic, that her and Rory was nice folks – though I don't think Pa fell in with that."

"Well, no matter what Pa says, you'd like them," she said defensively, "especially Rory." She lay on her back and tucked her arms beneath her head, thinking how she'd shape the rest of her story.

"You say that like you know him, I mean better than just meeting him casual-like, at a picnic or that run-in down to the river."

"We got to talking at the dance, is why. He came over and sat down, almost squeezed me off my bale. I thought he was curious about my scar and all, but after a while I could see he liked me. He treated me like a friend, someone he cared about. He told me some things too – said he doesn't want to run cattle any more'n you want to herd sheep, but like you, his pa expects it and he's pretty much stuck for a while."

"That's a lot to tell a girl he only met but twice."

They lay on their sides, facing one another, July chewing on a sprig of hay. She dipped her head to her chest and smiled. "Well, this is the hard part, see?"

"You can tell me," he said, his face serious and true. "I'd never go singing it to town like Lilly would."

"Okay, but you got to promise – you can never tell a soul, Richard, else I'm dead."

"Hope to die, July. I won't tell."

And so she told him of meeting Rory at Valentine; how they'd arranged it that day at the celebration and how'd she'd played possum just to get her hat back.

"You mean that old bowler?" said Richard.

"It wasn't just the hat, silly."

"No, I guess not," he said, realizing, as July's tale unfolded, there was something dark and mysterious and altogether unknowable about his sister – a sort of courage that lived deep within her and a determination he feared he lacked. She told him how, with some coaxing from Rory, she'd walked into that ghostly house at Valentine, how Rory had told her he wanted to one day live with her there, and how she'd grasped his hands and squeezed them.

"He kissed me," she confessed. "And I kissed him back."

Richard studied her hard, for he'd never looked at his sister as a suitor might. When he'd thought to look at her at all he'd seen only a child, a skinny girl with knobby knees standing in the shadow of their father. Now he saw her as someone altogether unfamiliar, a sort of glowing miasma on the brink of womanhood. And though he was happy for her – for truly, he was – he was hurt too, for now she had someone while he had only the dark tangle in his heart.

"You love him?" he wanted to know.

"I do."

"What're you planning to do, then?"

"I don't know. I'm still mulling it over." She chewed the little sprig of hay more vigorously now, and stared at the rooftop. "Worst part is, I got no idea how he's doing – I haven't seen him since just after Independence Day, and here the leaves are turning brown. Won't be long till frost begins to light on Ma's garden."

"Well, what's wrong with him that he hasn't snuck out to see you?"

"He broke his arm on his way home from Valentine – horse fell on it after we'd said our goodbyes. It just worries me to think of him walking around with some useless old thing dangling at his side."

"Will you still love him if he's crippled?"

"I'd love him if he didn't have any arms at all."

"Then you got nothing to worry about." When she didn't respond, he told her he'd ride into town if she wanted him to, see if he could get Preston Forbes to talk about Rory. "I'll be sly about it too. He'll never guess I'm asking for you."

"He's too smart for that, and even if he weren't, he'd pick up on it real quick. He's sweet on me – gazed at me all sheep-eyed when he told us about Rory falling off his horse. I reckon now he'll watch me like a hawk."

Richard flopped back against the hay. "Why, Doc Forbes is Tom's age, ain't he?"

"I don't know and I don't care. I'm not going anywhere near him."

"How will you find out how Rory's doing?"

"I don't know," she said, exasperated. "For all I know he's forgot about me. Most boys can't even remember their multiplication tables past the age of nine, and here he hasn't seen me since summer."

"I don't expect he's studying arithmetic, July. If he told you he loves you, he's thinking on you plenty."

Chapter Fifteen

And he was. In all the time he was away from July he spent his afternoons daydreaming of her, the feel of her mouth on his, her breath soft and warm against his skin. He longed to get a message to her, to let her know he'd not forgotten her and to hear she'd not forgotten him. But his broken arm kept him at the ranch. Silas showed him no sympathy at all and spent the better part of two weeks complaining about the accident, going so far as accusing Rory of breaking it on purpose. "You wouldn't be the first to bust a bone just so you could stay home and play cards," Silas told him. But when Rory insisted he'd done no such thing, that he needed both arms to tote his camera, Silas waved him off and sidled toward the house.

Two months later the argument surfaced a second time, and when Silas walked into the kitchen, the heels of his boots scuffing Lydia's hardwood floor, she flat out told him she wanted him to leave the boy alone. "All the hollering in the world won't make him a cowboy," she scolded.

"Don't I know it," he flared. He slapped his hat against his thigh and sat at the table, leaning his elbows against it. He looked at Lydia as though he expected something more from her, a logical explanation for why his son had gone so wrong, though what he got from Lydia was far from satisfactory.

"Dinner isn't for an hour yet," she said, offering nothing more. She leaned over an open sack of flour, which she'd propped on the floor next to the cupboard. Into the sack she poured a cup of buttermilk and dumped a fist-sized lump of lard, mixing the concoction with her hands.

Silas watched her with the same consternation he always had. In seventeen years of marriage, and after the birth of four boys – only the last of which had lived – she still refused to dirty a mixing bowl if it wasn't necessary.

Lydia formed a small doughy ball with her fingers and added more flour. She placed the biscuit in a pan to breathe. Silas preferred rolled biscuits, but with just a few men at the table that afternoon it was too much trouble to go to. In a few weeks all the boys would be home again – Mads and Slack and the rest of them – sometimes there were as many as a dozen of them crowded 'round the table – and she'd again spend the bulk of her morning preparing their noon meal: boiled potatoes and fried steaks with brown gravy, beans and ham hocks, canned peaches, and two kinds of pie. Only then would her husband get his rolled biscuits and his fresh-churned butter too.

She wiped her hands on her apron and looked at Silas. He hadn't moved since he'd sat in the chair, just tied himself there and set his mouth in a stubborn pout. "I didn't raise my only boy to work as a picture-taker," he complained.

"You didn't raise any girls at all," Lydia said, "but do I hold that against you? Because it seems to me you hold everything about Rory against me. You blame me for coddling him and worrying too much I'll lose him like I lost the others." Silas started to object, but she told him to keep still. "Maybe I am to blame. Maybe I could have encouraged him to go your way more and mine less. But I don't think there's anything wrong with a boy wanting something more than what his pa has. Leastwise, something different."

"I didn't want more, and it suits me fine."

"Ranching is *all* you wanted, Silas. It's all you've ever wanted."

His face took on the melancholy expression that Lydia had seen too much these days. "You don't know what I want," he muttered, and turned his face away.

Lydia got up and walked back to the flour sack on the floor. "The world is changing, Silas," she said, dipping her hand into the bag for another go at the biscuits. "If you don't change with it, you may as well find yourself a bury hole and climb on in it."

Times *had* changed, and it rankled him.

Yet the odd thing was, if he'd taken a magnifying glass and peered into his life, he would have seen it wasn't so different from

Isaac Caldwell's. Not so many years ago, either one of them could have hitched themselves up on a fence rail and gazed across Idaho, where huckleberries grew plentiful as bitterbrush and sheep and cattle grazed to their hearts' content.

Now, though, Idaho carried the scepter of a territory, and soon enough the crown of statehood would weigh its proud head down. It hurt Silas to see homesteads springing across the countryside, their little towns clogging the valley and making it difficult, if not impossible, to graze so much as a gopher.

The influx was relentless. Men as far away as Virginia smelled water in Idaho's big rivers and once they moved in they immediately set to digging their ditches and diverting the resources into their settlements. All along the Snake River canals were dug, and once the state got some money behind it, those trenches were certain to zigzag Silas's way, turning the whole damn valley into one giant potato bin.

And here was Lydia, lecturing him about change. He knew what she wanted – an apple tree here, a purple fig there. Why, she'd plant a whole damn orchard if he let her, but he wasn't about to concede. No, he aimed to keep his cattle and his ranch. What he wanted – what he needed – was his competitors gone.

That his own son saw the range disappearing, that he planned to profit from it by photographing the settlers moving in, set Silas's temper to boiling. Father and son both knew it was only a matter of time before they came to blows over their disagreements, and when the day finally came that Rory refused to ride the range with Mads, Rory knew too he could hold his own against his pa. He was almost as tall as his father now, and until he'd broken his arm, just as strong. Since he was eleven he'd been helping Mads and the others cull cattle from a herd on open ground – fat steers, strays, old cows, whatever needed to be sorted, and he'd done it well. But doing a job well and liking it were two different matters.

And now that he'd met July and decided to marry her, the notion he'd get himself situated in town with a shop of his own blossomed into full-fledged desire. But opening a shop took money and no banker would give a boy his age – even one who stood at the brink of manhood – a loan to open a place of his own. So he earned it and saved it, and when no one was looking, buried it in the barn under a pile of rangy blankets.

Each day his arm got a little better. When he first broke it he kept it in a sling. And when it began to heel he exercised it, slowly bending the elbow to and fro until he could move his whole arm freely again. After finishing his chores, he pulled himself onto his Indian pony, rode toward the hills and spent long hours photographing the open range, the animals in and above it, and the settlers who now called it home. Most of them had never seen their likenesses in a photograph before. Such a couple was a man and woman who'd trudged to Idaho from the Plains. They sat in their kitchen on a wooden box situated on a bare dirt floor, tins of sugar and salt lining the shelf behind them. A pan of bread rose on the open oven door. The man preferred to look straight into the camera and told Rory so, but Rory suggested he hold a block of wood and pretend to carve it. "You'll look more natural if you do," he told him. He posed the woman with a spoon in her hands and angled her so a small ray of sunlight danced across her hair.

He developed the photograph at home, then rode back to deliver it. And when he gave it to the woman she stared at it without a word. Her mouth curled up and tears flooded her eyes. "We've scraped out a life in the territory," she told her husband, "and this is the proof we done it."

From one of the many tins on her shelf top, she plucked the two dollars Rory required for payment. Before he left, the woman's husband stopped Rory outside and asked him to come back before Thanksgiving. "I'd like a picture of me with my mule," the man told him.

But none of Rory's photographs – not the hawks or homesteaders or rosy valley landscapes – compared with his portrait of July. He often took it from the drawer in his bureau to look at it as he lay in bed at night, holding it close to the lamplight and tracing its smooth edges with his thumb. He ached at the sight of her, and yet it was with profound joy that he studied her gently parted mouth, the slight dip of her chin toward her chest as she gazed up at him with liquid eyes.

It seemed he'd waited forever to see her again, and when the occasion finally presented itself one October afternoon, he got on his horse and rode toward Morning Tree. The hills loomed purple in the background; the sky gleamed black and blue above it. Hundreds of geese fluttered like silver streamers against the dark clouds, and all across the valley the grass shimmered like golden grain. He worried the sky would open and soak him to his bones, but by the time he arrived at July's school the sun had pushed the clouds aside and warmed the autumn breeze. He positioned his horse behind the trunk of a cottonwood, and without dismounting waited for July to show herself.

She didn't see him when she burst through the door, holding her books and laughing with Emeline. Her curls tumbled over her shoulders and spilled almost to her waist now, and her skin gleamed warm as sunrise. She filled the picture in his mind like the frame of his camera, and it was through that lens that he saw her bright, nervous smile when she first caught sight of him. She said something to Emeline then quickly walked his way. She'd never looked prettier, nor happier to see him.

He slid from his horse as she approached, and though he wanted to clutch her tight as a pillow he stood back, for she needed no tongues waggling about his presence that day.

"Hullo," he said, when she'd come so close he could smell her. He was dizzy with her scent, a mix of lavender and sweet sage.

"How's your arm?" she asked straight off, shy like she'd never seen him.

"Better, but it ain't my arm I come to talk about."

She was quiet a while, said, "I was afraid you forgot about me."

"No, I ain't forgot you at all. You're all I've thought about since that day at Valentine."

"July!" called Raymond. "Who you talkin to?" July looked around to find a dozen classmates peering in her direction, Emeline among them. July's friend neither spoke nor moved, but stood, transfixed, and watched with a sort of trembling curiosity. One of the older boys whispered something into Raymond's ear. Raymond giggled. "Is that yer sweetheart," he hooted, joining the other children in raucous laughter.

"That's my brother, Raymond," July whispered, leaning in. "What'll I tell him?"

"Tell him yes, we're courtin."

"I can't tell him that."

"You said the same thing about walkin into the house at Valentine, yet you did it, didn't you?"

"I also said my pa would skin me alive if he knew I was seeing you." With that, she turned around again to peek at her brother.

When he stuck his fingers in his ears and waggled his tongue at her, she turned back to Rory. "He'll tattle, for sure."

Rory shifted, looked over at the eyes staring their way. "I've been takin photographs, July," he told her, "savin my money too." He spoke quickly, as though his words were sand, racing through an hourglass. "I should have enough to set out on my own next summer. I won't be able to open a shop for some time yet, but I figure if I keep at it, come June I can support myself – you too if you'll let me." He pulled her behind the tree, held her face in his hands and kissed her. "I wish I could marry you now."

She wrapped her arms around his neck. "I'll wait, since I got to," she told him, burying her face in his shoulder, "but it hurts my heart to do it."

He hugged her hard, lifting her from the ground. "I wish we could stay like this forever," he told her, but a minute was all they had. Raymond again called from the steps of the porch. "Yoo-hoo July – whacha doin back there with that Morrow boy?"

Gently, July pushed away, only to have Rory pull her in again. "You got to let me go," she insisted. "If Pa finds out I was kissing you behind this tree, he'll lock me in my room and throw the key into the Weiser."

"How's he gonna find out?"

She nodded toward Raymond.

Rory stepped out from behind the tree, then looked back at July. "What'd you say his name was? Raymond?" She nodded. "Hey, Raymond," he called. "Come on over a minute. I got somethin for you."

Raymond stepped back, as though worried all at once it might be a pounding. One of the older boys gave him a shove. "Go on," the boy urged, "see what he brung ya." Ray shuffled forward, his gaze on his toes. When he reached Rory, he looked up and blinked.

"Please don't clobber me. I don't care what you and July was doin back there, honest I don't."

"Oh Raymond," July chided. "He's not gonna sock you."

"What's he gonna do, then?"

Rory reached into his shirt pocket. "I want you to have this," he said, handing Raymond a photograph. Raymond scrunched his nose, studied the photo hard. "What is it?" he said, not taking his eyes from it.

"It's a butterfly – one they call a swallowtail. You like it?"

July stepped forward to see it too, marveling at its lifelike quality, its checkered wings and the eyespots near the tail. "Why, Raymond, it's just like the one you put in your jar last summer, remember?" She turned to Rory. "How did you know he likes bugs?"

"I didn't," he confessed. "I brought it for you."

"But I'm keeping it," Raymond announced. He'd still not taken his eyes from it, and held it now in both hands.

"What'd he give ya, Ray?" called the boy on the porch.

"A picher," Raymond hollered.

There was a murmur from the children, and the boy called back, "Well, what of?"

Raymond didn't answer. He merely stood, admiring the butterfly and tracing its wings with his finger. "I can almost feel its powder," he told Rory, his husky voice filled with wonder. "Just like velvet."

"I'll give you another one, too," said Rory, "a photo of a bird – a chicken hawk on a fencepost. But you got to make me a promise, first."

Raymond quickly agreed, as he was prepared to promise Rory anything.

"July and me are sweethearts," Rory told him, "but if your pa finds out, he won't let July see me again. So you got to promise you won't tell him I was here."

"I won't tell."

Rory tousled Raymond's silky blonde hair and gave him a nod.

"When will you give me that bird picher?" Raymond asked.

"Soon as July tells me you've kept your promise."

"Raymond," said July, "go show your friends your butterfly while I talk to Rory for a minute."

Raymond scooted off, his feet shuffling in the dust. He cradled the photo in both hands as though it were a saucer of milk, and he didn't want to spill a drop. Before he got to the porch, the little knot of children gathered around to peer over his shoulder, and to point and hoot over what Rory had given him.

Now it was July's turn to pull Rory behind the tree. She took his hands into her own, drew him near, and looked into his face. "Your eyes are green as a river, you know that?" He blushed and looked away, brought his gaze back to July. She held his face steady in her hands, as he had once held hers. "When will I see you again, Rory Morrow?"

"Tonight, if you'll let me. I'll follow you home and sit at your table for supper." He laughed and shook his head, wondering aloud how her ma and pa would react to that. His smile faded as reality set in. He wrapped his arms around July and crushed her to him.

She let him hold her for a long moment, and when the children on the porch began breaking off into groups and calling their goodbyes, she gently pulled away. "I got to go now, and so do you." She urged him on with a nod of her head, but he didn't move, just stood there, his wiry frame made slimmer by the slight hunch of his shoulders, the resigned tilt of his head as he watched her back away. At last, he turned and pulled himself up on his horse. For the longest time he sat twisted in his saddle, looking back at her as she walked away. July waved goodbye, holding her hand in the air even after his horse had galloped off. She nestled Raymond under one arm and started the long walk home.

When they rounded the corner and headed toward the corrals, July noticed Tom had stretched a beaver pelt against the side of the barn.

"Finally got him, eh, Tom?" she called. He looked up from the wheel he was greasing to call a hello. Setting his bucket down, he walked over to examine the pelt with July. Raymond scooted off, eager to inspect his photo in the privacy of the barn.

"Seen this old mama at the creek yesterday," Tom told her. "Trapped her this morning just after breakfast – I don't know where the youngun went." He stood back a moment to admire the skin. Leaning in, he blew the fur apart, where it was thickest and finest. "Feel of it," he said, nodding at July. She stroked the prickly fur of its back and its soft sides, asking what he planned to do with it.

"Hadn't thought on it," he shrugged. "You got a use for it?"

She really didn't, but thought it might come in handy as an additional bargaining tool for Raymond. She told Tom it would look nice on her bed, maybe keep her toes warm when it was cold outside.

"It's yours, then. Best let it dry a while so it don't stink up the place. Your ma wouldn't take kindly to that."

When she thanked him, he nodded, slipped his hands into his pockets and turned to walk away.

"Tom?" she said. He stopped to gaze at her with his lively, dark eyes. "She's your ma too, you know."

"I know." He made a peculiar little movement with his mouth, but never said another word about it.

*   *   *

Toward dusk, as July sat at the kitchen table, hunched over Richard's poetry book, she looked up to peer at her mother in the next room. Eliza sat in a rocking chair next to the hearth, knitting a wool scarf for Tom. It was to be a Christmas present, which he would have figured out on his own had he ever thought to ask what she was doing. Her face was content and relaxed, her forehead free of the furrows that so often signaled a headache. She rocked slowly as she worked, pausing every so often to hold up the scarf and examine her progress.

July felt a pang of pity for her mother. How many times had she baked Tom's favorite sweet cake then walked all the way to the creek to deliver it only to find him sitting and contemplating all that was wrong with the Caldwells?

They all sensed his unhappiness, yet never discussed it – just more or less accepted he'd always hold them at bay, as if loving them – Eliza and Isaac, in particular – was too risky a venture. It wasn't hard to figure out Tom was afraid he'd lose them, as he'd lost his own parents, that he didn't want to again suffer the pain he'd known when he was ten. Secretly, July worried she might one day lose her ma too, especially when she looked into her mother's sad eyes. July didn't think she could survive losing someone she loved, and prayed she'd never have to.

Richard came in and sat next to her, asked what she was reading. "A Red, Red Rose."

"My favorite," he beamed, and immediately set to reciting it.

"O, my luve is like a red, red rose, that's newly sprung in June. O, my luve is like a melodie, that's sweetly play'd in tune. As fair art thou, my bonnie lass, so deep in luve am I. And I will luve thee still, my dear, till a' the seas gang dry."

"That's delightful, Richard," Eliza said from the other room. "As many times as I've heard you tell it, it still brings tears to my eyes."

July and Richard exchanged a glance, a look that on Richard's part, at least, expressed sympathy for his sister's predicament, for he understood how much the poem now meant to her too.

Richard got up to go to his mother. "We should all love someone that much, at least once in our lives, don't you think, Ma?" He sat at her feet and draped his arms over her knees.

"How the Lord has blessed me," Eliza marveled. She leaned over to kiss his head and run her fingers through his hair. "All these children and not one of them lost to sickness or in childbirth."

"Ma?" asked July, setting her book down and walking into the room. She too sat at her mother's knee. "Did you ever love anyone before you loved Pa?"

There was the slightest hesitation between the time Eliza clucked her tongue and when she actually spoke. "Goodness no," she said, "but then I hadn't been on my own long, or out in the world much before I married your father." Her expression turned pensive, but she kept her eyes on her knitting and never once looked up. "Wouldn't have mattered if I had," she went on after a while, "your pa was the one for me. I knew it the minute I met him."

"What if he'd been a Gentile, though?" July probed. "Would you have loved him, still?"

Eliza set her knitting in her lap. "What would I have in common with a Gentile?"

"He wouldn't want six wives," Richard put in. "Or even two or three."

The tips of Eliza's ears flared red. "Your pa was never interested in taking another wife," she told him. "It's mostly the higher-ups that go in for it."

July grew impatient with the direction the conversation was taking and tried to steer it back again. "But what if you'd met a Gentile first?" she persisted. "Would you at least have got to know him?"

Eliza gripped her yarn, which had tangled a bit, and gave her head a shake. She couldn't bring herself to confess her old attraction to Lucas Franzen. Just thinking on it set her hands trembling and her head hammering. "I wouldn't get to know him," she insisted, her voice filled with a quavering assurance, "for what would be the point?"

The question took July aback. "The point would be marrying the man you loved."

Richard glanced first at his sister and then his mother, his eyes filling with an earnest need to know. "Didn't you ever wonder if you were doing right by marrying Pa? If there was another out there who might have loved you more?"

"What has gotten into the two of you? All these questions, I swear." Eliza quickly stood, the rocker swaying with the movement.

"The world's full of folks we *ought* to marry," Richard went on. "Seems to me we ought to cipher who we're best suited to."

"Meaning what, Richard?"

"Meaning a Mormon don't necessarily fill the bill."

"If your pa hears you talking like that, he'll whip you till your toenails bleed."

"See, now, that's the problem," Richard went on, his voice climbing a notch higher. "We ought to be able to talk about it. With each passing day people get farther apart, and if we never talk on what's eating us we'll be shouting our troubles from Ohio."

Eliza spoke as sternly as July had ever heard her. "You won't meet a Gentile but a Mormon, and you'll marry within the Church – it's not only the Lord's law, but your father's. Shout *that* from Ohio if you want."

Richard stood. He stared a long moment at Eliza, and though he might have stormed from the house, he walked quietly toward the door. Before passing through the threshold, he turned to gaze at his mother. She held a look he hardly recognized, and in that instant he realized she might have wanted to do a fair bit of shouting herself, once. Yet he knew she hadn't. She'd done what the Lord had commanded.

Chapter Sixteen

July found Richard in the loft. She climbed up and sat with him, the scent of hay and manure and milk in her nose, the song of bullfrogs in her ears.

Richard wasted no time at all, told her straight off he had a mind their mother had feelings for a Gentile once. "Every so often when her and Pa get tangled in their words, mention of a cowboy comes up. You ever notice that?" July thought on it a minute, said why yes, she did. "I think there was someone before Pa," Richard went on, "and I think she got riled tonight because we hit a nerve and it stung her."

"You think Ma actually *loved* a cowboy?"

"And I think he was a Gentile."

"Hoo!" said July, lying back and scrunching low into the hay. "A cowboy and a Gentile…not much would offend Pa more than that, I guess."

"But it makes sense, don't it? She don't want us to get hurt like she did, and so she puts it to us like it's a sin to love someone other than Saints and herders."

"You think she still loves that cowboy?"

"I think she loves Pa, though it rankles when he teases about fetching another wife to home."

"He wouldn't fetch another wife any more than he'd take on another you or me," July scoffed. "We're handful enough."

Later, when she thought on her mother's cowboy, she wondered if he truly existed. And if he did, was he gruff and grizzled like Silas Morrow, or fair to pleasing, like Rory? It seemed July's mind was always on him. She pictured his smooth, smiling face as she stood in the kitchen, stirring walnuts and chopped dates into her mother's Christmas fruitcakes. And when she drove the wagon for her pa, she imagined Rory riding along the snow-covered hills as Richard and Tom pitched hay onto the ground for the sheep. Every now and then he'd stop to capture the special sparkle of the season with his camera, and after that he'd keep on going, wind his way through the dense fog that clamored along the Weiser. In her mind's eye she saw him perfectly: a solitary figure bundled in a jacket, its collar trimmed with felt, his hat situated low on his forehead to keep the drizzle out.

It was a romantic scene that July played in her head time and again. Into this tapestry she wove a portrait of Rory selling photographs, saving his money and whisking her off to the little house at Valentine. She saw them, in time, setting up a real home in town with a shop next door and a dozen green-eyed children playing on the floor near the fire.

Where her sweet imaginings were less clear was with marriage itself – the need to break from her family to wed not only a Gentile but the son of her father's enemy. Isaac Caldwell would sooner see his daughter banished to some Mormon's cabin in Labine than married to the son of Silas Morrow. Plain as day July could see her pa on a rampage and so she turned her thoughts from him and settled them squarely on Rory. Her pulse quickened at the recollection of their first kiss, and even now her body tensed at the memory.

She understood the way love worked, for at the tender age of nine she'd watched, with deep concern, a ram mounting a ewe. "That buck has upped and hitched himself to that old ewe," July informed Tom. "Get him off, will you?"

Tom looked up, smiled. "He ain't hurtin her, July."

"Yes he is," she went on. "He liked to break her in two." Though she'd witnessed these antics all her life, she'd never comprehended what the coupling meant. She finally put it together when Tom said, "He ain't hitchin no ride July, he's makin babies."

She leaned in, studying the twosome hard. It appeared Tom might be right, for the ram didn't seem to be going anywhere, despite all his freeloading. She hopped off the fence and scurried into the house, her eyes fixed hard on the dirt.

"Where you goin?" Tom chuckled.

"Far as I can get," she told him, and that was the end of that.

Now she was about to celebrate her fifteenth birthday, and later that summer, Rory would awaken to the dawn of his seventeenth year. That she anticipated the feel of his shoulders beneath his shirt, the press of his naked chest against her own bare skin, was as natural as blackberries budding in the meadows.

She savored these thoughts all through the holidays, when the pressures of everyday life were eased for a while, when the house was festooned with red and green streamers and the Christmas tree with birds' nests, popcorn strings, and the pinecones Pun fetched from the forest. Eliza knitted stockings for each member of the family, Pun and Daniel included, and stitched their names with embroidery floss in fancy white lettering.

Christmas morning, when the house was as cold as the mountain's shadow, Raymond was the first one up to check the toe of his stocking. He found ten cents there, wrapped in crinkle paper. Not twenty minutes later, Daniel, Pun, and Tom wandered into the house from their shack behind the barn, eager to warm themselves by the fire and check the toes of their own stockings.

Lilly too dove into her sock, squealing when she discovered a box of her favorite hard candies and a small bag of nuts. Richard found two slices of poverty cake in his, an offering from their mother. He thanked her and tenderly kissed her forehead.

July checked her stocking last, worried she'd find a miniature porcelain doll or some other item to dispute her blossoming womanhood. But when she reached in and pulled out a hand mirror, she glanced at her mother and smiled. "Thank you, Ma."

"Thank your pa," Eliza told her. "It was his idea."

That her father had thought to give her such a grownup gift hit her hard. She fought back tears, and when she looked up to thank him, she saw he was a bit watery too.

"Hell sakes," he groused. "Can't a father give his child a gift without her leakin like a rooftop?"

July stood, walked over to him, wrapped her arms around his neck. "I love you, Pa," she whispered in his ear. In return, he patted her back and gave her a brusque but telling hug.

Two days later, on her birthday, Tom hitched up the Go Devil – a wooden sled he'd built with long, slick runners – and piled the children inside. He drove to the frozen pond on a low spot by the river, where Lilly and July skated and the boys built a snowman. Tom broke out the grain shovel he'd stashed at the back of the sled, and where the snow had frozen and formed a solid crisp floor, they each took a turn riding down the icy, white hill. Raymond was the lightest and had hardly skidded a foot before the shovel began to twirl. He tumbled into a snowbank. Even Tom gave it a go, and when he too bounced off, landing hard on his rump, they all bent in laughter, their voices pealing across the hillsides.

On the way home they interrupted a marsh hawk's meal of a bufflehead, a diminutive black and white duck some called a butterball. Tom spotted the hawk first, pointed out the feasting bird to the rest of the crew. The hawk hunkered down as Tom approached, dropped its shoulders and puffed its wings like a parasol, then took to the sky in flight.

Tom pulled the sled around for a better look, and they all leaned over to inspect the grisly scene. The hawk had clipped off the duck's head in a tidy little snip, dropping it some six inches from the body. The flesh was stripped clean from the bird's neck, its bony spine exposed. The duck's head showed purple and green hues and a little white wedge below the eye.

"I never seen a duck with a blue bill," Raymond put in. His eyes wandered from the duck's head to its body. The torso was almost entirely intact. "Why didn't that hawk eat the rest of him, Tom?"

July spoke up before Tom had a chance to. "We scared him off, is why."

"Will he come back?"

"Maybe, maybe not," said Tom. "But if he does, he'll only eat the breast – next to the neck, it's the best part, I reckon."

No one said much after that, thinking, as they were, on the way the world worked, how one minute a fellow could be flying high in the sky, happy as a horned lark, and the next some hungry old hawk would pluck him from his cloud and tug out all his feathers.

And so it went, those short winter days of December and January. Each morning, July dutifully helped her mother around the house, but by late afternoon she was itching to dash outside to join Daniel and Pun on the Go Devil. Twice a day, the men circled the fields in Tom's sled. He'd hitched a sleigh to its back and stacked a good amount of alfalfa there. It was their job to pitch the fragrant hay onto the snow, then holler at the sheep to come get it. They didn't have to holler loud or long, for the fluffy white balls came wobbling on skinny legs to gobble it. "Ha!" snorted Pun through the icicles on his mustache. "Sheep eat like pigs – chomp, chomp, chomp!" The notion that anyone would liken a sheep to a pig got

July to laughing so hard she nearly had to change her drawers before sitting down to supper.

She loved tending the ewes in the softening twilight. Each night, she stood in front of the setting sun, evaluating the expanding bellies of the pregnant ewes, wishing them well as their sweet babies grew inside them.

But it seemed the men had no time for tender musings. By February, Isaac and the others were busy sorting ewes into two groups: those likely to lamb first, and those who would wait awhile. The first group Tom kept at the sheds near the river – wooden structures with heavy canvas covers draped over the top – where new mothers and lambs were held in rows of pens – or jugs, as sheepmen called them – to protect them from late spring snows. Isaac was an innovator in this regard. Most Mormon sheepmen lambed in the open and prayed for pleasant weather, but seeing Isaac's success, they soon imitated his methods and increased their flocks twofold.

Once the ewes popped their wee ones, the fuzzy infants butted their mother's udders to start the flow of milk. Sometimes a mother rejected her babe and it was up to Tom to collect the little bummer and carry it to the sheds, his lean form a silhouette against the low-lying sun, his broad hands carelessly toting the floppy lamb as if it were a rabbit he'd throw on his fire for supper. He wasn't a sentimental man, and didn't believe in coddling babies. But hard as he sometimes was, he refused to watch an animal suffer, and every now and then he'd bring a lamb inside so Eliza and Raymond could feed it and warm it in a blanket.

July's pa hired three extra hands to help with the workload – men willing to toil day and night for four weeks and hardly any pay. Eliza saw to it their stomachs took in what wages Isaac couldn't pull from his pocket, feeding them simple food and lots of it. Sometimes she pitched in too, spelling Isaac and caring for the lambs born at night, situating each newborn with its mother and watching to see the youngster suckled. Richard, relishing his time at home, worked side by side with Tom. Overnight, it seemed, his thin arms grew bulky with corded muscle and his shirt took to stretching across his chest. And it seemed to July that his personality was melding with Tom's some, so that they often moved and acted as one. Perhaps Richard would find a place on the ranch after all.

A week or so after the first of the lambs were born, the air was redolent with tar and turpentine. July likened it to the coming of spring, for it meant the worst of winter was over. She sat atop a wooden post in the corral and watched as Richard and Tom leaned over the docking table, a special setup that made the lopping of tails and testicles easier. Tom held a pocketknife in his bloody hand, while Richard hoisted a sturdy pair of blades. As soon as Pun set a ram lamb onto the table and laid it on its back, Tom cut the end of the testicle bag, squeezing the sack with his thumb and index finger until two little walnuts popped up. He grabbled both testicles with his teeth, pulled them out, then bit the two cords instead of cutting them.

As though by rote, Richard stepped forward with his shears and snipped the lamb's tail about an inch from its body, then dabbed a bit of lard and turpentine on both the stump and testicle bag to stop the bleeding. Here Raymond, now eight, was pressed into service. He no longer cried at the sight of the damaged lambs, but neither did he undertake his role with eager interest. It was his job to brand the lambs' backs with paint, and as he did so he willed his gaze to settle anywhere but on Tom's bloody lips and fingers. Job complete, Daniel grabbed the critter and hefted it to the ground. Somehow the animal found the wherewithal to wobble to its feet, waddle from the corral to the sagebrush, and hunker beneath the branches.

The days passed in a blinding haze of heavy work and appetite. Eliza could scarcely keep up, for everyone responded to the call of her dinner bell as eagerly as the locusts of Mormon history, sucking marrow from their drumsticks and gravy from their spoons. Still, she refused to put up with bad manners, for they weren't sitting on the ground at a picnic but at a table in her home. Raymond was abruptly excused when he let loose a robust burp. "No fair!" he objected, shooting from his bench. "I haven't got my custard yet." He perched himself squarely behind July, crossed his arms and pouted.

"You know the rules," Eliza admonished. "I won't hear another word about it."

The temporary workers wiped their mouths with the backs of their hands and exchanged worried glances. "'Scuse me, ma'am," said the scrawniest of the three. "Our manners is rusty too, and if we committed a violation we apologize." The men nodded in unison, eyes wide, mouths quavering nervously.

"Don't worry," she told them. "You'll get your custard, but Raymond knows better, so he'll do without."

Raymond's face crumpled and he marched from the room and out the door. The group sitting at the table looked out the window and watched him run across the yard, heading for the sanctuary of the barn. July suspected he'd console himself with a good cry and the comfort of his photograph.

As it turned out she had underestimated her little brother. He'd had himself a good cry, all right, but he'd also grown weary of his picture and decided he wanted a new one. While the two of them sat alone at the table after breakfast the next morning, Raymond informed her in his husky voice he was tired of keeping Rory's secret, and if Rory didn't give him a second picture soon, he'd tell their ma and pa what he'd seen behind the cottonwood at school. He scrunched his flat nose and added a second threat. "And I'll tell Pa that Rory told me to keep quiet about it too."

"That's mean, Raymond," July said, her voice a low scold. She gave him a look, the one with the tightly furrowed brow that her pa had practiced on them when he was angry. Raymond worked his mouth convulsively, as though battling some inner demon, and July thought him chastised until he stamped his foot and blurted, "Rory promised me a new picher and I aim to get it." His eyes brimmed with tears and he sagged, knowing he might never get it at all.

Rory had made Raymond a promise all right, but how could he possibly keep it? He couldn't come around with her pa and his men to home, and whatever difficulties Rory battled back at his own ranch in Badger surely made the trip impossible.

July clasped Raymond's hands, the same pudgy hands she'd clasped so many times when he was just a sprout, when he'd sobbed over the nicks the shearers made to his favorite grandma ewes. "I can't see Rory for a while," she told him, "but I'll tell you what. You know that beaver pelt Tom gave me? The one I keep at the foot of my bed?"

He sniffed, gave a little nod.

"You can have it if you'll keep Rory's secret a little longer – until I meet him again and he gives me another picture to give to you. But it might be a few months, you hear?"

Raymond tucked his face in. "I don't want a pelt. I want that hat you got."

"What hat?"

"The one you got hid behind the trunk in the barn."

He was a sly one, Raymond Caldwell. "Is that where it is?" July said in her own crafty way, even as her cheeks burned red. "I've been looking all over for that thing."

"It don't look missing, it looks hid."

"It's not hid," she flared. "I lost it, but if it's so all-fired important to you, take it."

He scooted out the door before July changed her mind, then pranced around with that hat on his head for five days without once taking it off. And from the time the rooster started in at sunrise until the evening's shadows stretched along the valley, July wore a path from the kitchen to her bedroom window, peeking outside, watching for signs she'd been discovered. She expected to find her pa stampeding toward the house, eyes fixed hard on the ground, razor strap in hand. Yet it wasn't her father who'd figured her out, but Pun.

The day before, when Raymond and Pun stood talking in the yard, Pun had patted Raymond's bowler, then drawn back ever so slightly in reaction to something Raymond said. July saw it from her window, held her breath when Pun glanced up at the house and studied it, a look of disapproval crossing his face. She'd dipped behind the curtain, leaned against the wall and prayed, *I promise I won't lie again, Lord, if you'll let me keep my secret.*

But when Pun kept his lips stitched tight all afternoon, July knew her secret was his now, and that soon enough he'd take advantage. The next morning there he was, ready to make his move. She'd just mopped up the last of her eggs when he ordered in his clipped little accent, "Come, Jew-rye, we hoe ground, get ready plant gahden."

Richard looked up from his sausage. "But Pun," he said, "the ground ain't anywhere near thawed yet."

"No matta. Jew-rye strong as ox now." He turned to her, squinted, and spoke so quietly that only she heard. "Dumb as mushroom too."

July marched to the garden and spent the next hour whacking solid ground while Pun stood by, singing. "Put ya shouldah to da wheel, push along." It was her father's favorite work song, the one he'd sung in the buckboard on the way to the picnic in Morning Tree, the one he was likely singing now in the machine shed while he slapped tar on the axel of his wagon.

"Very funny," she said, leaning on her hoe.

"Don't lean hoe," he admonished, "*push* hoe." And then he chuckled.

Chapter Seventeen

In bed that night July lay awake until well past midnight, her back and shoulders aching. Her mind spun with what Raymond might tell their pa. She wondered when her little brother would again loosen his tongue and what details he'd spill when he did. If he told about the hat, July reckoned she'd come right out and admit she lied. She'd tell her pa she missed her bowler so, she could barely stand it. The admission would earn her a strapping, though she was fifteen and well past the point of spanking. But if Raymond told her father about Rory, how he'd kissed July behind a cottonwood when the leaves were still shivering on the trees, her pa would lock her in the root cellar and drop the key down some well. That'll teach you, he'd tell her later, rattling his finger in her face, though he had no idea at all how determined she was, how she planned to marry Rory the moment he came to fetch her.

She began to grow sleepy and though she longed to mull on Rory a while longer, she closed her eyes and quickly fell into that hazy place that straddled the dream and waking worlds. Maybe it was because she intended to keep the full story from her pa – the part about meeting Rory at Valentine – that the devil slipped into her room as she lay snoozing. He trod heavy into her nightmare, ripping back her covers and binding her heels with a thin strip of rawhide. His face was hidden by the room's dark shadows, but his hands, rigid and ropey and black, were plain as if July had viewed them in sunlight. His breath, when he leaned in close and hissed its scent, smelled of burnt hair.

"What're you gonna do?" she cried.

"Eat ya," he said. He glanced upward as though admiring the view, then turned slowly back and flashed a shimmering knife.

July's eyes popped open with a start. She didn't move a muscle, just shivered and shook and flared her nostrils, for she thought Satan might be outside her bedroom still. She wished her pa were with her now. He would face Satan outright, tell the devil in his stern voice his presence wasn't welcome. "By the virtue of the holy priesthood vested in me, I command you in the name of Jesus Christ to leave." And Satan would do so, because strong as the devil was, not even he could overcome the power of the priesthood.

July wasn't a priest but she could pray, and pray she did, clasping her hands across her bosom. "I won't lie to my folks like I have in the past, no matter what it costs me," she swore. "Just keep me safe, Lord, and give me peace of mind."

As July's heart slowed and her sweat cooled, she heard the call of a night bird. She tipped her ear toward the sound, and when the creature hooted a second time, she gathered her courage, crawled from bed and quietly lifted the window. Gray clouds skidded across the lavender moon, and the owl's woodsy notes echoed over the treetops. Owls were almost always bad omens, but to July the night bird brought comfort and a strange sense of relief. Oh how she longed to reach out to it! Before she got the chance though, it hopped from its perch and flew directly at her, dipping up and over the rooftop. She slipped into her boots then and flew outside, running toward the garden. The air stirred warm and windy, carrying with it the scent of newborn leaves. She lifted her face to the trees and calmly breathed it in.

The owl called one last time before thumping away in the darkness. July filled with a gentle peace then, and soon returned to bed. She believed the Lord had sent the creature to tell her all was forgiven. Her parents, though? They were a different story, and she'd have to seek their forgiveness on her own.

*   *   *

To July's amazement they gave no notice to the hat sitting on Raymond's head. Weeks passed as they gazed far beyond it, concentrating instead on the farm and the fields. Her father attached his team to a plow and tilled from dawn 'til dusk while her mother cleaned the kitchen like a woman possessed. Raymond set about scrubbing the lanterns in each room and July to carding the wool in the mattresses. Lilly, now seventeen, finally left home to work in town as an assistant to the seamstress Mrs. Abrams. "I'll see New York yet," she whispered in July's ear before stepping into Mr. Abrams' buggy, amending the remark by adding, "Soon as I've earned enough money to board the train, that is."

July never doubted Lilly would get to New York City, nor did she once consider that Rory wouldn't come fetch her like he promised. She knew now his word was as good as the gold Pun sometimes talked about, and she believed with all her heart he would one day appear at her doorstep, a bouquet of lupine and red clover in hand, to make his request to her parents. They'd refuse him, she was sure of that, and how she'd persuade them to change their minds she hadn't worked through her head yet.

She wished she'd taken Lilly into her confidence, asked what to do before Mr. Abrams picked her up in his fancy two-seater. But she supposed she'd said too much already, telling all to Richard and ensuring Raymond he'd get everything he wanted, if only he'd keep his mouth shut.

She sat gloomily on the front porch, contemplating her growing list of worries when she spied Preston Forbes riding up the path toward the house. He sat straight in his saddle and stood up in his stirrups, then flung his leg around in that saucy way he had when hopping from his horse. He was up to no good, that much was clear. He was a Mormon in need of a wife, and no matter how he couched his arrival, July knew he'd come to get one.

He glanced her way, ran his hand through his thick, curly hair. "Hello," he hollered as Isaac and the others gathered around to greet him. Only July stood apart from the tangle so eager to make him welcome and hear his stories from town.

Eliza bid him inside and pointed to a chair in the kitchen. Preston sat, claiming to have stopped by the ranch on his way back from Badger, where he'd just finished tending Mads Larson. "Seems Silas Morrow's had a run of bad luck this year – first there was his boy with his broken arm, and now this deal with Larson."

"Bad, was it?" said Isaac. He raised a hopeful brow.

Preston nodded. "Shot a cougar up to Blue Ravine. Didn't happen to kill it, though, and when he grabbed it by the scruff of the neck, it tore his hand up good." He directed his next comment to July. "No one brought him in nor called me for a week, and by then gangrene had near set in. I had to amputate two fingers." July sucked her breath in, for the thought of anyone losing even one finger to a doctor's saw made her weak in the knees. "Silas should have sent for me the minute it happened," he went on, "like your pa did for you, July. It's to your father's credit you're alive today." He neglected to bring up his own handiwork, knowing no doubt Eliza would do it for him.

July had to admire his skill in currying favor with her parents. "Pun helped too," she put in. "I was burning with fever until he whipped up his creams and ointments." Not wanting to sell her mother short, she added, "Ma's prayers and Pun's medicines, that's what did it."

Eliza walked over to Preston and placed her hand on his forearm. "Let's not forget Doctor Forbes' contribution," she said. "Truly, he's the one we need to thank."

Tom was the last to join the crowd in the kitchen, having only just finished his chores at the sheds. He shook Preston's hand, and when Isaac shared the doctor's story about Mads, Tom stood for a minute, eyebrows twitching as he absorbed the news. "Right or left?" he said.

"Pardon?" Preston asked.

"Hand. Was it his right or his left that got tore up?"

"Right, I believe. Why?"

Tom glanced at Richard. "That day he threatened you up to Brundage, which hip steadied his holster?"

"Right," said Richard, without hesitation. The encounter with Mads was seared on his brain, and not something he'd soon forget.

Tom gave Richard a sly smile. "Don't reckon he'll shoot up any sheepherders' camps for a while, yet." Chuckling, he strolled through the kitchen and out the back door.

Everyone sat in silence, not quite certain where to next steer the conversation. Preston again glanced at July. He cleared his throat and coughed politely into his fist. The cue wasn't lost on Eliza; it was she who sensed the real reason for his visit, she who suggested July and Doctor Forbes retire to the porch for a cup of hot chocolate. "I'll make yours with top-milk, July," she said, knowing she liked it that way. When July reminded her mother she hadn't yet finished her chores nor carded the mattress on Lilly's old bed, Isaac rose from his chair. "Take our guest to the porch," he said firmly. "Your mother's fetching hot chocolate."

July glanced at Richard, saw the distress in his face. There was little he could do to help her without revealing her secret, and so he said nothing when she led the doctor away. She sat in her father's wicker rocker, angling herself in such a way that she was as far from Preston as possible. She declined to even look at him when he sat on the swing by himself. Back and forth he went, the springs squeaking with each annoying sway. July sat firm, staring into the distance, her mouth set in a resentful knot. She felt his eyes on her, wandering up and down her shirtwaist. He, too, no doubt, wondered about the scar between her breasts.

He leaned forward, twirling his hat with both hands. As though reading her thoughts, he said, "You know, July, I'm not so awful as you think."

She looked over at that, viewed him with harsh eyes. "And I'm not so good as you think."

"I don't believe that." He offered a small smile. Seeing she was serious, he said, "How bad can you be? You're a Mormon, aren't you?"

"Not a very good one. I've lied to my folks twice now, and committed questionable acts."

Preston's hands slowed their twirling. When it seemed he'd make no reply to her confession she told him she didn't understand why he kept coming to the ranch. "You can have any woman you want in Morning Tree," she told him. "Lilly's crazy about you, though she's going to New York soon and you've missed your chance with her."

"What are you talking about?"

"I'm telling you Pa won't give you permission to marry me, if that's what you're here for. I'm only fifteen, you know." She said nothing about sixteen being a more suitable age – the age when she'd likely marry Rory – seeing as how she had no interest in steering Preston's thoughts in that direction.

"Who said anything about marriage?"

Her cheeks flared. She thought maybe she'd misread him, but then she spied the tremble of his bottom lip and knew he couldn't feign surprise much longer. "Why'd you come if not to court me?"

"To tell your pa about Mads Larson." He ran a finger beneath his collar, stretching it from his throat.

"I guess that makes us both liars then."

There was uncertainty in Preston's voice when he spoke again. "I'd not realized you were so mature, July. You've grown a great deal this year."

"Did you think you were proposing to a child?"

"No, no, never." His whole body began to quiver. He rose from the swing and bent to his knees at her side. Taking her hand and holding it, he said, "I understand if you don't feel ready, but I'll wait for you forever if you'll have me."

Gently, she pulled away. "I'm sorry, Preston, I don't love you."

He again reached for her hand, gripping it tighter now. "You'll learn to love me, I know you will."

"Preston –"

"I love you, July," he said, edging closer. "My arms ache to hold you – my lips – "

"I don't want to hear it," she said, pushing him away.

He gripped her arms in a desperate clasp and pulled her toward him. Quickly, before she could object, he placed his hand behind her head, drew her near, and kissed her with a ferocity that rattled her teeth. With his lips crushing hers, she pushed hard against him, wrenching her mouth away. He grasped her harder still, and when her garbled protests became cries, he let her go as quickly as he'd grabbed her. She lurched forward, landing hard on her hands and knees. "Good Lord," he said, scrambling to help her up, "I'm so sorry, July. I never meant to – "

"Get away!" she spat, pushing to her feet while wiping her mouth.

Isaac bolted through the kitchen door, Eliza at his heels. "Hell sakes! What's all the commotion about?" His eyes traveled from July's disheveled hair and the red splotch smudging her mouth to the frantic expression worn by Preston Forbes.

"I won't marry him!" she screeched, as at last the truth came spilling out. "I'll never marry him! Rory Morrow's already proposed, and he's coming to fetch me in June!"

Eliza's face turned ashen. "You don't know what you're saying, July."

"I do know. I've known since the day I snuck to Valentine to meet him." She looked frantically around the yard, and spotting her youngest brother, said, "How do you think Raymond got my hat? He found it, is how – found it behind the trunk in the barn, where I hid it." Her eyes flicked from her mother's to her father's. "I'll tell you straight out I didn't go to Valentine to find it, I went to meet Rory, for I knew that day at the picnic there was something between us – something special, Pa, like you *used* to have with Ma."

That last part slipped out unexpectedly, and July knew in an instant she'd gone too far. Isaac took one step forward and slapped her so fast she scarcely saw it coming. The blow sent her reeling. She tumbled to the ground and landed on her hip, her hair cascading across her face. Preston again lurched forward to offer his hand, but Isaac plunged his fist against the doctor's chest. Preston hesitated. "Mount your horse," Issac ordered, "ride on out of here."

Preston glanced across the yard, saw Tom striding toward him.

"I'll leave of my own accord, Tom," he told him. He placed his hat on his head, gave it a pat, and walked sternly toward his horse.

Daniel and Pun now joined Richard and Raymond in the middle of the yard, the four of them watching Preston's departure, intending to gauge his courage by the dust his horse kicked up. They expected to see plenty of it, but to everyone's surprise hardly any rose at all. He rode calmly away, as though the encounter with Isaac hadn't rattled him one bit.

One by one, the quartet looked over at July. Seeing her sobbing on the porch, her tears wetting the wooden floorboards, wrenched their hearts. Slowly, they turned their accusing eyes toward her father.

Isaac's brow thickened and his face turned dark. "You all got work to do," he flared. "Get yourselves to it."

Chapter Eighteen

Had Rory known July was sporting a red spot on her cheek where her father struck her, he too would have tapped his hat on his head and mounted his horse. But he wouldn't have dallied on his way to the Caldwell ranch, as Preston Forbes had dallied when he'd left, but flown with the speed and determination of a hawk, his eye on the prize that was July.

But he didn't know, and so he bided his time until he'd see her again, when his pockets would bulge with the cash he'd earned from selling his farm-folk photographs. He'd made money – more, in fact, than he'd dreamed possible. But despite the coins spilling from the tin box he stashed beneath the blanket in the barn, his pa gave him no kind words nor encouragement.

"If you're bent on a worthless profession," he told Rory, "you can work it on your own." He'd made these noises before, threatening to throw Rory from the house, but always with the assumption photography was merely a distraction – a hobby that kept his son from the real job of raising cattle. Deep inside, he always hoped the boy would come around, but when Rory took up picture-taking full time, riding off for days to pose farmers with their mules, Silas laid down the law to his son and to his wife too.

Lydia held her ground. "You make him go, I'll leave too," she warned him. "Then who will cook for a dozen men with bellies big as washtubs? Blink Neely and Slack Jaw? They can't even break an egg into a fry pan without juicing up their shirts." No, as long as there was breath in Lydia Morrow's body and spirit in her son's soul, she'd never turn him from home. And if Silas believed she would, why, he had no more sense than a bucket of rocks.

By the time the plump-bodied warblers had sent their young ones from their nests, Rory had traveled seven hundred miles, crisscrossing the state, stopping at ranches outside Boise and beyond, photographing men and women eager to show the folks back home what they'd made of their lives. Everywhere he went, the surging immigrant population welcomed him, inviting him to sit at their tables in their makeshift tents, to enjoy meals of ham hocks and beans, and slices of hot, buttered bread.

He saw firsthand how the burgeoning settlements threatened the livelihoods of men like his pa, and marveled that his own father lacked the foresight to plan ahead, to ask himself every now and then how his family would survive if the open range dwindled, then disappeared altogether.

Smarter men had gotten out of the cattle business and started new operations in Council or Mesa, where they grew apples in orchards as big as the old places they once had up to Badger. But Rory supposed his own pa would never go for that. He held no more esteem for apple growers than he did photographers, and in his eyes both were worthy of little more than scorn.

So many times, as Rory rode up the dirt trail that led to the Caldwell's house, he'd paused at the fork in the road. Countless times he'd nudged his horse toward her place and then turned back, not wanting to ruin with a misstep what might be his only chance to see her. And so on this afternoon, too, he again held back, unaware July sat alone in her room, the spot on her cheek blooming into a bright purple bruise.

When he was but a mile or two north of the fork in the road, he spied a wagon ambling toward him. Three figures sat crowded together on the seat up front, the two on the left shimmering in puffy blue bonnets. As the wagon approached, Rory recognized the girl in the middle as July's friend, Emeline Houston. He recollected how she'd gotten teary over the news his pa had whipped him that day at the pond, and who had watched July so tremulously from the school's porch last fall. She sat between her parents, her back straight, her smooth, white face as curiously expectant as the last time he'd seen her. She struck him as the delicate type, a girl who'd disintegrate as easily as fluff from a dandelion if spoken to too harshly.

He called up his best manners when he stopped to tip his hat. "Hello Mrs. Houston, Emeline." He nodded to the women. To Emeline's father he said, "Hello Mr. Houston. What brings you out today?"

"Trip to celebrate my sister's birthday," came the man's reply. "And what about you, young Morrow? The bridge at Valentine is still out and you're a good twelve miles from home. What are you doing so far from Badger?"

Rory patted the pack in which his camera was stored. "I'm off to Mesa to photograph the apple growers." He let his gaze slip toward Emeline, whose cheeks now flushed pink, then looked again at her father. "Photography is my specialty, and I'm better than most at portraits. I'll take your wife's, or your daughter's photograph, for two dollars – any setting you like. I aim to hang my shingle in Morning Tree one day, and when I do, the same photo will cost you double."

Mr. Houston chuckled. "You're quite the businessman," he mused. "A boy with your gumption will go far. Seems a tragedy to waste a career on so trivial a pursuit as picture-taking when you could be working for me."

"Solomon," chastised Mrs. Houston, "where would we be without photographs? Why, they're the records of the world we live in." She looked at Rory and smiled. "Of course we'd be delighted to have you take Emeline's portrait, dear. Come to the house next Tuesday and we'll offer you supper, as well."

"Thank you," Rory said, again tipping his hat. "I'll be there."

Mr. Houston gently tapped the reins against his horses' backs. "'Tis a pity you won't work for me, boy," he called over his shoulder as the team trotted forward. "You'll never get rich that way."

"I ain't aimin' to get rich," Rory hollered back. "I'm aimin' to start my life – and maybe a family." When he raised his hand in farewell, Emeline turned in her seat to look at him, her chin dipped low, her eyes filled with something akin to possibility. Her expression so surprised Rory that he sat, unmoving, his hand suspended in mid-air, while she held her eyes on him.

It was this expression, so queer and yet captivating, that he sought to mimic as he arranged Emeline in the parlor of her house. He situated her in a tall wooden chair, a paisley curtain tacked to the wall behind her to soften the reflecting sun. The light filtered across the left side of her face, highlighting her hair and shadowing her right cheek. Her eyes shone vivid as a mountain stream, her mouth, sumptuous as a strawberry. Had he met Emeline before July he might have been tempted to reach over and caress her cheek, yet pretty as she was he suspected her too fragile a flower, too easily crushed, to endure the love he held inside.

Before Emeline got the wrong idea about why he'd come to Morning Tree and who, exactly, it was he planned to marry, he told her he was saving his money to wed a Mormon, although he didn't say who. He hadn't officially proposed to July and didn't want to let the cat out of the bag since it would come as a shock to July's father.

Emeline's mouth puckered, and in her voice Rory heard questioning surprise. "But you're a Gentile, like me."

"I'm willing to convert," he told her, and then just like that, came out with it: "I'm marrying July." He saw emotion brewing behind Emeline's eyes; saw too she loved July as much as she ever had, though the news hurt her some.

He had no words to console her, and in fact was beginning to burn a fever in the small, tight room, which now seemed to draw no air at all. He'd done nothing to encourage Emeline, had no wish to hurt her, either, yet here she was, perusing him with doe eyes he'd never invited.

Not knowing how else to cool the prickly sensation on his neck, he gathered his equipment, declining Mrs. Houston's invitation to stay for supper. He excused himself with the lie of a forgotten appointment, embellishing the story by pulling his watch from his pocket, glancing at it, and clucking his tongue at his carelessness.

"You'll come again, though?" Emeline asked as she walked him to the door.

"Of course," he said, not meeting her gaze. And when he at last looked up, took notice of the way she chewed at her bottom lip, he told her kindly he'd deliver her portrait in person.

The incident at Emeline's fueled the fire in his belly, made him think how much he missed July, how his arms ached to hold her. Though he'd told her that day at the schoolyard he'd not fetch her until June, he couldn't wait a minute more to see her. If he didn't inhale the sweet sage of her hair, kiss the delicate curve of her mouth, he'd go as crazy as that woman to Valentine. And so this time, when he approached the fork in the road, he yanked his horse onto the prong that led to the Caldwell's place and raced hard toward her.

It was Tom who spotted him first, Tom who had the advantage of recognition. He'd seen the boy when Lilly pointed him out during the Independence Day picnic and knew what he meant to July. Anyone who knew Isaac also knew he would never beat the devotion from her heart, nor force her to marry Preston Forbes.

Tom hadn't liked seeing July sprawled across the ground at her father's hand – none of the boys had – and they'd all leaned a chilly shoulder Isaac's way for days afterward. Tom had even thought about it a time or two while lying on his bed in the bunkhouse. He had decided there must be something decent about the boy for July to risk everything in announcing her plans to marry him; he wasn't even a Mormon – which, to Tom's way of thinking, elevated him all the more.

He raised a hand as Rory's horse approached. "Hold up there, fella," he called. "What's your all-fire hurry?"

Rory pulled back on the reins, stopping short of Tom. "I'm here to see July," he announced. "Don't be thinkin you'll stop me, either." His horse shifted on all fours, sensing perhaps, Rory's need to go.

Tom pulled a bandana from his pocket, swiped it across his face. "I ain't thinking any such thing," he said. "What I'm wondering though, is how long it'll take Isaac Caldwell to shoot you from your saddle." He let that sink in. "You're Silas Morrow's boy, ain't you?"

"What if I am?"

"Then you're in a chunk a trouble, young man. I seen you at the picnic – we all seen you, making eyes at July – and that's your first problem, see? You're a cattleman's son, here to call on a sheepman's daughter. That ain't likely to set well with July's pa. Second problem is, you got no gun on your hip."

"I got a Winchester strapped to my scabbard and I know how to use it."

"Third problem," said Tom – and he let this sink in too – "is July's not home and you'd be dying for nothing."

Rory had not counted on July not being there when he finally came to fetch her. "Where is she then?"

Tom leaned on his shovel. "Well, let's see. It's the middle of May, so my guess is she's halfway to the mountains with Richard by now. Isaac sent her off with the whole lot of them, figuring she'd take to her horse, looking for you, if he left her home. She told her pa and everyone else she loved you, even though Doc Forbes is set on her, wanting to ask for her hand."

"She told her pa she loved me?"

"And that she wanted nothing to do with Preston Forbes." Tom watched Rory's face shift and then brighten as the boy calculated some inner doings. "If you're thinking of pointing that pony to the high country," he went on, "you best think again. Daniel's got no qualms against shooting kidnappers."

"Daniel?" said Rory, his face folding with confusion. "Who's he?"

"Herder – and a tough biscuit too." Tom neglected to mention that Pun for the most part was a pacifist and Richard, while a thoughtful young fellow, was more likely to pack poetry than a pistol, though even if he pulled a gun he'd never shoot July's intended. As for Daniel, Tom let Rory draw his own conclusions.

"Tough biscuit or no," said the boy, "I got to see July."

Tom nodded. "I see you're determined but you best take my advice. Ride on out of here if you love her, for a dead man don't make that good a husband."

Rory looked to the ranch then back at Tom, grunting in frustration. "When will she be back?"

"First of November – somewhere along there."

"Why, that's five months from now!" Rory cried. "I can't wait that long." And with that, he yanked his horse around and galloped toward Badger.

What the boy was after Tom couldn't say, but he guessed it had something to do with a little money stashed in a box somewhere, and maybe a slim gold ring to go with it. That Isaac would never grant them permission to marry was simply what it was, so there wasn't much point in stirring July up by mentioning Rory's visit. Tom felt it only fair, however, to let Isaac know the boy had been around, for once Silas Morrow learned his only son was bent on marrying a Caldwell, it would be the Civil War all over again. Isaac would need time to situate his cannons, although God help him, he'd likely make a mess of the battle plan.

Chapter Nineteen

Before Tom loaded the wagon and mules with supplies, then left for the lower elevations of the sheep camp, he told Isaac about Rory. As predicted, the man stormed from the machine shed to the middle of the yard, hurling tools and tar buckets until they littered the ground like a hailstorm. "I won't have it!" he shouted. "Tie her up if you have to, or lock her in the barn – just keep her away from that cowboy!"

"I'll keep an eye on her, Isaac, but I don't see what good it'll do. If she aims to marry him, she will."

Isaac's face softened, the anger shifting to pain. Tom saw by the furrow in his forehead and sad dip of his eyes he understood he'd someday lose July – that perhaps he'd lost her now. Even so, Tom's heart stood hard against him, for the man hadn't the good sense to compromise – to at least hear July and Rory out. Isaac would sooner say goodbye to a daughter than allow himself some wiggle room, for his need to control his wife and children was greater than his love.

Tom saw too that though July wasn't his blood sister, though she hadn't yet drifted as far from the Church as he had, she was more like him than anyone else in the family. She attended Sunday meeting with her folks and abided by the Word of Wisdom, but even before her accident she'd never flung herself upon the Elders, seeking their prayers when a worry worked her mind. She was far more likely to put her problems to the trees, looking for God's answer in the whisperings of their leaves. She wasn't one to shape the doings of her daily life like her ma did either, filling the well of her longing with good deeds just so she could glide through the gates of the Celestial Kingdom.

When he watched her five days later, wandering the sheep camp, listlessly offering water to the crew and wearing a face that would make a hangman cry, he suspected she'd decided to stick to home and make her pa happy. Tom hated to see it come to that, for in trying to help Isaac do battle with Silas, he began to think he'd stuck his toe on the dark side and cheated July out of a choice. Had she known Rory had come to fetch her she would have worn the flesh from her heels to get to him. But ensconced as she was in a haze of ignorance, she spent long days preparing meals for the shearers.

The men were sturdy and rough. July sat on a boulder, apart from them, watching as one of the bigger shearers – a fellow with thighs the size of tree stumps – opened a ewe's fleece at the shoulders and clipped the creature close, careful to leave just enough wool to protect it from the chill of night and blistering sun of day.

Later, Tom caught her staring at him too, as though he were a traitor. While she couldn't have known he'd betrayed her, he thought her gaze heavy as an anvil and so he turned from her and went hard about his business. When one of the men refused to work with Pun, saying the Chinese were as disgusting as sheep scab, Tom fired him. He told the man's friend he himself could stay, so long as he kept his trap shut and his nose low to the ground. His voice was a warning as much as his words, and for the rest of the day the man worked with his head down.

July looked at Tom a little more kindly after that. When she wasn't cooking it was her job to help Richard gather the fleeces and secure them tightly with cord. Richard stuffed the bundles into long burlap bags hanging from tree limbs, tromped the wool down until the bag was tightly packed. Pun, the smallest of the men, numbered each bag and painted it with Isaac's brand. Daniel and the others heaved the nearly three-hundred pound sacks onto a series of wagons commissioned for the task of hauling them to the train depot in Weiser.

One of the shearers, a fellow whose face was caked with dirt and damp with sweat, looked old at thirty-six. Though his back was broad and hilly with muscle, his eyes were lined and weary. "Twenty years is a long time to wrestle these critters," he groused one day at dinner. His friends didn't speak, but their own faces said as much. They all looked exhausted, worn down from shearing and the strain of living, traveling from ranch to ranch and town to town, spending no more than a month or two at their own homes each winter.

On their last day of shearing, the men finished early. Tired as they were, no one wanted to start the long trek home, so they put together a boxing match, hoping to liven things up.

"Too tired head home," observed Pun dryly, "but plenty energy fight. Just like American." He stepped back and shook his head, crossing his arms over his chest.

"You ought to get in there, Pun," said Daniel, "show em what you're made of."

"Made of steamed radish," Pun said with a snort. To demonstrate, he held up one thin arm and jiggled the soft flesh beneath it.

"Hell, I'll get in," said Tom.

"Me, too!" hollered the fellow who'd spoken up at dinner.

They pulled their shirts over their heads, rolled up the sleeves of their long johns, and snapped their suspenders in place. Daniel bound their knuckles with socks while Richard gathered a rope; he and three others held it taut at the corners.

"This here's your ring!" Richard called.

Tom and the shearer went at it, and Tom promptly took two swift jabs to the jaw. His head snapped back before he righted himself. "You're packing quite a punch, there, fella," he told the man. While the shearer congratulated himself, Tom leveled a good one at his nose. Surprised, the man stumbled back. Blood poured down his chin. He sputtered, wobbling to one corner. He climbed out of the ring to the good-natured jeering of his companions.

A second shearer bounded in. "I believe I can take a little a that," he boasted, cocky as the first.

Tom smiled, bouncing on his toes before lunging unexpectedly. The shearer was too quick for him though, and caught him hard on one eyebrow. The flesh split open, and this time it was Tom who skittered back. He hit the rope and bounced forward, his hands whirling slowly. He was having a fine time, tottering in a rhythmic to and fro, circling the man, holding his fists high to protect his face. Every so often his right arm shot out and clipped the man on the ear. It wasn't until the blood from Tom's wound began dribbling into his eye that he slowed at all, and even then his right arm kept on going.

"I kin split that other brow for ya," the shearer taunted, reeling from Tom's punches. "Just step in closer, is all."

Tom obliged, but before the fellow could get his swing squared away, Tom clobbered him under the chin. The man spun like a top and crashed to the ground.

Pun put an end to the ruckus by hopping into the ring, grabbing Tom's arm and raising it high. "Tom winner boxing contest," he announced, dropping Tom's arm and climbing from the ring. To anyone who would listen, he added, "In China we have more dignity – fight wit mind, not fist."

"In that case," called a shearer in the back, "try thinking your way out of this!" He hopped into the ring and motioned for Pun to join him. Pun shook his head. "C'mon, little man," the shearer sneered. "Like Dan'l said, let's see what you're made of."

Pun scowled. "Not want fight."

"Sure you do," puffed the man, his fists stabbing the air.

It was all too much for July. She didn't want to watch these men smacking and jabbing each other, bloodying one another's noses. If they had any idea what it was to be slapped down in earnest, made small in front of those they admired, she doubted they would have crawled into the ring in the first place.

Pun watched her as she got up to leave. He was about to follow when the man in the ring scurried up behind him and punched him in the kidney. Pun folded sideways and groaned, holding this position while the man danced around him.

"Come on," the fellow goaded, slugging Pun on the shoulder. "You must got some mad in ya somewhere." He bounced around Pun and glared at the crew. "I know I do. I got some mad stored up for this bug-eatin Chinee." He bounced in front of Pun, punched him again. "That was my buddy you got fired, Mongolian," he sneered, and again he punched, the blow to Pun's shoulder sending him wobbling a few steps back.

Tom stood to intervene, took one step forward.

"He can take care of hisself," said Daniel, blocking Tom with one arm. "I seen him practicing once when he didn't know I was watchin."

"Practicing what?"

"You'll see."

"Not want fight," Pun repeated. He stood straighter, spread his legs almost imperceptibly and set his feet firmly on the ground.

The man raised his fist and paused, as if aware all at once of a change in the air. The hesitation cost him, for in that moment Pun stirred the air with both hands. In a peculiar little motion he brought the edge of his palm hard against the man's throat. The man gripped his neck and staggered back, his tongue dangling like a lamb's.

"What the hell was that?" asked Tom.

"I don't know," Daniel admitted, "but I'd like to learn me some."

Poised for a second attack, Pun asked the man if he wanted more. Tears spilled from the shearer's eyes. He shook his head. The older man, the man whose nose Tom bloodied earlier, stepped forward and glared at the injured man. "That's what you git for struttin like a rooster," he told him. "Maybe now you'll keep your banty old backside in the henhouse, where it belongs."

Tom sent the man packing with the pay he'd earned, just as he had his friend. When the shearer slunk off, his fingers clutching his throat, Daniel walked over to Pun. "Say now," he said, gripping him on the shoulder, "you reckon you can teach me that?" Hearing this, the man with the bloody nose turned and said, "Me, too?" And then the whole crew sidled over, wanting to know Pun's secrets. Before the day was over he'd taught them all a trick or two, and come suppertime they were in fine spirits. To celebrate Tom's victory and the last day of shearing, Tom and Richard slaughtered an old ewe and cooked her up with some steamed potatoes while Pun shaped an apricot pie.

The moon was halfway up the sky by the time he brought a plate to the tent and offered it to July. She was laying on her bedroll, her back toward the open flap that was the door. "I'm not hungry," she said, "but thanks for thinking of me, Pun."

He squatted on his haunches, settling in next to her. "Got pie," he cajoled, "mix in plenty sugah too. Tom say taste like home." He smacked his lips, attesting to its goodness, but when July made no move to roll over he set the plate on the ground. Sighing, he said, "Pun mad at faddah once, too, and faddah mad at Pun."

July rolled over, and then leaned on one elbow. "What did you fight about?"

"Faddah make Pun feel foolish." He went on to tell July how he'd approached his father, informed him he planned to head to America to make his fortune, return with his satchel of gold. "Faddah say, stay China, where muddah cook rice, sistah rub feet, and enemy's skin same color. But I proud man, full of good ideas" – here, he tapped his head – "so I tell muddah, sistah, bruddah – all of dem goodbye. But to faddah I say nothing, just turn and walk away."

He drew his feet beneath him, situating himself so he sat more comfortably on the ground. "When boat land America, Pun see some what faddah say true. No muddah cook rice, no sistah rub feet. Just devil with dog breath yelling 'Get back on boat, Chinee – go home where belong!'"

"Why didn't you then, if they hated you so much?"

"Want prove faddah wrong," he said. "By time save money, decide go home, fadda die…" Pun's voice trailed off at the memory. When he spoke again it was to tell July he wanted very much to return home, pay his respects to his father and give what he'd earned to his mother, but to do so meant he'd never be able to return to the United States again. By then it was the law instead of some devil's breath that would keep him away.

July's eyes widened. "There's a law that says you can't come back to America?"

Pun nodded. "See what saying, though? When go from faddah, important tell goodbye."

She pulled a long face and lay back down. "I don't know why. My own pa's never listened to a thing I've said."

Pun thumped her on the head. "What's mattah you? Faddah loves Jew-rye. Want her come home soon."

July harrumphed. "I'll believe it when I see it, but I sure won't hold my breath."

Chapter Twenty

Pun's conversation with July didn't have the impact he'd hoped for, for instead of nudging her closer to her pa it set her farther from him. It put her mind to working long and hard about how she could make money, too; how, if she had a camera, she'd take photos and sell them for a dollar. If she and Rory pooled their money there was little doubt they'd have enough to get married *and* set up shop in Morning Tree, maybe as soon as September.

This particular shearing crew might well spend money on a photograph, and as she thought on it, she pictured the scenario in her mind's eye: twenty or so characters standing tall inside a shed, shirts bloody and hair mussed, shears glinting in beefy hands. They'd gladly release a portion of their wages to capture their likeness on film, to gaze proudly at a photo so they could one day point to a sunburned face and say, "That one there, that's me. Sheared upward of a hundred sheep a day, I did, in the mountains of Idaho."

Revisiting this reverie the next morning, she devised a plan to find Rory by slipping away, pointing herself in the direction of the Joshua River and then the Weiser, where she'd mingle with the shadows of the cottonwoods and travel undetected.

She decided to make her move the next day, while Tom readied the mules for his trip home. She hid a few slices of mutton in a handkerchief and tucked it under her belt, told Pun she was off to hunt ginseng. She looked around the camp and bid each of them a silent farewell – Tom, as he arranged the packs on the mules and tightened their cinches, then Daniel, as he headed over a hill with his band of winsome sheep. To Pun she issued a loving goodbye, and to Richard she braved a smile. He sat with Tick and Bug, tossing them bits of roasted meat. Tick sat with her bat ears up, her mouth open and legs trembling. She caught the morsel with a clap of her jaws, swallowed before she'd even chewed. Bug sat slightly behind her mother and waited her turn, scooting forward in increments of an inch or two, hoping to be noticed. "I see you," Richard told her, and then he threw her a scrap too.

July stood on a slug of granite as wide as her father's buckboard. Gazing at the valley below, she took in rusty willows meandering along glimmering streams. Higher up, where the ground turned rocky and the dirt red-brown, junipers sprouted among the sage, and as far as she could see, yellow flowers spilled like buckets of fool's gold.

She turned, breathing in the sweet pine air. Looking toward the mountain, she saw snow pulling away from the sun, tucking its cool arms into the mountain's blue-black ridgetops like a turtle ducking into its shell.

And that's when she saw him – a man on horseback.

"Richard," she called, her voice uneasy. "Are any of our shearers wearing cowboy hats?"

"Two or three, I guess. Why?"

"One of them's riding like the wind in our direction."

Richard tossed a last scrap to Bug and looked up. He squinted hard. "That ain't a shearer, July," he said, standing slowly. "That's Mads Larson." He whipped around and hollered at Tom to fetch his gun.

Tom's thoughts were on his chores at home, how they were piled high as a haystack, when he heard Richard's cries. He looked up to see the boy gesturing toward July. Thinking she'd met up with a wolf or maybe a she-bear, he jerked his rifle from its scabbard and bounded her way. It wasn't until he'd scrambled halfway there that he realized Richard wasn't pointing at July at all, but somewhere just beyond. His eyes scanned the distance. He too spotted the cowboy.

Richard jogged over to the rock, his face etched with worry. "That's Mads Larson, Tom. He means business."

"July," Tom said evenly. "Go on past the mules and hide yourself. Richard, run and get your gun."

"I can shoot as good as he can," July protested. "Maybe better."

"I ain't got time to argue now. Go."

July hopped from the boulder and took off for the mules. But instead of hiding behind the animals as Tom directed, she slipped behind a lodgepole pine not far from where they stood. She wanted to witness Mads' threats for herself, to tell Rory how Mads wasn't the straight shooter he thought he was, how he'd spilled toward them, angry as a flashflood, and tried to intimidate Richard with his rough ways.

He was a feisty one, roaring into camp. He must have spotted Tom and Richard poised on the rock, rifles steady in the crook of their arms, for he tugged hard on his reins and halted. He took in the scene – the mules, the band of sheep browsing on the hillside, the sturdy young men defending their turf – and viewed them darkly. He nudged his horse with his heels; the animal snorted and then slowly trotted forward. Mads' eyes glinted dangerously at Richard. "I told you last fall to keep your pa's woolies off this mountain, yet here you are again."

"We're the ones ought to complain," Tom said. "Morrow's cattle all but ruined the range last fall, long before you come whining to the boy here, about the damage our sheep done." He gestured toward the mountain. "What your steers haven't chomped down they've stomped, spoiling the stream banks and filling the ditches with mud. I ought to know – I mucked enough of your slop to build a mountain tall as Brundage."

"That's a sad song, Blakely, but I ain't here to listen to your troubles. Ain't here to deliver no warning, neither. I'm here for one thing, and that's to tell you to get out."

Tom slowly raised his rifle and pointed it in the vicinity of Mads' stomach. "Get out, yourself."

Even from her spot behind the tree, July saw Mads' face grow tight as a carcass and white with rage. She saw too the blood pulsing through his neck. When he lightly pulled on his reins with the three remaining fingers of his right hand, his horse took a few steps back. Mads turned his head and gazed at some unknown object. He held that pose for several seconds. The reins fell from his fingers. All at once he jerked his Colt from its holster and pulled the trigger. A shot rang out. Tom stumbled back, his finger snagging the trigger as the gun's barrel snapped up. The bullet hit Mads in the face, tearing off his nose and a good sized chunk of his chin. He tumbled backward, over the horse's rear end, and landed on his back, arms splayed, one leg clamped awkwardly beneath the other.

Richard stood, mouth hanging, his breathing short and shallow. He didn't move until July dashed out from behind her tree and ran toward him. She threw herself around him and clung to him, sobbing into his neck.

He wrapped one arm around her, and together they stumbled toward Tom. It wasn't until he moaned that they realized he was alive, that Mads' bullet hadn't pierced Tom's heart, but his shoulder.

Chapter Twenty-One

That Tom lived was in some ways the undoing of all their lives, for had he died along with Mads, Silas's men might not have retaliated but talked among themselves and agreed, in some common desire not to let things get out of hand, that one eye given for another was vengeance enough, and let things go at that.

Instead, Blink Neely rounded up a dozen hands from various cattle companies around Badger and brought them in on a meeting at Silas Morrow's ranch. The men gathered in the barn, listening hard while Blink railed against Tom Blakely. Blink told the men Mads' death was neither an accident nor cruel design of fate, an opinion the men seconded, their fists punctuating the air. "Tom Blakely murdered Mads," Blink insisted. "It's plain and simple as that."

Slack Jaw stepped forward. "If Mads shot first, like Caldwell claimed, he'd of hit Blakely in the head, not the shoulder."

The men chorused their agreement, never stopping to consider that with two fingers missing, Mads' aim wasn't what it used to be. They looked to Silas for some sign he was with them. All this time he'd been sitting on a stool, his forearms propped on his knees, his gaze fixed on the ground. His hat shadowed his face so that no man could read his thoughts but there was no reason to believe he didn't grieve Mads as much as they did, that he too wouldn't seek revenge.

"I never thought I'd see the day a sheepman nudged me out of Idle Valley," he said at last, "but I believe that day has come."

"Oh, it's come," said Blink, agreeing, "'less you do something about it."

"We can wipe Caldwell out," said a man in the back. "All the rest of them too."

"Then what?" came a voice from the dark. It was Rory. They'd not seen him leaning against the wall, absorbed as they were with their plotting. "Will you wipe out the squatters too? The farmers and Chinese, the Mormons up to Morning Tree? Where will it end, Pa, for once you start, you won't be able to stop."

Silas's head snapped up. "I washed my hands of you, told you to git." He sat firm, but his face gave way, and anyone could see it pained him to repeat this truth.

Blink Neely wanted to know what the Mormons and Chinese had to do with it. Silas told him it was none of his concern, but Rory wasn't about to let his pa off so easily. "Not thirty minutes ago I told Pa I aim to marry July Caldwell," Rory said. "Pa told me no son of his would lower hisself so, and to pack my bags and go. As you can see, I ain't gone yet."

The news that one of their own would wed the daughter of a sheepman astounded the men, and they stood with their mouths open.

Rory turned to his father. "I was in the middle of gatherin my things when your posse rode up. I don't know what you're plannin, but I'm not going to let you hurt July or her family – you best get that through your head right now." It was as bold as he'd ever spoken to his pa, and he wished he'd done it long ago.

"How you gonna stop him?" came a voice from the back.

"And all the rest of us?" said Blink, stepping forward. "How you gonna do that?" The men in the room pressed toward Rory in a collective shadow. "Silas," said Blink, pausing, "you best lend a hand or turn a cheek, 'cause we don't aim to let Rory run off and tell Caldwell we're a-comin."

One of the men, a big-chested fellow with a scar across his nose, slipped through the crowd. He hadn't spoken up before, but now he roughly told Silas he wanted no part of the ugly scheme. "It ain't right, what you're suggesting, and you know it well as I do." He glanced at Rory, his eyes filled with pity. When he looked back at Silas, those same eyes turned cold and he strode out the door.

Silas watched the man climb on his horse and ride away. He turned to Rory. That his son refused to flinch, that he stood tall and proud despite the cruelty around him, set Silas's teeth to grinding. If he couldn't teach his son a lesson maybe Blink and the others could. He slowly stood, and then he too walked out the door.

* * *

Tom laid in Lilly's old bed, naked from the waist up, his shoulder wrapped in gauze. Preston Forbes had put him to rights again. Isaac had ridden into Morning Tree to fetch him, saying hardly a word even after they'd gotten back to the ranch, for neither he nor Eliza had forgotten so soon the incident on the porch. Yet Preston refused to yield to Isaac's stern stare and performed his job expertly. He spoke only to request hot water from Eliza and to ask her assistance in administering the chloroform so he could dig deeper for the bullet lodged below the tip of Tom's collarbone. July had nothing to do with Preston, making herself scarce and taking refuge in the loft. Birdy nickered from her stall. July gave the horse a pat and kissed her nose before climbing the ladder. She found Raymond sprawled on his belly atop the hay, his chin resting on his hands. His brows were knitted in a tight knot, and there was a mournful glint to his eyes.

"What are you doing up here, Ray?" she asked softly.

"It's my fault Tom's shoulder's bung up," he said, his mouth quivering.

She crawled up there with him, nestled into the hay and wrapped one arm around his shoulders. "Now, that's just silly," she said, and this little bit of tenderness set his eyes watering. He laid his head on July's lap. "If I hadn't found your bowler and stuck it on my head, none of this would a happened. Pa wouldn't a sent you off, and Tom wouldn't a gone runnin after no she-bear."

He'd gotten his story mixed up somehow, but none of that mattered now. "Hush," she told him, though her voice was kind. "I made my own troubles, Ray. It's got nothing to do with you. I lied about meeting Rory at Valentine – asked you to lie too. I should have told Ma and Pa the truth from the get-go."

"So it's *your* fault Tom's hurt?"

"No, it's Mads Larson's fault. He shot Tom, and when Tom's arm flung back, his gun went off and the bullet hit Mads in the head." She was quiet a moment. "Neither of us is to blame – it's just this awful thing that happened."

"Is Tom gonna die?"

July shook her head. "Doctor Forbes is with him now. Likely Tom'll be digging ditches before you can count to ten."

"I already done that," he said, tears springing anew. "I done it twice now, and he still ain't up. He ain't even awake yet."

"It's just an expression," July told him. "It might take longer than that." She lay back against the hay, despairing over the turn her life had taken. Tom's too. And she worried over Richard, for he was alone in the hills again, stuck in the circumstances of his life. They were all stuck, it seemed: she and Tom, Richard and Pun. Even poor Lilly, who continued to talk of New York City but still hadn't boarded a train. And all of this happening without the comfort of Rory's arms around her.

She thought on him long and hard, as Raymond lay next to her. She was all set to go to Rory that morning at Brundage, so why couldn't she just go now as she'd planned to do before? She sat up, thinking she could, of course, and would, the minute she had the chance to get away. She'd sneak off in the night if she had to, leave a note for Raymond so he wouldn't feel she'd up and left him, although certainly she had.

She heard the screen door slam, followed by the sound of Preston's horse clomping from the ranch. Raymond had fallen asleep on her lap, and after a while she tenderly moved his head onto a small pillow of hay, then left him to his nap in the barn. She crawled down the ladder and went inside, asked after Tom, peeked in to see him. Eliza stood in the doorway with her, saying Doctor Forbes had done all he could – "just as he did for you, July." Even now, Eliza worked like a warrior to forgive his forceful advance on her daughter.

They both turned to the sound of someone wheeling up in a buggy. It was Brother Kilker, come to provide a blessing for Tom. He'd gotten word of Tom's injury through the local grapevine, and figuring Isaac would forget to call him this time too, rode out of his own accord. July and Eliza watched as he anointed Tom's forehead with oil. Eliza closed her eyes and bowed her head, but July quietly stepped away from the door and padded toward the kitchen. The sun had dipped behind the hills, and the evening's shadows had crept into the house. She lit a lamp in the parlor and two in the kitchen and set a kettle of water on to boil. Standing at the window, she stared at the golden-green hue washing across the landscape. The Magic Hour, she'd called it. It hurt to look back to that happier time, when she and her family had broken out in song on the way to a picnic, when they'd eaten fried chicken and licked their fingers and gazed with wonder at the stars. Truth told, she'd never known a day of true unhappiness until her father slapped her to the ground. Even then, it wasn't the beating that hurt, but the knowing: he'd never open his heart to Rory, not in this lifetime or the next.

Though it was little more than a week since her pa had struck her, she felt she'd aged ten years. She ached inside to think of it, this growing up she'd done in so short a time, and all of it without Rory. But soon enough he'd see the woman she'd become.

She was in her room when her ma called her to supper. Brother Kilker joined them for the evening meal, having missed out the last time he came to minister to July. He took Tom's usual place at the table. Eliza twice called Raymond in to eat and was about to call him a third when July told her mother Ray had fallen asleep in the loft, though he might have stirred since then.

Eliza peeked out the kitchen window and looked toward the barn. Seeing nothing of Raymond, she walked to the door and stepped outside. A gust of wind picked up the corners of her apron as her eyes searched the twilight for her son's gangly form. Raymond's hearing was selective, like all boys his age, and it seemed he only came running when she threatened to hide him with a switch. She opened her mouth and inhaled, fixing to let loose just such a threat, when the low rumble of thunder tickled her inner ear. She glanced up, expecting signs of a storm. Seeing only stars, she realized too late it was no dust devil but the hooves of horses. Taking its meaning instantly, she screamed for Isaac to come.

An army of masked men rounded the corner and rode hard toward the house. They started shooting at once, aiming for the animals in the corral. Two of the marauders split off from the group, lit torches and tossed them into the barn. Hay piled in stacks near the stalls ignited at once.

Eliza tore across the yard, yelling Raymond's name. One of the men – a burly figure with a blue bandana draped across his lower face – thumped her hard on the shoulder with the butt of his rifle and knocked her to the ground.

Isaac burst through the door. Taking the steps two at a time, he fired wildly into the night, and might have hit a cowboy had his toe not snagged a gopher hole. He crashed to the ground, hitting so hard it knocked the wind from him entirely. July bounded out next – Kilker at her heels – spotted her mother on the ground and all but flew toward her. Just before she got there, Eliza scrambled to her feet, her shoulder drooping, and loped toward the barn. The fire's blue flames raged up the walls and licked the roof. Black smoke curled out the door. Birdy snorted and screamed, but there was no sign of Raymond, no sound from him at all.

Eliza again shrieked Raymond's name. There was no answer, just the whoosh and roar of the fire. She covered her face with her forearm, dipped her head, and plunged inside. Her skirt's hem, torn and dragging, quickly began to smolder. July jumped into the doorway, one forearm covering her mouth and nose, and snatched her mother's arm. Eliza turned on her, clawing and slapping and wrenching her body, but July hung on until Isaac ran up and roughly shoved her aside. Grabbing his wife by the scruff of her neck, he flung her from the building, her skirt ablaze. Kilker grabbed a blanket from a fence rail and threw it atop her, rolled her to and fro along the ground in an attempt to extinguish the flames.

Isaac again charged the barn. Shielding his face from the heat and flames, he too screamed Raymond's name, screeching until his throat burned and his mouth went dry and he could screech no more. Mired in smoke, he grabbed a rung halfway up the ladder and jerked himself up. The air was an acrid mix of scorched leather and burning tack, of smoldering hide and hair. Birdy snorted and Brigham screamed, and both horses reared in their stalls. Leaving Eliza, Kilker rushed inside. Threw open the doors and slapped the rears of both horses, shoving them toward the clearing. The animals jerked and resisted, and it took a second slap and then a third, to finally get them going.

The heat seared Isaac's skin. Flames scooted up the sides of both walls and met in the center of the ceiling, forming a canopy above the loft. Inhaling sharply and holding his breath, Isaac ducked his head and charged up the last three rungs. He spied Raymond, lying on his stomach. A chunk of cinder fell into the hay just as he clutched his son's ankle, and the whole space ignited with a whooshing sound and the sudden explosion of flame. The force sent Isaac reeling, and he fell ten feet to the floor, landing hard on his back.

Dazed, he sat up on one elbow. Kilker shot into the barn, hitched his fingers under Isaac's armpits and dragged him from the building. The roof groaned and then collapsed. For the longest while, no one moved nor spoke. Eliza sobbed, turning her face and plugging her ears, for the hissing embers were more than she could bear. Isaac sat still as stone. And when the fire died, Isaac got up, moving stiffly, and gathered Eliza into his arms. Inside, he and July tended her burns while Brother Kilker rode for help. Three days later he assumed, as well, the lead in preparing Raymond's funeral. In between, he sent the sheriff to the hills to fetch Richard and Pun, knowing Daniel could handle the sheep for a week while Richard buried his brother. Kilker no longer cared what became of Tom Blakely. It was Tom who had stirred this hornet's nest, and as far as Kilker was concerned, he could go to hell. That Raymond Caldwell gave his life to settle the score between the Caldwells and Morrows was a despicable thing, and if it happened that Tom did not pay some terrible price, then someone else would have to. "I saw a masked man on an Indian pony the night of the burning," he told the sheriff. "I think you should know the horse looked a lot like Rory Morrow's."

Chapter Twenty-Two

July sat in the parlor in front of the pot-bellied stove, empty now of coals during this last warm spell in May. Abigail Kilker, Brother Kilker's first wife – and only wife he claimed, now that the Manifesto forbade polygamy – tried to persuade her to eat something. Abigail's insides filled with pity to see the girl's silent shock, the way she did not weep. For losing a brother of eight when you yourself were just fifteen was akin to losing a limb or an organ – perhaps even a heart.

Eliza walked stiffly into the room, her legs bandaged, a crisp cotton skirt covering her burns. She was dressed in black, from the rise of her stiff collar to her starched, puffy sleeves. Her shoes were black too, polished and not yet dusted with dirt. Lilly, who'd come back home from Morning Tree, sat across from July, sipping Pun's special tea. He was there too, cut loose from the pine tree around which Morrow's men had bound him. Two days he'd sat like that, a circle of dead sheep bloating all around him. The sheriff took the herder for dead, as his wrists were ringed with ripe, purple bruises, and his body shriveled with thirst. His queue was gone, hacked off at the back of his head, and his face and neck covered with crusty scratches. Now, he shuffled between the kitchen and the drawing room, waiting on the Caldwells and their guests, anything to keep his mind off the quiet in his head, the peculiar, closed-lip silence of the sheep as one by one, Morrow's men clubbed them to the ground.

"Where is Richard, Pun?" Eliza asked through thin, parched lips.

"Outside," he said, nothing more. There was no point in letting her know Richard was helping Isaac and the others load Raymond's casket onto the buckboard. It had taken Isaac nearly two days just to gather his bones from the charred wood and ashes of the barn, but she didn't need to know that, either. In another minute more, they'd haul Raymond to his burial site. "Get Missus tea?" Pun asked, but Eliza shook her head.

"And Tom?" she said, straining as she looked out the window. "Why is he out of bed?"

Pun shrugged, not wanting to tell her of Tom's struggle to rid himself of his blankets, of his need to wander over to Raymond's bury hole and help as best he could, even if it was to shovel dirt one-handed.

The front door squeaked open. Isaac walked in, the heels of his boots echoing in the room's silence. "We're ready, Mother," he told Eliza, walking softly toward her. She pushed herself to her feet and took his hand, leaned against him as she shuffled out the door. They'd bury Raymond under a stand of cottonwoods, near the spot where July had heard her owl calling. She thought about that bird now, how her chest had gently thudded when she realized he'd come to tell her all was well, that God had forgiven her and her family was safe. But she must have mixed up the Lord's message somehow, for nothing had gone right since then.

A warm breeze stirred the trees and the scent of smoke lingered in the air. Eliza, Isaac, July and Richard gathered next to Raymond's casket while Tom, Pun, Daniel, and the handful of mourners from town stood alongside Abigail Kilker. Brother Kilker stood beneath the boughs of the old tree, the shadows of its leaves dancing across his face. He read a passage from Romans 8:35-39:

> *Who shall separate us from the love of Christ? Shall tribulation, or distress, or persecution, or famine, or nakedness, or peril, or sword?*
>
> *As it is written, for thy sake we are killed all the day long; we are accounted as sheep for the slaughter.*
>
> *Nay, in all these things we are more than conquerors through him that loved us.*
>
> *For I am persuaded, that neither death, nor life, nor angels, nor principalities, nor powers, nor things present, nor things to come,*
>
> *Nor height, nor depth, nor any other creature, shall be able to separate us from the love of God, which is in Christ Jesus our Lord.*

"Amen."

The group chorused its own quiet amen and somberly watched as the men lowered the casket into the ground. It was a simple box stained the color of pecans. July inhaled the smell of fresh pine, where just this morning nails had pierced the coffin's corners and sealed its lid forever. That scent, combined with the smell of rich dark earth, filled her senses and for one brief instant brought Raymond to life again. She thought of his sweet, soft hair, the way it caressed her lips when she kissed his head, and of his gravelly voice. She thought of his love of creatures great and small, and how he'd yearned for that second photograph from Rory.

It was this recollection that finally summoned her tears and cleansed her with relief. She cried until she could cry no more, then tossed a handful of dirt onto Raymond's coffin. Head bowed, she turned to wait on Richard while he did the same. She dabbed at her eyes and looked up, her clear, moist gaze settling on a familiar shape leaning against a tree in the shade.

Seeing Rory's face, she sucked in her breath. His cheeks were cut and bruised, his lip badly split. She tilted her head to take it all in, her legs wobbly as willows. He stepped forward then, told her with his eyes he'd come at last to fetch her. And when he reached out, she walked over to him, crawled into his arms and laid her cheek against his shoulder.

"I'm so sorry," he murmured, holding her to him. "I tried to stop them, I swear."

She took his face in her hands, kissed it tenderly. "I know this wasn't your doing." She didn't speak to his bruises, knowing without asking they had something to do with Raymond. She knew too he'd tell her in his own time, and when he did she'd listen.

She wrapped one arm around him and led him toward his horse. He leaned on her, clutching his ribs as he limped along.

Isaac stepped up from the graveside, his face pinched in anger. "You go with that boy you won't be coming back," he said, but oh, how his voice wavered.

July paused, turned to face him. There was no anger in her voice, only sad acceptance. "I love you, Pa, but if you don't want me back, I won't come."

He pulled a stiff face, but his eyes began to water. "Git on out then," he cried, and flagged her away.

July looked to her mother. Eliza stood, a fistful of skirt in each hand. She hesitated only a second before stumbling toward July on her burnt legs and throwing her arms around her. She plied a single desperate kiss to July's cheek. "No matter what happens, I love you, Julia. I always will."

"I love you too, Ma." July held her mother in one last embrace, then slowly let her go. She turned to Rory. "I'm ready," she told him. He helped her into the saddle, pulled himself up behind her, then gave the horse a nudge.

Chapter Twenty-Three

It wasn't the departure July had imagined, the fantasy she'd first sculpted in her mind where Rory stepped onto the porch, fresh-faced and smiling, asking for her hand. Nor was it the ugly fight with her folks she'd later come to expect. Instead, the parting was slow and sad, lacking altogether the fanfare she'd envisioned, but the drama too.

That she'd lost Raymond only added to her sadness, as she thought about her little brother every day now, remembering the feel of his silky head in her lap and the sound of his small, rough voice. All these months she'd waited to be with Rory, yearned to be at his side, and now that he'd finally come for her she wondered how she'd let go of Raymond's memory long enjoy to make a life with the boy she loved.

She leaned against Rory's chest, let the warmth of his body surround her. In time, a bit of happiness crept in. She closed her eyes, told herself Raymond rested in God's house now, that he'd find a new life there. And sure as God wanted Raymond to be happy, he wanted the same for July.

Rory must have been comfortable in their silence, for he held July in a grip that spoke of his love. When he shifted in the saddle, July turned and asked if she'd leaned too hard against him.

"No, no," he said, pulling her closer still.

They rode like that for three miles before he told the story of his bruises. "It wasn't Pa's doing," he said without preface, "and yet it was." Once he got those few words out it took a while for the rest to come. "Blink and Slack Jaw and the rest of them – men I never seen before – met in Pa's barn. I could hear the ugly things they were plannin and stepped in to put a stop to them –"

"What ugly things?"

"Killing your pa's sheep, burnin his barn."

July dipped her chin to her chest. When he didn't go on, she guessed he thought she couldn't stand to hear it. "I can take it," she told him. "Tell me the rest now."

He leaned forward, placing his cheek near her ear. "None of them could put it together that Tom didn't draw first, for Mads wasn't one to miss and if he'd a mind to kill Tom, he would of. I heard them speculating on it, talking about how they'd put your pa out of business, and that meant killing sheep. I stood up, told them outright it was the wrong thing to do – we didn't have your pa's side of the story yet."

"And they beat you for that?"

"Riled them pretty good," he said, nodding. "They weren't about to give me the chance to take off and warn your pa. They even told my own pa to look the other way while they sawed off my horns. He did too, just left me there to fend for myself while they punched the stuffin out of me."

July gripped his knee, told him she wished she'd been there to help him. He kissed her head, said he wished so too. They again fell into a rhythm of silence though surely the hardest thing had already been said. It would have been easy to talk if they'd a mind to, so after a while July asked him how he found out about Raymond.

"Wasn't till the sheriff come out to pose a few questions to Pa that any of us realized Raymond was in the barn that night. News hit my pa hard, I'll tell you. He could approve a beating all right, but he'd never say 'go' to a killing, especially of an eight-year-old boy." July felt the breathing in his chest grow tight. When she turned to look at him, it was with red-rimmed eyes. "That's something, Rory, to know they didn't torch our barn knowing Ray was in there."

Rory's face shifted and bitterness singed his voice. "Don't cut them no slack, July. They liked to kill me and might have killed Pun too if he'd resisted."

"Did the sheriff arrest them – Blink and Slack – any of those other fellows?"

"Naw, he had no proof. That Mormon, Kilker? He told the sheriff he saw a masked man on a horse that looked a lot like mine, but when

Pa yanked me out of bed, pointed to my face and said, 'Does this look like a boy who was in any shape to ride?' the sheriff said he guessed not, and let it go at that."

"Didn't he ask how you come to look like that?"

"He did. I told him a bull run over me and he bought it. That's the way it is up here, July. Cattlemen got more pull than sheepmen – and it sure don't help that you're Mormons."

"Why'd you lie, though? Why didn't you tell the sheriff Blink gave you that beating?"

"I didn't care enough to, I suppose. I wanted out of there, and the minute I got wind of Raymond's funeral, I wanted to be with you."

*   *   *

The circumstances under which July now returned to Valentine were entirely of her own design. For the first time she had no reason to fear the little house with the pink stone windows. She let it exist for what it was, a haven for her and Rory, a shelter in which no one disturbed them, but left them alone to learn what made the other one tick.

Rory slid from his horse first, offering July a hand. Before they took so much as a step inside he asked her to wait a minute. Pulling a slim length of rawhide from his pocket, he quickly fashioned a braided ring, clipping the loose ends with his knife. He slipped it onto her finger. "It'll be like we're married," he said. "Soon as we can, we'll ride into town and have the reverend make it right."

July fingered the little leather circle and smiled. Though she didn't want or need anyone's permission to be with Rory, it gave her a bit of comfort to imagine their union was real. "I want to put something on your finger too," she told him. She asked for his knife, cut a little strip of fabric from the hem of her slip and rolled it into a slender tine. Wrapping it around his finger, she tied it in a knot and made him promise he wouldn't take it off.

"I promise," he said. He kissed her gently on the mouth before he led her into the house. Before she'd even put water on to boil or built a fire in the stove, she shook the dust from the quilt and guided Rory into bed. While he lay there under the covers with his eyes closed, she dabbed his lips with a cloth dipped in the stream behind the house and lightly kissed his bruises. He opened his eyes to gaze at her and with one hand brushed the hair from her face. His finger lingered at her jaw, traced a line from her ear to the silky valley of her throat. He thought her skin as soft as a bird's breast, and rubbed a circle on her neck with his thumb.

She brought her hands to her collar and slowly slipped each button from its hole. Shrugging the blouse from her shoulders, she bent to remove her shoes next, then sat up, reached around, and unbuttoned her skirt. When she stood, it billowed to the ground and landed in a soft heap at her ankles. She stepped out of the fabric and stood before him in a chemise and petticoat, a shaft of light revealing the shape of her slender thighs and delicate curve of her hips.

Rory's gaze traveled slowly upward to the indentation of her waist, then over to her breasts, small as peaches, settling finally on the raised ribbon of flesh starting at her collarbone and disappearing beneath the fabric's lacy hem. July watched his eyes drift to her scar. She brought her arms to her breasts and tried to hide it. A hint of sadness crossed Rory's face. He reached out and took her wrist, pulling her onto the bed.

His fingers fumbled for the button on her drawers. She stiffened slightly and he hesitated, fixing her with a gaze that said he meant no harm. Her eyebrows folded in an apology of her own. "I don't know what to do," she told him. "Nor how to do it, either."

"We can wait, if you want to."

"No," she said, her mouth resolute. And then she smiled. "I'm ready."

"Me too." He grinned a bit too broadly, splitting the crack in his lip that had just begun to heel. July leaned over and kissed it, sucking it as gently as a kitten. Rory slipped the strap from her shoulder. She again brought her arms up as if to cover her scar, and when her eyes welled with tears he told her there was nothing about her he wouldn't love.

"How do you know? You haven't even seen it yet."

"If you can love me lookin like I do, I guess I can love you too." He struggled to sit up on one elbow, gave her a nod. Slowly, she sat up too. Closing her eyes, she took a breath, pulled the chemise over her head then lay back down and tugged at her drawers. Pulling them from her hips, she dropped them over the side of the bed, onto the floor.

The scar, still bright and swollen after all these months, began at her collarbone and ran across her stomach to her left hip. More stitches than Rory could count fanned from each side of the little red rope, and even though they'd started to fade some, the evidence of what she'd endured pierced his heart. He kissed her stomach, ran his fingers over her body and between her breasts, where the scar cut deepest.

Quelling hot tears, July dug her palms into her eyes and heaved a quivery sigh.

Rory righted himself, took her hands into his own and kissed her lashes. "Don't cry, July. You're the prettiest thing I ever saw, and no scar's ever gonna change that. I love you, hear?" Her tears abated, and she told him she loved him too. "Then help me get my shirt off," he said, smiling. "I'm too sore to raise my hands above my head."

She sat up, grasped the bottom of his shirt while he bent forward so she could get it up and over. He grimaced, and she asked if he was okay. "I am," he said. He motioned with his chin toward his pants. "But you got to help me get these off too." She managed a small grin as she loosened his belt and told him to raise up some. He hoisted his backside and she pulled his pants down in one smooth motion. His underclothes came next.

July glanced at his chest and the small folds of flesh that constituted his belly. She tried to hide her surprise as her eyes drifted southward. Oh she'd seen Raymond scooting naked around the house after his Saturday bath plenty of times, but he'd been a child, not a man. Rory was a man, and she found his form intriguing and a little frightening, all at the same time. Even so she longed to kiss him the way he'd kissed her, with her mouth traveling across his body.

He took her in his arms, slowly edging himself on top of her, bracing himself with his elbows and asking if she was all right. She told him she was. He buried his face in her neck, taking in the smell of her. His breathing picked up some when she kissed the tops of his shoulders and the corners of his mouth. He released the weight of his arms and sunk into her, as if sliding softly under water. She gave a little cry, and it seemed she'd hardly moved before he shuddered and it was over.

*   *   *

His ribs grew stronger every day, and ever so slowly his bruises began to fade. His lip healed and he kissed July at every opportunity: in the evening, as she warmed herself by the fire he'd built near the creek, or during the day, when she peered into his camera. She'd taken an interest in seeing things the way he saw them, told him when she looked into the lens, gazed beyond the stream and over by the river, she could easily imagine her pa's sheep gathering at the water like Latter-day Saints at a baptismal fount. Said she could see Pun too, and Tick and Bug, and all the trees leaning soft in the wind. "Is that the way it works?" she asked. "You see things like you want them to be, then fix them till they suit you?"

"More or less," he said, nodding. And then he smiled, looking at her with the eye of a photographer, saying he just might make her his assistant one day. She asked what she'd have to do. "Just stand there and look pretty," he said, and she laughed, propping one hand on her hip like they did in the catalogues, and saying it would be the easiest job she ever had.

"I mean it," he said. "Not just anyone can take a picture. You got to see the world in a particular way, and I think you got that talent."

He told her about the time he'd sat in a rocking chair on his porch to home one evening, petting Dunkel's head and contemplating the setting sun, the way it cast a reddish gold on the horizon and set the grass to shimmering like velvet. Told her too how he'd tried to describe it to Mads while they all sat to supper during a cattle drive and how Mads had only snorted. "He turned to Blink and said, 'What's Rory talkin about?' and Blink said, 'Don't ask me, I ain't never seen gold, nor velvet, neither.' Right about then, Slack puts in how he seen gold once but it weren't the color of the hills. I told him it was because he wasn't lookin right, then I got up, smacked my hat against my thigh, and set it my head. I didn't speak to none of them for a week after that." He was quiet a moment. "But you see what I'm sayin? Those boys got no gift at all – but you? You got an eye, July." He kissed her nose and smiled. "If I'm not careful, you'll be better'n me one day."

July could hardly believe it. No one had ever told her she'd be better than them at anything, and here Rory had not only said it, but believed it too. How she loved him for it.

And so it was they spent their days at Valentine in a haze of happiness, rising with the sun to watch birds flit among the trees and to sip tea from Mrs. Valentine's porcelain cups. Rory had packed enough supplies to last a month, and with the few pots and pans they'd found in the cabin they had all they needed to prepare a meal or bake a loaf of bread. They were short of sugar, though, and with Rory's birthday coming up, July fretted she didn't have what she needed to make him a cake.

"Don't need a cake," he told her. "All I want is for you to ride into Morning Tree with me."

"What'll we do there?"

"Ask Mr. Houston for a loan. If he gives it, we'll set up shop, get married, and move into a room in the back." She threw her arms around his neck and very nearly broke it. "Lord," he told her, "you're easy to please." And it was true, for the life they lived at Valentine was heaven. They made love every evening beneath a canopy of jeweled stars, and sometimes, in the afternoon, on a blanket in the sun. Rory found a spot behind the house that was sheltered from the wind as well as from strangers, if one ever happened by. July willingly tried it out, since she'd lost some of her shyness about her scar. She found the more she lay naked in the middle of the day, the lighter the old injury became. Rory came around with his camera once, threatening to take her picture. She screamed and threw a rock at him, hollering that her pa would have her hide if he knew.

"How's he gonna find out?" Rory teased. He lay down beside her and nuzzled her hair. "You and me will be the only ones to see it."

"Lying around naked is one thing, posing is another. Lilly's the actress, not me."

Rory rolled onto his back, forlorn. "I don't give a lick about Lilly – you're the one I got eyes for, July."

"Don't be mad," she cooed, laying her head on his chest. "I just don't feel right about it, is all." When he looked her way, she smiled. "Maybe by summer's end?"

"We'll be in Morning Tree by then."

"So I'll lay naked on your bed."

"I'll hold you to it."

"I bet you will." She tugged at his pants until he finally shucked them and flung his leg over hers.

There wasn't an inch of his body she hadn't fallen in love with. The part she liked best was the little notch on the inner rim of his left ear. She kissed it, said it was her favorite. Tracing it with her finger, she told him it looked like a mouse had taken a bite there.

He laughed. "That ear ain't anywhere near my best feature." July smacked him, and then she laughed too.

Twice, they walked down to the river to see the progress there. Men from town had cleared away the debris from the fallen bridge and begun work on the new one, although to July's eye, it looked a long way from completion. The bodies of the sheep were gone now too, their flesh having returned to the earth and air and river. That was the Lord's doing, July thought then, and she was grateful.

Rory, less so. When July stripped from her clothes and jumped into the water, he went nowhere near her, but stood back on the bank, refusing to dip so much as his big toe.

"C'mon," she coaxed, "I'm going to teach you how to swim."

"I got no interest in swimming."

"You fall out of a boat again, Mads won't be there to save you."

"I got no need to get in a boat – you'll do my fishin for me."

"Hell I will," she teased, and Rory's eyes widened at this small curse of July's. She whipped one arm across the top of the water, trying hard to splash him, but he was too quick for her. He jumped back, hollering, "You're gonna have to work a lot harder than that to get me wet, July."

She charged toward him then, inasmuch as she was able, being naked and barefoot and too slow for Rory, who taunted her from the beach with an odd little dance that got her laughing so hard, twice she doubled over and clutched her side, telling him to stop. When she finally caught him, it was only because he'd let her, and then she wasn't strong enough to budge him. She promised she'd get him yet, if she ever caught him near the water. He pulled her close and kissed her wet face, telling her not to hold her breath as there was no way it was going to happen.

And so their sweet days passed. The day after they were at the river, the clouds rolled in and the air cooled, and it rained in the afternoon. They stayed in bed during the worst of the storm, intending to merely rest their eyes and listen to the hail as it drummed the rooftop, and then fell asleep for an hour. When they awoke, the world smelled clean as fresh-washed linen, and they got up to finish their chores. July was picking plums from a tree near the creek and Rory was on the roof, patching a hole where the rain leaked through, when Lilly rode up, sloshing through a puddle. "Lilly!" July cried when she saw her. She raced toward her sister, scattering the damp plums she'd gathered in her apron. Lilly hopped down from her horse and ran toward July. They met in a whirling embrace and held on tighter than they'd ever done at home.

July held Lilly at arm's length and gazed merrily into her eyes. She pulled her in again and squeezed. "How did you know where to find me?"

"Richard told me," she said, though she insisted July needn't worry. "He spilled your secret because he knows I'm the only one who can help." She looked up to the roof and waved at Rory. "Hello!" she called. "We haven't properly met."

Rory stood stiffly, as his ribs hadn't fully mended. Smiling, he hollered, "I'll come down and introduce myself."

July brought the conversation back to where it started. "But I'm fine, Lilly. I don't need help – Rory and I are getting along just fine."

Rory hopped from the ladder. He clutched his side as walked over, extending his right hand, which Lilly clasped politely. She told him he looked much better than he had two weeks ago; that he was, in fact, the picture of health. He thanked her, said he felt better too. There was a silence, and July thought she detected a certain strain on Lilly's part now, as though she were uncertain how to proceed. It wasn't like her to hesitate, trained as she was in the art of performance. That she already had one foot on Broadway was a given, so why she wavered now July couldn't say.

"Tom sends his hello," Lilly said at last. She swiped at the perspiration on her forehead, as the day had gone somewhat steamy, then abruptly asked if they could go inside, where it was cooler. She walked toward the door without waiting for a reply.

Rory glanced at July. She shrugged and raised one eyebrow, as if to say, "That's Lilly for you." July and Rory followed her inside, then stood while she sat at the table in the corner, her shoulders hunched, her gaze on the floor. All at once, her face puckered and a tear trickled down her cheek and tumbled to her lap.

July stepped forward, dropped to her knees, and rested one hand on Lilly's. "What is it? What's wrong, Lilly?"

"I'm not here to help you, July," she confessed. "I know you don't need me – you've always managed just fine on your own. I'm here to tell you Mother's sick."

July held her breath.

"She fainted on the back porch a few days after you left," Lilly went on. "It was Tom who found her. He yelled for Pa, tried to get him to fetch Doctor Forbes. Pa said there wasn't any need, said Mother was grieving over you, July. Tom threatened to fetch him anyway and Pa cussed like a wild man. He hopped on his horse, brought Doc Forbes to the ranch, himself. And, oh, July, Preston was so good to Mother. Looked her over and up and down, tender as could be. Even cradled her head and fed her a spoonful of Laudanum when there was nothing else he could do."

"Nothing he could do?"

"She's dying, July."

July stood, set her mouth in that tight way of her father's. "She's not dying. She fainted because of Raymond – her heart's broke, is all."

"It's the headaches, it's been the headaches all along."

"People don't die of headaches, Lilly."

"No, but sometimes they die of what causes them. Preston said there's a growth inside Mother's head, some sort of pressure, I guess. He doesn't know for certain, but he says the symptoms are all there. He saw it once in San Francisco, said he doesn't think she'll last the summer."

July covered her mouth with her hands.

"You've got to come home," Lilly told her. "Mother needs you, July."

"Pa won't have it," July cried. "You heard him – he'll see me dead first."

Rory stepped forward, reaching for July. She stumbled toward him and clung to him. "Come with me," she begged. "Don't make me go alone."

"I can't, July – you know I can't. Isaac will make things ten times harder on you if I do."

"I won't go without you."

He pulled her in, crushing her in his embrace. "Tend to your ma, do what you need to do. But come back to me, hear? Come back the minute you can." He hated the words as they slipped from his mouth, hated what it meant to let her go so soon after he'd fetched her to their own little house. Their home at Valentine.

Chapter Twenty-Four

The warm hues of evening – the oranges and azures of sunset – filled Eliza's room. A candle flickered on the table next to her bed, for anything brighter hurt her eyes these days and made her head throb. She was sleeping just now, her slim form childlike under the covers. Sickness had beaten her as badly as any cruel cowhand and banged her up so she'd never get out of bed again. Never lay a hand on July's forehead or sit at her bedside, nor rinse a Mason jar for poor little Raymond, dead and buried hardly a month before his mother would soon join him.

July sat on a straight-backed chair in the corner of the room and watched her mother breathing. She thought her ma's face free of the familiar little crease that had in recent months settled between her brows, and almost let herself believe her mother might recover. But then she glanced at her ma's eyes, saw the dark footprints imprinted below their sockets, and understood how little time Eliza had left.

July bowed her head and closed her eyes, wishing she were outdoors where she could have a proper conversation with the Lord.

Isaac stood in the doorway, perusing his daughter in prayer. "You should be on your knees, thanking God I didn't turn you away like I said I would."

She opened her eyes, took in the bitter set of his brow. "You can turn me out anytime you want, though a daughter should be present for her mother's funeral."

He worked his mouth as though he had something hurtful to say, but kept still. His anger must have taken him to a quieter place, for

he slipped his hands into his pockets and leaned against the wall.
Everything about him seemed to sag, and July regretted, all at once,
the tone she'd taken with him.

"If you'll let me stay," she tried again, "I'd be grateful. I might
be of help to Richard and Lilly."

"I won't have that boy in my house," he said, aggravating her anew.

"I didn't say a word about Rory, did I? He won't come – he
knows you hate him."

"Silas Morrow is a bad seed," Isaac went on, "and where
wickedness grows, evil sprouts."

"Rory took no part in Raymond's death, he told me so himself.
Said no one knew Raymond was in the barn. Those men meant to put
us out, yes, but not to kill anyone. That's why they didn't shoot Pun."

"They killed three hundred sheep – clubbed them and shot them
and knocked them down like they was nothing!" She looked away
without speaking. "Did Rory tell you who gave him that licking?"
Isaac said, "cause it weren't Mads Larson's ghost."

"I won't say what's stuck in my craw because you're my father,"
she whispered harshly, "but I'll tell you again I love Rory. Soon as
we can, we'll marry."

"See your bags are packed then, 'cause you'll be leaving after the
funeral." He turned and left, as he'd done so many times before.

There was a sound from Eliza's bed, a whimper and a sigh. If she
heard the cruel quarrel between her husband and daughter she gave
no sign. She looked at July and smiled. "I waited for you," she
whispered, reaching for July's hand. "I hung on just for you." July
got up and went to her mother, fell to her knees and buried her face
in her ma's bedclothes. Eliza took July's warm hand in her cool one
and brought it to her lips. "My precious, precious girl."

"I don't want you to go, Ma," July told her gently. "I've hardly
got over Raymond, and now you? We got our whole lives to live, you
and me."

"I'm tired, July, and Heavenly Father's calling." She smiled, and her
face shone. "I hope He saved me a spot in the Celestial Kingdom."

"He saved you a spot, I know He did," July told her. But the
words came out coarse and jagged, as she tried not to cry.

"Promise me you'll live a good life so you can join me there."

All her life July had heard too much about heaven. "Don't try to
make me good, Ma," she said. "It's not possible."

Eliza must have thought it true, for she nodded and looked away. "Problem is," she said softly, "you love a cowboy, and I tell you now it'll be the end of you, as it pert near was of me." She looked at July. "Yes, I loved a cowboy too, and after all these years your pa still can't let it go. I've told him a hundred times I love him and would marry him again if he asked me to. Don't think I ever convinced him, though. Deep inside I think he always believed I loved that cowboy more."

"What happened between you and your cowboy? Why didn't you take up with him?"

"He couldn't take to the notion the Lord was real. Told me God wasn't a being – spiritual or otherwise. Said when we die it's a lot more likely we'll lay in the dirt than drift on up to heaven." She raised her head just the slightest bit, tears welling in her eyes. "Can you imagine – eternity spent in some deep, dark hole, underground?"

July stroked her mother's forehead. "That's not going to happen, Ma." She kissed her mother's cheek, told her not to worry. Eliza closed her eyes and lay back down on the pillow, exhausted by the effort of getting those few words out. After a while she fell asleep, her breath soft and even.

In her old bed that night, July thought on the things her mother told her. Richard had been right – their ma *had* loved a cowboy once, and a Gentile at that. It explained perfectly why their pa had spoken so surly upon mention of Silas Morrow and every cowboy like him. And now that she had fallen for Rory it must have crushed her pa's soul, for surely he believed a woman he loved had let him down again.

Knowing it didn't make it easier, though, and July resented this new burden weighing on her soul. In the morning when she awoke, it was to a sour stomach and troubled heart. When she went to help her sister tend to breakfast, her voice came out harsher than she'd intended. "That pan's too hot, Lilly. You're burning the eggs and stinking up the kitchen."

"I didn't ask for this job," Lilly flared, slamming the spatula onto the counter. "I've already got one job in town I hate – I don't need two."

"You won't be put out long. Soon as Ma's in the ground, you'll collect your wages from Mrs. Abrams and be on your way to New York City, for all that sobbing and carrying on you did at Valentine was for my benefit, to get me home and keep me here, so you can do as you please."

July looked at the faces of the men at the table expecting to see sympathy there. Instead, she found worry in their eyes; fear that in sixty seconds she and Lilly would both clear out, that no woman would sit at

Isaac's fire again. Any fool could see they wanted July to stay, for Lilly had never been theirs to begin with. They'd never come right out and ask her to stick close to home, though, for they knew she loved Rory. Instead, they would let their long, sad faces do the begging for them.

"Don't look at me that way," she hollered. And then she stomped from the kitchen, letting the eggs turn black in the pan.

She escaped to Eliza's room, fell hard to her knees and grasped her mother's hand. "I love Rory so much, Ma, yet when I look at Richard and Tom – when I think of Pa out here on his own – I don't know what to do." She gripped her mother's hand tighter. "Tell me what to do."

Eliza's breathing, slow and steady, never faltered. If she held any pearls of wisdom for her daughter, July never knew. For in the gray light of dawn two days later, Eliza Caldwell died.

* * *

Pun and Daniel set Eliza's bury hole not too far from Raymond's, dug it east to west, as was the custom when Daniel was a boy. "We'll stick her feet facing west," he told Pun, "so when she sits up on the morning of the resurrection, the eastern sun'll warm her face."

"Hmm," said Pun. He stared hard at the ground, for a thought had just occurred to him. "We set Raymond in wrong way."

"I thought a that," said Daniel, nodding. "But Isaac was the one what laid him out. I don't see how we can turn him around now."

Pun shrugged. "Raymond like sun on back of head. Is okay."

While the men readied the ground, Lilly and July prepared their mother for burial, dressing her in her best white organza and combing her hair. They worked without speaking, for Lilly's feelings were smarting, though July didn't care. She had no interest in making things easy on Lilly. That her sister could put aside Richard and Tom's welfare – not to mention their cranky father's – infuriated July, for why was it her duty alone to tend to the men in the family? It seemed everything made July angry these days. Angry or sick. She hadn't felt well for a week now, a lack of spirit due to her mother's illness, and profound grief upon her death. It sorely hurt her that Rory hadn't braved an appearance despite his argument that showing up at the ranch would make things worse for her. What was worse than losing your brother and mother in the same six weeks, and then your betrothed, too?

July fretted that while she was away from Rory he would change his mind about her – see folly in his plans to marry her – though it was the workings of her own mind that worried her more, for she was fixated now on whether to go or stay, whether the men could live without her. When she sought Richard to ask his advice she found him sitting at the creek, crying as he'd never cried before. She didn't approach but stood behind a cottonwood, listening as the sobs poured from his body in great, hulking hiccups.

Without a sound, she crept backwards, then turned toward the house. Chewing her lip as she walked, she prayed this wasn't her mother's way of telling her to stay, yet deep down she knew that was her ma's wish, exactly.

As if Rory had read her mind somehow – as if her thoughts had seeped into his heart and sent him soaring her way – he appeared at the ranch the next day. He spotted Tom at the ditch, just where he'd found him the first time they'd met, only now the man wore a sling and all that was strong and determined and spry about him seemed absent. Rory didn't hesitate to ask him to fetch July, knowing he'd now get no argument. And when she came to him, she bounded into his arms and he twirled her around as though he'd not seen her all summer.

"Lord how I've missed you," he said, his voice catching. He breathed in the smell of her, buried his face in her hair. She let herself go in the feel of him, his arms so tight around her. She kissed him full on the mouth.

He looked up toward the house, took her by the hand and led her to a tree. Ducking behind it, he pulled her close. "I don't want your pa to see us – I ain't ready to be shot at yet." She wrapped her arms around his neck, and when he tried to pull away to properly kiss her, she held on tight. "July," he teased, "you're about to strangle me." Still, she hung on. And when it became clear she would not release him, would not look at him, it frightened him. He wrenched her arms from his neck. "I reckon I know you as well as the flurries in my heart," he said, his chest pounding. "If you got something to tell me, you best tell it now."

She clamped her mouth, gazed at him through tear-threaded lashes.

"Dear God," he said, his voice rocky with fear. "Don't leave me, July. God in heaven, don't do it."

"I don't know what to do," she cried, walking a circle in the dirt. "I can't leave Richard and Pa to wander the house without me – they haven't got anyone else."

Rory didn't say a word to that, just shook his head and stood there. "Is it your kin you love, or me?" he asked evenly, "'cause there's no way in sand you can have us all."

"You!" she cried, reaching for him, clinging to him now. "It's you I love, Rory – but you can't imagine what it's like – the state of them, sitting around, watching me, worrying what I'll do. I can't walk away, not yet. It would kill them, and me too."

He flung her arm away. "They'll learn to live without you, but what am I to do? If I live to be a hundred, I'll still pine for you."

"It's what my mother wanted."

"Your mother's dead, July! She don't want nothin from you now."

"I just need time, is all, get them settled in. I'll make it clear I can't stay, and soon as things calm down, I'll –" All at once she stopped, for the irises ringing Rory's pupils gleamed dark and unfamiliar.

"You'll what?" he spat. "The longer you stay, the tighter their grip will hold you. Don't you see?"

"No," she whispered. "I don't see at all."

"They'll turn you against me, July – get you to believing I'm no good for you." He shook his head and kicked the dirt. "Hell, I'm afraid you believe it now."

"I don't believe it, not for a minute." She wrung her hands, thinking hard on what to do. "What if I tell Pa that no matter what, we're getting married – that if he wants me to stay at the house he's got to welcome you too."

"He ain't gonna welcome me. Not now, not ever – he hates the Morrows, July. He'd rather see me dead than married to you, livin in his house."

"Well, what do you want me to *do*?"

"Stand up to him. Tell him to get his own goddamn life, that he's lived his life already."

July's eyes filled with tears, and she shook her head. "It's not a fight with him I'm having, it's a fight with you. I've got to stay, and I need you to help me find a way to make it all work out."

Rory clenched his jaw. "Seems like you got it figured fine without no help from me." It wasn't until he'd walked over to his horse and climbed on that July understood how done he was, and that he was really going.

"That's it?" she hollered, storming after him. "After all we've been through, you're leaving?"

He turned and looked at her, hard – though not so hard she couldn't see the hurt in his eyes – then rode off without so much as a nod or goodbye.

Chapter Twenty-Five

With the help of Brother Kilker and some of the townsfolk, Isaac began rebuilding his barn, and in time, Daniel and Pun returned to the hills. With so many sheep dead now, Richard was no longer needed to help herd. Isaac wouldn't have parted with him, anyway. He'd already lost Raymond and Eliza and would do whatever he could to keep Richard to home. Where July had once taken on the role of coaxing her brother from his melancholy moods, Tom now did what he could to coerce a smile from Richard's lips. He showed him how to build a waterwheel along the Weiser, how to construct the buckets that dumped water into a sluice box, and how to properly set the boxes so they emptied into Isaac's ditch. Gradually, Richard began to thrive under Tom's tutelage, whereas July withered, dry as an ancient garden.

Likely she missed her ma, Isaac told himself, and little Raymond too. What she thought about the Morrow boy he couldn't say, since he hadn't asked and didn't care to know. On some level he sensed something more was amiss, for July now looked as peaked as Eliza had on her worst days, when she'd complained her head felt swollen as an overripe melon. He worried July had taken on Eliza's sickness and even thought about pulling Pun back from the hills to make his special teas. In the end he held tight, for when he spotted her lingering near the privy and heard her bilious heaving, he drew the only conclusion he could. She wasn't suffering from illness but a malady far worse; that it wouldn't kill her was of little consolation and Isaac neither spoke of it nor acknowledged it, choosing, for a while, to deny its existence.

Not two weeks after Rory had shown her his stern, straight back, July knew a baby was on the way. She estimated it would arrive in May, but not having a woman in whom she could confide meant the date was but a guess.

As one day folded into the next, the angry wall she'd erected between her heart and Rory began to crumble, for it was loose as sand to begin with. She missed him so, it seemed the ache in her chest might burn a hole clear through her skin. She couldn't imagine him never coming back, nor not insisting on filling the role of father to their child, once he learned of her condition.

He'd been right all along.

The heartbreak she could have saved them both if only she had listened. Richard was on his way to living his life without her, constructing some new future under Tom's instruction. And her pa – well. He surely suspected she was with child, for every time he looked at her, his eyes filled with scorn. She knew better than anyone he'd no more allow Rory's baby to toddle around his house than he'd allow Rory himself, and it was this knowledge that finally allowed her to let loose her pride and return to the man she loved.

* * *

The next morning, not long after the brown rooster crowed, she saddled Birdy and rode to Badger, guessing Rory had gone back home. When she came up and over the ridgetop, her eyes took in a flat expanse of land dotted in sagebrush and bunchgrass. There was a barn next to a corral and a pond clotted with cattails; it was a grand old body of water, nearly twice as big as her pa's and three times as tempting, but the dock Rory had spoken of had fallen into disrepair; it leaned slightly to one side, and held a gaping hole in the middle, where the planks had rotted through and fallen out. She supposed no one used it anymore, although it was easy to see why Rory, as a youngster, had fallen victim to the pond's charms.

She angled Birdy toward the broad circle, thinking back on the story Rory had told her about the licking he'd earned there. She thought too about that day at the river, not so long ago, when she'd wanted to teach him to swim. He'd refused to let her, and she understood now that they each possessed their own fears: Rory's happened to be water. Hers was her father, she supposed. Disappointing him.

The air was warm and still, and a bullfrog trumpeted in the distance. She watched a turtle skim just beneath the water's surface. It poked its head up, hauled its unwieldy body onto a clump of dried grass at the pond's edge, negotiating its heft with a stout shove from its foot. Its slippery brown back was wide as a dinner plate and July thought it the biggest turtle she'd ever seen. After a while, she turned her gaze toward the house, where a line of trees stood; Lombardy poplars guarded the place like tall, slim soldiers.

It could have been Mormon country, so familiar were its lines. Though no poplars lined her own pa's ditches – for they lived where cottonwoods, willows, and aspens thrived – he'd always longed to grow some. She took in the yellow two-story house, the front porch, supported by slender white beams and adorned with a low picket fence. Her pa would have thought their own porch grander in scale, with its depth of nearly seven feet and its sloping roof that shaded visitors from the hot summer sun.

Nudging Birdy, she passed under a wooden banner pronouncing the place the SILAS MORROW CATTLE COMPANY. The ranch was eerily quiet and July saw no sign of Rory at all. It never occurred to her he wouldn't be there and her heart sank at the prospect she might miss him altogether. Uncertain of her welcome, she approached the house slowly, Birdy's clopping feet echoing in the stillness. Then the gate scraped against its hinge and Lydia Morrow walked out, a basket of sorry looking vegetables perched on one hip. She startled when she looked up, squinted as though trying to put a name to the face.

"It's me, Mrs. Morrow. July Caldwell."

How the woman had changed. Her hair, once lustrous as a horse's tail, now rested dull upon her shoulders. Her cheeks, thin and sallow, gave the appearance of a considerably older woman. July could see she'd been through a trial. "I've come to say hello to Rory," she told her. "If you'll let him know I'm here?"

"July Caldwell," said Lydia, her face just now flickering with recognition. She hesitated, wary perhaps, of what July wanted. And then she seemed to take in all of July, and her face softened. "Get off that horse and come inside," she said. "You look wilted as these carrots."

July slipped down from Birdy and followed Lydia toward the house. The woman strode strongly ahead, despite her weak appearance, and without turning asked July if she'd ridden all the way from Morning Tree.

"Yes, ma'am, I did." July followed the woman inside. The parlor's curtained coolness settled on her cheeks and calmed her churning stomach. Lydia nodded toward the sofa, told her to sit a spell while she set the vegetables in the kitchen and washed her hands.

July sat, leaning back and closing her eyes while she waited. The house smelled of linseed oil, reminding her of the times her ma had assigned Lilly the chore of dusting and polishing furniture. How Lilly hated that task – although not as much as laundry. And until July had taken over the washing she'd never appreciated how hard it was. Nothing spelled drudgery like stacks of soiled underwear.

"You all right, dear?" Lydia asked when she walked into the room. The wariness she'd demonstrated earlier left her now, and July supposed it had much to do with her own peaked appearance.

"I'm fine," she said, opening her eyes and sitting straighter. "The ride just tuckered me out."

Lydia handed her a glass of water, then sat in a rocker and gently urged the chair to and fro. "I was sorry to hear the news of your brother, and your mother too." Her forehead folded and she glanced at her lap, and July saw real pain there. All this time July had imagined Rory's mother hadn't known the entire story, but then Lydia confessed she'd left Silas for a while after learning of Raymond's death. "I asked him straight out if he was responsible, given the goings on between him and your father. He said he hadn't a thing to do with it – the night your barn burned, in fact, he was sitting here with me – and I wanted to believe it." She chewed her lip, thinking, July supposed, on the words she'd put forth next. "But there was no explaining the welts on Rory's face, the bruises on his skin, and I knew he'd taken a beating in somebody's defense." She looked up at July.

July's eyes welled. "My pa's."

Lydia was quiet a while – so quiet that July thought the conversation might be over. And then Lydia told her that after she'd left Silas, she thought she might not come home again. "But the truth is, I know my husband. He's ornery and stubborn and hard as the devil, but he'd never kill a decent man nor deliberately harm a child."

"Except Rory, that is."

Lydia's breath caught at the remark and her eyes too grew watery. "My only boy, and I let him down."

"As did I," July told her, her heart heavy. "That's why I've come today."

Lydia looked straight at July, but no longer seemed to see her. "Since the day of his licking, Rory doesn't tell me anymore what all he's up to. A day or two after his lip set up, he took off – though I told him he wasn't in no condition to travel. He spent a few weeks I don't know where, and then he come home not long ago, all down on himself, said he'd been to Valentine. I asked if he planned to make his home there, but he said no, he wanted to get on down to Boise." She sighed, thinking back on it. "He always talked of wanting to see it again, and sure enough, he threw everything he owned on his horse the next morning, packed a mule too, said he might as well be off since there was nothing left for him here. I suppose that's where he is now, Boise. Though he might have dropped on down to Oregon or California."

July clutched her hands and stared out the window. "Did he leave a forwarding address, someplace I might write him?"

Lydia shook her head, and if she heard the little quiver at the back of July's throat, she never said a word.

*   *   *

July talked to the trees on the way home, talked like she'd never talked before, prayed to God for a sign – anything to tell her where Rory was and when he'd come home, for he couldn't possibly have meant to leave her for good.

Each day she strolled her father's porch, gazing longingly at the hills and watching the horizon for Rory's familiar form. Every so often a rider appeared in the distance and for a moment July's heart raced. And then some bulky body would come into view and she'd let out a cry, departing the porch in despair. Her pa told her with his frosty gaze he knew full well what she was waiting for, though she never said a word to him about the ache she felt for Rory.

She told Tom though, and found it a comfort he was willing to listen.

"Will you ride into town?" she asked. "Check the mail and see if I've got a letter from Rory?"

He kindly did so, hoping for July's sake a letter from Rory *had* come, or at least a card with her name on it. Into Morning Tree he traveled, ignoring the saloons he'd sought in his younger days, when he'd had things to prove and a notion he'd up and leave this Mormon family, though he was twenty then, twenty-six now, and still hadn't done it.

When he returned, empty handed, he offered to go again the next day, and the day after that one too. Each time, July stood waiting on the porch. Not once did she ask if his saddlebags contained a letter, for she always seemed to know his terrible answer. When she shut her eyes – squeezed them hard to keep from crying – he told her – and rather harshly too – "May as well give up, July, ain't no letter comin." And then he apologized, saying it wasn't her he was angry with, but Rory.

Without a word, she turned her back on him and ran toward the privy. Tom sat back, listening to the sound of her stomach turning inside out, realizing all at once July was going to have a baby. The notion should have yanked him from his horse – mad as he was with Rory – yet even Tom knew the young man wouldn't abandon July with a child on the way. Rory simply didn't know the whole story, and that made July's situation all the sadder.

When July came out, wiping her mouth with her sleeve, Tom climbed down from Brigham. "Maybe we oughtn't give up on Rory just yet."

Something in her face shifted then, and she walked up to him, wrapped both arms around him. Leaning her head against his chest, she let it all go, the grief inside, and cried hard into his shoulder. He patted her, and seeing she wouldn't soon let go, rested his chin atop her head and told her to have at it.

The next day was his last trip into town. He rode home, smiling like he never had before. "July!" he called from a quarter mile out, waving a letter like a banner. He hit the yard and pulled the reins back hard, hopped from his horse and rushed into the house. July was making Isaac's bed when he bounded up the stairs. "It came," he whooped, "the letter you been waiting for."

July stood motionless, unable to speak or hear.

Tom handed her the letter, and she took it, holding it with both hands. "It come from Boise," he said, pointing to the postmark. "What's Rory doing there?"

July sat on the edge of the bed, and with trembling hands opened the letter. She was confused for a moment, as it seemed there was nothing inside, but when she turned it over and shook it, a little ring spilled out. It was the ring she'd made for Rory at Valentine, the one she'd given to him before they'd come together the first time, giving so tenderly of one another. She sat forward in the slightest little lean then, and Tom thought she might keel over. "July?" he said, stepping forward. "What is that thing, and what does it mean?"

She got up, walked unsteadily toward the door. Twice she faltered, and it wasn't until Tom grabbed her elbow that she at last looked his way. "It's a message," she said. "A message from Rory. It means he's not coming back."

*   *   *

She passed the next few days in a haze of hurt and disbelief. Laundry piled up on the back porch while she sat out front, gazing mindlessly across the yard. Every so often she glanced over to find Richard casting mournful looks her way. Tom had no doubt told him about Rory, and would have told Pun too, had the Chinese herder been home. Just as well he was up in the hills with her father's sheep, as he might have approached her with a mysterious cup of tea, a stinking black liquid he'd leave on her nightstand, along with a quiet but stern warning of what to expect, should she decide to drink it.

But she would not drink Pun's tea – nor any other poisonous beverage – for she wanted Rory's baby as much as she wanted him. No sooner had she let herself imagine that her Pa might actually welcome a baby after all than he stomped up the steps, regarded her with cruel eyes and then berated her for sitting around all day like a stump.

"This ain't no free ride," he told her. "You can sit just as easy over to Mrs. Abrams', if that's what you've a mind to do. Least you'll earn a wage there."

July raised her chin and drew her lips tight. She might have risked a comment or two, but by the time she drew up her courage her pa had stomped away. From the corner of one eye, she saw Tom and Richard watching from the barn. They talked low between themselves, walked over and sat next to her.

"You can pretend it ain't happin, July," Tom said, glancing at the stretching seams of her dress, "but sure as the world, you got a baby comin."

"I know I do," she told him.

"I hate to think what Pa will do once he hears he'll be a grandpa," Richard put in. "Have you even got a plan?"

July nodded. "I just never thought I'd have to act on it – I believed with all my heart Rory would miss me as much as I missed him, that he'd come fetch me like he did at Ray's funeral." Neither Tom nor Richard spoke, for July needed no reminder she'd never see

Rory again. "I reckon I've waited as long as I can though, and now I've got to do what's best for my baby."

"That plan you got," said Tom. "We ain't gonna like it, are we?"

"No, Tom, you won't like it. And I don't like it, either."

* * *

Preston sat at his desk, a mahogany rectangle in the back of the room. There was a hutch too, on stilt-like legs, with three shelves and glass doors, behind which he stored cotton and gauze and a row of special medicines. There was Arnica, for sprains and bruises, and Belladonna for coughs, and there was Laudanum and Paregoric, both of which contained tincture of opium and which, respectively, relieved pain and diarrhea. His chloroform inhaler was there too, positioned alongside a pile of clean handkerchiefs. On the opposite side of the room, next to a curtained window, stood a cushioned table on which his patients lay while he cleaned their cuts and bandaged their wounds. When the office was empty he kept the curtains open so he could see onto the street and watch the passersby, and when it was full he shut the curtains, as well as the door, affording his patients every possible privacy.

The office was in his home, a single-story structure that had once punctuated the end of town like a period following a sentence. In the few short years since he'd bought the place and set up his practice, a drugstore had sprung where sagebrush once grew, and beyond that Mrs. Abram's dress shop sprouted. Despite this, Preston didn't feel at all crowded, for the bigger the town the more residents in need of a doctor.

He was in the process of revising his fee bill when he paused to gaze out the window. The price for amputating a toe or finger was now ten dollars, but Preston thought twelve more appropriate, given the cost of wrapping that an amputation required. He was about to put this to paper when a woman with a cascade of brown curls slipped past, a woman whose profile he'd recognize anywhere. Her pace slowed, and he held his breath, waiting for the tinkle of the bell that signaled her entry. When it came, he sat, paralyzed, unable to bring himself to stand to greet her. He merely looked up, his heart thumping against his chest, and waited for her to step into the room.

She walked timidly around the corner, purse clutched at her stomach. "Hello Preston."

"Hello July." He laid his pen on his desk and folded one hand atop the other to still its nervous trembling.

She nodded at a chair across from his desk. "Do you mind if I sit down?"

"Of course not." He rose, indicating the seat with a flourish. "Pardon my lack of manners, July, it's just that, well, I'd not expected to see you again. Ever." He thought her complexion pale, and that she looked unwell. He didn't try to disguise his concern but immediately asked if she'd taken ill.

"No, nothing like that." She looked up briefly without meeting his eyes, dropped her gaze and absently fingered the clasp on her purse.

A quiet moment passed, and although the silence was awkward, he soon relaxed. The look on July's face and the anxious way she sat before him told him her visit wasn't easy. Assuming it had something to do with her family, he leaned forward and told her he was sorry to hear of her mother's passing. "She was a wonderful woman, so kind and attentive – she clearly thought the world of you, July." She thanked him and he nodded, saying nothing more. He didn't wish to dwell on the sad topic that was Eliza Caldwell.

He embraced this second silence, as it gave him the opportunity to peruse July as he never had before. Even after all this time he still thought her lovely as a wildflower – so much so that he considered it a shame her parents had named their first child Lilly. If they'd known what was coming they surely would have reserved the name for July.

Though her face had grown thinner since he'd last seen her, her figure all but swelled now, her hips round, her waist small, her breasts firm beneath her bodice. He was consumed with desire – the same yearning he'd endured for eighteen months now, and when she began fidgeting in her seat and glancing out the window, he worried she might leave without revealing what she'd come for. He seized the chance to help her. "I'm guessing you're having a hard time sleeping?"

"Well, yes," she nodded.

"And eating too."

"Yes, that's true too – but it's not why I've come, Preston."

He sat up. Blinked. "What is it, then?"

She shifted slightly, and turned her face toward the wall.

His heart flamed with compassion. "I can't help unless you tell me what's wrong, July."

She laid her purse on his desk, and for the first time since she'd entered the room looked him square in the eyes. She started, paused, began again. "After Raymond died, I left for Valentine with Rory," she told him. "I was there a month when Lilly came with word our mother was sick, so of course I went home to be with her. I thought I'd stay until the end of summer, till she died, and then I'd go on back to Valentine. But she left us sooner than we thought – before any of us could get used to the idea – and once we buried her, Richard, especially, had a hard time getting on his feet again." Her eyes welled with tears, but July being July, she brusquely wiped them away.

"I wanted to go, I'll tell you plain," she went on, "but I stayed because I thought Richard and Tom and Pa needed me. Wasn't long till I realized Rory needed me more though, but by then he'd left, gone I don't know where."

Preston stiffened. "You've come for sympathy, then? Is that it?"

"I've come to tell you I'm sick in the morning and sick in the evening – that I can't eat and can't sleep – that you're the only one who can help me now." All at once she brought her hand to her mouth and looked around. "Your privy? Point me, quick, please."

He stood, hurried around his desk. "There's a bathroom here in the house," he said, grasping her elbow and leading the way. Just inside the door, July fell to her knees and vomited in the toilet. Preston watched in shock, stepped back and quietly shut the door. He stood in the hall, his face hot, his mind reeling with the realization July was going to have a baby.

And then oh, how the tables turned.

Flushed with power, he leaned against the wall and crossed his arms. When she opened the bathroom door and emerged, he smiled smugly. "I see you're in a bit of a predicament," he said, his voice concrete with knowing.

"It wasn't like that," she said, objecting to his spiteful tone and the meaning behind it. "I loved Rory when we made this baby, and he loved me too."

"Well, where is your beloved Rory now?"

"Boise," she said quietly.

"And he *isn't* coming back."

July glanced at Preston with red-rimmed eyes.

He pushed off from the wall. "Why have you come?" he demanded. "What do you want from me, July?"

"You want to hear me say it? Ask if you'll have me and beg if you won't?"

"Oh, I'll have you – you knew that the minute you stepped in the door. But I'll insist on one thing before I make you mine." She clenched her jaw and bit her tongue, though she had a thousand words to hurt him. "We'll consummate our marriage the night we're wed," he went on, "and you'll return my affection with vigor."

A chilly silence settled between them. "I'll do it because I have to," she said sharply, "but don't expect too much, Preston. I'll surely disappoint you."

*   *   *

With Lilly in New York and her mother in the grave, July had no one to help her on her wedding day. Pun was in the hills with Daniel and Tom – whom Isaac had again called upon to herd rams up to the ewes – or he would have been there to plait her hair or curl it with a hot iron and pile it high atop her head.

Richard found her sitting on the edge of Preston's bed, looking particularly forlorn. He knew he'd been no help at all since their mother died, and that if it weren't for his carrying on and Tom's slagging about so she'd be with Rory right now, celebrating the impending birth of her child. He aimed to make it up to her, if he could. Walking into the room, he told her Rory wasn't the only one with an eye for a pretty girl. "I too got a notion how a woman should look in a wedding dress – how a crown of chrysanthemums should sit on top her hair."

July's eyes misted at the mention of Rory's name. Richard said he was sorry, that he hadn't ought to brought it up. "It's all right," she told him, though she truly ached to think of Rory crisscrossing the country by his lonesome. She worried that his anger would fester, one day turning him into a cruel and indifferent man, like his father. And once he learned she'd married Preston Forbes he'd shut her out forever. She didn't want that for either of them, yet she had no idea how to prevent it. All she knew was she loved him, and more than anything in the world she wished it was Rory she was marrying that day, instead of Preston Forbes.

Richard wove her hair into a loose braid, as he'd so often seen Pun do, then wrapped it around her head. Throughout the little circle he inserted flowers of yellow and gold, until she glowed lovely as a sunset. Her hair complete, he asked her to stand and step into her dress.

July glanced at Richard with reluctant eyes, and he read her look at once. Despair, it was, and regret too. Right then and there he thought about telling her to call the wedding off, for surely they could figure out some way to appease their pa and keep July to home. But deep down he knew it wasn't possible, and hard as it was to tell it, he owed her the truth. "Try not to think on it," he said. "Just put one foot in front of the other and move forward." She did as she was told, and climbed solemnly into her dress.

He'd never seen her so lovely. She all but shimmered in her floor-length skirt, with its pleated bib and lacy hem of ivory silk. Her feet were decked in matching slippers, and in her hands she carried a spray of the same delicate flowers that adorned her hair. Richard's eyes glistened when he told her he loved her, and was proud as he could be.

She hugged him tight, lingering a moment in his embrace. "I'd best do you proud, for I got no one else to please."

Preston's parlor was the site of the ceremony. The room was small and crowded, filled with July's family and Preston's patients, and a few from church who'd come to join in. July took her place beside Preston. He stood tall beside her, his back straight as a stovepipe, his jaw set firm. A stranger might have guessed something was amiss, for though a smile crossed his lips when he first saw his intended, July kept her eyes on the floor.

Brother Kilker, who a number of weeks ago had risen to the rank of Bishop, officiated. He opened his black leather book and said a good many words – so many in fact, July's knees started to wobble, for the scent of Preston's shaving soap set her stomach churning. And then Kilker finished his sermon at last. "By the power invested me by the state of Idaho and the Church of Jesus Christ of Latter-day Saints, I pronounce you man and wife." He needn't have nodded at Preston, for the man quickly leaned over and kissed July, a kiss more passionate than proper. Anyone could see it was a statement: he meant to tell the world July was his now – that he'd no longer step aside to accommodate an aging sheepman nor a boy named Rory Morrow.

Richard stepped forward first. He engulfed July in a warm embrace and hung on tight. And then he turned to Preston. In consideration of his sister he shook the man's hand, though it charred his heart to do so. Isaac stepped forward next, and he too shook Preston's hand. He might never forgive the man for his behavior that day on the porch, but he admired him for stepping up when likely no one else would. Were it not for Preston Forbes, who knew what would become of July? Thinking on this, Isaac turned toward her, brushed her cheek with his dry coarse lips. "It's for the best, you know," he whispered in her ear.

She glared at him. "You've known about the baby all along and still you refused to take us in? Me and your grandchild?" His silence was her answer. "I'm not here but for you," she scolded. "If you'd opened your heart after Ma died – let me live the life I wanted – I'd be married to Rory now. As it is I'll spend all my days with a man I don't love." Isaac's face folded at that, for July's words might have been Eliza's. Feeling no pity at all, she snapped, "And don't you dare say one word to me about cowboys."

Isaac was set to launch his own attack when Abigail Kilker approached, offering congratulatory kisses to July's cheeks. But instead of firing his bullets into July, Isaac turned his anger toward this innocent woman, wondering aloud and none too sweetly when Kilker planned to pull his wives from the pantry. "No point in denying they're in there," Isaac taunted. "Manifesto or no, he might as well parade them." And then he had a fine idea. "If he's got an extra to spare, why don't he send her over to my place when he's done with her? With Eliza and July gone, my house is all but ruined and I could surely use a housekeeper."

"Pa," July put in sharply. "You've got no call to talk to Abigail that way."

"It's all right, July," said Abigail. She turned to Isaac, her eyes hard. "Your pa's still grieving the loss of his Eliza, and doesn't quite know how to handle it."

"What I'm grieving and what I ain't, ain't none of your business."

July sighed. Looping her arm through Abigail's, she led the woman to the far side of the room. "I'll thank you to keep this quiet, Abigail," she whispered. "Truth is, he isn't himself right now. He's angry at me, not you, and I reckon he can't think for the turmoil in his head."

Abigail turned to July, and with questioning eyes, said, "What did you do to anger him so?"

"No matter, it's nothing I can fix now, anyhow."

The wedding frolic ran clear till morning, with men and women dancing in the kitchen, their frivolity spilling into the back parlor. Isaac had left hours earlier, and Richard, just before dawn. Dirty dishes were strewn about and the carcasses of seven chickens lay atop the table. Some kind soul had thought to pile them neatly so that July might easily scoop them into a waste bin. Preston stood, hands on hips, and surveyed the scene. "I'll help you with all this later, July," he volunteered, "but now we'll slip off to bed. I'm exhausted, and I expect you are too." He didn't look at her when he said this, nor did she glance at him.

And so their relationship began, with Preston pretending July was a willing partner, and July shutting from her mind what that notion cost her.

* * *

In the earliest days of their marriage, Preston ensured that July made good on her promise, demanding the enthusiasm she might have showered on Rory. "Louder," he insisted when she moaned for his enjoyment, and "Harder," when she pressed her hips to his. Despite his determination to make her pay for having rebuffed him all those months ago, he found in time his heart wasn't truly in it. It wasn't July he resented but Rory, and it remained his mortal fear he'd never please her the way the Morrow boy had.

After all this time – after tolerating July's cruel invectives and harsh treatment – he still loved her, and there was something in his soul told him he always would. He didn't know yet how he'd feel about the baby, for so much depended on whose flame flickered behind the child's eyes.

Not a month after their wedding night, when July had said no more than a handful of words in all the days since then, Preston made a stab at amends. He showed July a new politeness, letting her lie back in bed at night to quietly grow her baby. Though she continued to say little, he thought she appreciated the courtesy, as it seemed she was warming to him some, demonstrating her gratefulness with a variety of small gestures. Once, when he'd mentioned that his mother – dead some six years now – made the finest bread pudding he'd ever tasted, he walked from town one afternoon, his nose following the scent of cinnamon and sugar, to find a small dish of pudding sitting at his place at the table. After he'd scooped the last drop with his spoon and slipped it into his mustached mouth, he told July it well bested his mother's. She offered a rare smile, and immediately set to mixing a second batch.

Another time, when he stooped over a kettle of hot water to boil his instruments, he grabbed the pot's handle without thinking and burned all four of his fingers, sparing only his thumb. When he cursed and dropped the pot against the stovetop, boiling water sloshed onto his shirt and singed his chest. July mixed a potion of camphor and lanolin, dabbed it on his fingers and trunk, commenting, though not unkindly, he seemed a mite careless, for a doctor.

And then there was the time he spent half the night stitching up the drunk who'd tottered through a plate glass window. July waddled into Preston's office, her belly round and hard as a boulder, and offered to hold the mask while Preston chloroformed the man. "Not necessary," he sweetly told her. "He's nearly unconscious from the whiskey, as it is." July looked around the room. Finding it a mess, she bent, with some difficulty, to retrieve the bloody sponges from the floor. Without a word she walked from the room, only to return a short time later, everything rinsed and evenly distributed on a small white tray.

It brought Preston great joy to believe July was coming around, and then Solomon Houston came to see him about an ingrown toenail, and the myth was quickly dispelled. The man sat in his suit on the examination table, looking much like a toad perched upon a wall. His short legs dangled from his rotund body, and his portly hands sat clasped in his lap. Preston sat on a stool and rolled it toward the table, where he grasped Solomon's sockless foot, poking and prodding it, while July looked on.

By now she was a regular fixture in Preston's office, assisting here and there with patients whose problems were minor. She'd memorized the contents of the hutch and when Preston called for a ball of cotton, she expertly plucked it from the shelf, watching as he moistened the material in clear liquid, then stuffed it between the offending nail and fold of inflamed flesh. The sharp scent of solvent stung her nose.

Solomon winced. "You're quite the assistant, Mrs. Forbes," he remarked through clenched teeth.

Preston looked up at his wife and smiled, pleased that a man like Solomon Houston should so admire her service. July smiled too. To Preston's surprise, she confessed to the man a curiosity about medicine she'd not realized she possessed. "I'd like to learn more, after the baby comes."

"You're a lucky man," Solomon told Preston. "My Emeline's been married two months now and if she's as blessed as your wife, she too will soon receive a visit from the stork." He laughed, then gave an involuntary jerk as a pang shot through his toe.

The announcement took them both by surprise, but it was Preston who offered a reply. "Why, congratulations, Solomon. I'd not heard the good news. Whom did Emeline marry?" At that moment July's heart quit beating, for she knew what the man would utter before the words issued from his mouth.

"Rory Morrow," he chirped. "He came to the house to take her portrait some time ago – I'd not realized he was interested in her but it turns out he was utterly besotted. No sooner had he returned from his sojourn than he proposed, and Emeline accepted."

With an almost imperceptible moan, July turned and walked unsteadily from the room.

"Oh my," said Solomon, watching her go. "Do you need to tend to her, Doctor?"

"She'll be fine, thank you." Preston made light of July's departure, saying she still suffered severe biliousness. "A bit of bread and milk and she'll be her old self again." The strain behind his smile went unnoticed by Solomon.

The man nodded. "I remember those days well. There was a time when I thought Mrs. Houston would eat nothing but milk toast, but look at her now" – he leaned in, conspiratorially – "appetite's as robust as a ranch hand's."

"I'm truly happy to hear of Emeline's engagement," Preston went on. He lowered his voice, adding, "but I must ask, aren't you at all worried about young Morrow's reputation? It's still not known who was responsible for July's accident, but rumor has it Silas had a hand in it – that he burned down Isaac Caldwell's barn too."

"I don't hold the son responsible for the sins of the father," Solomon told him.

"As it should be, I suppose," Preston said, nodding, though his tone held no conviction. He patted Solomon's foot. "Well. That cotton should do the trick. If it doesn't, come back and we'll talk about removing the nail."

"I'd sooner lose my hair," Solomon chortled as he scooted from the table and patted his frothy head.

When the chime above the door signaled Solomon's farewell, Preston washed his hands, scrubbing each nail vigorously and cursing beneath his breath. He strode into the kitchen in search of July, and not finding her there, walked with hard heels from the parlor to the bedroom, where she sat at the edge of the bed. She'd been crying, and was crying still, blotting her eyes and sniffing.

"How much longer will you spill these tears?" he demanded, his voice as harsh as her father's.

"What difference does it make? I married you, didn't I? It's your bed I warm at night."

"Against your will, yes."

"It took me by surprise, is all. I'll get over him one day, same as he got over me. Why, I'd think you'd be thrilled, Preston. Rory's married to Emeline, which means he'll never come fetch me now. You can throw yourself a party, for all the fun you'll have." She grimaced, and then lay back against the bed. "You've got no reason to worry or complain."

"I'll not spend one minute worrying, but I'll complain as loud as I like."

July clutched her belly and rocked to one side. "And will you chastise the baby, too," she groaned, "for our child is shortly coming."

*   *   *

The infant was a girl. The baby possessed a face as wrinkled as crinoline and a cry as hoarse as Raymond's. July smiled when she heard it, said it sounded like a chicken. She sighed and then her smile faded, as she'd lost a good deal of blood and was exhausted. She kissed the child's forehead, then handed her to Preston.

Although Preston had many times confessed he wouldn't know how he'd feel about the baby until he held it in his arms, July saw right away he loved this little one as much as he'd ever love his own. All those years of doctoring had taught him how to hold a newborn and he cradled the infant in the crook of his arm, cooed to her in a voice that astonished July, for she'd never known a father could be so tender.

"What shall we name her?" he asked.

She had a name in mind, but was afraid to put it out there. She picked at a ball of fuzz on her quilt, gazed at Preston with tired eyes. "I'd like to name her Valentine, if that's all right with you."

Preston's appraised the child, and must have seen that the name fit her well, as he caressed her cheek with his fingertip and gently kissed her head. "We'll call her Vallie," he said, and July said that sounded fine. She closed her eyes, needing to sleep, and Preston walked over to her, and brushed the hair from her face. "Get some rest," he told her, and then sat to rock their baby.

The following morning, Abigail Kilker came over to tend to July. She fed her chicken broth and warm dumplings, changed her sheets and plumped her pillows. And when little Vallie cried, she plucked her from her bassinet and handed her to July, whose milk was thin but abundant.

Those first two months after Vallie was born, July rarely left the house. Her recovery was slow and the weight she'd lost after delivery reluctant to return. But little by little she grew stronger, and when the baby was three months old, she took her for a walk in a pram Preston had ordered all the way from England.

The sun felt glorious on her face, and she wondered how she'd lived so long without it. She walked slowly on the wooden sidewalk, looking in the windows of the stores and taking in their smells. Someone across the street was baking bread, and farther on down, an apple pie with cinnamon. She'd heard tell Rory had opened a shop at the other end of town, but she was careful never to find herself too close to its boundaries. Oh she was certain she'd run into him one day, but by then she'd have a speech prepared – something to explain Vallie's premature birth, how it had come so unexpectedly that it had amazed even Preston. It was a lie but a white one – and would explain what she could never really tell him.

One day, while pushing Vallie near the general store, she paused to adjust the baby's blanket, which had bunched beneath her feet. As July leaned into the pram, she caught a glimpse of Emeline stepping from the store. July quickly dipped from view, praying Emeline would turn in the opposite direction, which, after a moment's consideration, she did. July sighed, relieved. She couldn't bear to face Emeline, for she'd prepared no explanation for Vallie's green eyes, nor for her complexion, so similar to Rory's.

Chapter Twenty-Six

Rory gave himself gladly to Emeline, for within days of returning from his trip to Boise – a journey in which he never ceased longing for July, nor regretting his stubborn, thickheaded ways – Rory learned she'd married Preston. He returned the favor in short order, proposing to Solomon Houston's daughter and marrying her in Weiser at the home of her grandmother. Here, Solomon paraded Emeline before the community while she smiled demurely, without pride or arrogance, and made her father proud. All the while, Rory wished July his bride, just as he wished it now. But because Isaac had twisted July's thinking – got her believing none of the Caldwells could live without her – she'd bent to his demands, turning herself inside out until she'd persuaded herself Isaac's wishes were her mother's. July must have believed Rory would never see the error of his ways, never come to fetch her, even though it was the first thing he planned to do the minute he returned from Boise.

By then, July had married Preston. In anguished desperation, Rory, in turn, married Emeline, and now the whole hangdog world was full of pretenders. At least that's the way he saw it.

How Emeline saw it, he couldn't say. If she examined the haste with which he proposed, if somewhere in her heart she believed he settled for second best and would someday grow to resent her, she never once questioned him. She merely steered the conversation her way when her confidence began to flag, asking him again to tell her he loved her. No sooner had he reassured her than she asked again, and then one day she quit asking and began pressing for a baby. Time and again he put her off, knowing in his heart he still hoped to get away, go back to the way it was before he and July went so far astray. A child with Emeline would only complicate things, yet when he saw her sitting forlornly at the window, her chin resting on one knee, he felt cruel in refusing her. Too, he knew he was living in a dream world, and so he granted Emeline the wish that would eventually become his own.

Yet a baby never came.

With each bright stain on Emeline's drawers she cried quietly into her handkerchief, telling Rory she didn't understand what was taking so long. "Women have babies all the time – more babies than most of them know what to do with. Why can't I have one too?"

He sat beside her, rubbing the small of her back. She was sweating some, the way people do when they're worked up with sorrow and disappointment, and her dress was damp to the touch.

"I love you," she said, and so he said it too, trying hard to mean it.

In the months since he'd opened his shop at the entrance of town, he'd come to feel a certain affection toward her; in time he supposed he'd call it love. But it wasn't the same as he'd felt with July, and likely never would be. He dealt with those old feelings by avoiding July, as he imagined she avoided him. It wasn't difficult – he lived and worked at one end of Morning Tree, she at the other. He'd heard she was helping Preston with his business and remembered when he and July once talked of her helping him in his photography shop. Now she was mixing medicines instead of developer's fluid, and the realization pained him. He tried not to think on it.

In time it got easier to concentrate on Emeline. When another month passed without a call from the stork, he persuaded her she was as normal as the next one, just a little nervous is all – which was why a baby hadn't come.

"I don't know how these things work, exactly," he confessed, "but maybe Doc Forbes can help?"

She knew what it cost him to suggest such a thing, for he'd never been friendly with the doctor. More than that though, she hated confiding in Preston Forbes for the simple reason the matter was personal, between her and Rory. She twisted her handkerchief into a knot. "I wouldn't know what to say or how to say it."

"I'll come with you, if you want. Help you get your words out."

Emeline felt a sudden burst of affection for her husband. She kissed his cheek and hugged him, told him that although she wouldn't dream of dragging him along, she was grateful he had offered.

"You'll go see him then?"

"Yes, I'll go, as it will give me a chance to see July and the baby."

Rory wore a casual smile, although his insides roiled at the idea of July toting some other man's child. Still, he wouldn't deny Emeline the pleasure of spending time with July, and so he told her, "Go – it'll do the two of you good to catch up on all the doings."

Emeline spent a good hour the next morning, readying herself for the visit. She curled her hair in ringlets and wore a crisp blue dress with petite white piping, then dabbed a little lavender water behind each ear. She couldn't wait to see July, for too much time had passed since they'd last exchanged their secrets. That July might not share Emeline's excitement never occurred to her, for they all made their own decisions in life. That July had chosen Preston instead of Rory made perfect sense to Emeline, given that July and Preston were Mormons. They had a kinship, a mutual tie, where July and Rory had no real bonds, beyond a brief courtship that went awry after July's mother died. July had been crushed by those tragic events, Emeline was certain. It hurt her to know how much her friend had suffered. But ultimately it was Rory who'd left July; who'd reached his hand out to Emeline; who'd proposed with all his heart and soul, and whose love for July was but a memory. Emeline told herself now that July had Preston *and* a baby, she was likely the happiest woman in the world.

It was on this gay note that she strolled over to Preston's office, stood in front of his door, uncertain whether to knock or merely step in. Her mother had never taken her to a doctor before, as Emeline hadn't suffered an injury or illness so serious that she'd required the services of a physician. Deciding it best to knock, she lightly rapped her knuckles against the wood and then waited for Preston to answer. Instead, it was July who came to the door.

Emeline didn't recognize her friend at first. Though she'd heard July's recovery had come slowly, she'd all but transformed into the ghost of her mother. Her rosy skin was the color of thin milk, and dark circles resided beneath both eyes. Sharp little points poked up from her collarbone, and her wrists, narrow as bird bones, jutted from beneath the sleeves of her blouse. But on her hip – oh! – a baby perched, sweet and plump as a gumdrop.

Emeline embraced her old friend at once, an embrace July hesitantly returned. The visit was entirely unexpected and July hadn't had time to prepare. When Emeline stepped into the house July all but held her breath, waiting for the woman to note the similarities between Rory's sunset complexion and the baby's – the hue of her eyes, green as mountain moss. She had assumed Emeline would draw a comparison immediately, yet to July's amazement Emeline merely held out her arms and wriggled her fingers. "May I hold her, July? Please?"

The tot smiled and bobbed on July's hip, shyly dipped her head into her mother's shoulder. July passed the child to Emeline, expecting at any moment the woman would come to her senses. She even called up the little speech she'd put together in her mind – the one she'd crafted one night in bed and had memorized for exactly this occasion.

But Emeline seemed to have no idea whose child she'd taken into her arms. "Look how beautiful she is," she marveled, her voice heavy with longing.

When the baby's mouth puckered and her little brows furrowed, Emeline patted the child's knee and assured her all was well. She looked at Emeline, then at her mother, and with the same puckered frown sat frozen and sucking at the air, fixing her mouth to cry. But she held still, comforted, perhaps, by Emeline's gentle cooing.

It was then July realized that the months she'd spent fretting over this encounter were a waste of time, for Emeline saw only what she wanted to see: Preston Forbes' baby, a child in a white cotton gown with matching booties, plump fingers in her mouth. Emeline kissed those fingers tenderly, tears sprouting in her eyes. "What's her name?" she asked, crying and laughing at the same time.

"Valentine – we call her Vallie, for short."

"Vallie," repeated Emeline, again kissing the child's fingers. She looked at July, her smile steadfast. "You named her after the place you and Rory were so fond of," she said, as though it were the most natural thing in the world. When July nodded, Emeline at last turned serious. "Much as I'd love to spend all day with you and the baby, I've got to talk to Preston." She blushed and looked at the ground. "I haven't been able to conceive and I was hoping he could tell me why." Here, she glanced up, met July's gaze full on. "What am I doing wrong that I can't yet make a baby?"

July hardly knew what to say. How could she tell her friend how to make a baby with the man she herself still loved? More to the point, how could Emeline ask? "I don't know," July stammered. "I imagine Preston could tell you, but he's not here – he's over to Langston, delivering a baby."

"Oh, no," Emeline cried, her voice filled with disappointment. "When will he be back?"

"I'm not sure. He's been gone two days now so it's likely a difficult birth."

"What if I come back tomorrow?" Emeline asked hopefully.

"I'm sure that's fine, but let me make an appointment so Preston knows you're coming."

"Appointment?"

"It's odd, I know. But with the town growing like it is he'll soon have to hire a second doctor. He can hardly keep up as it is." July asked Emeline if she'd mind tending Vallie while she looked for Preston's book.

Emeline gave the baby a squeeze. "Of course not. Take all the time you need."

While July searched for the appointment book, her heart pounding and her mind spinning, Emeline strolled the parlor. She showed Vallie each of the shiny trinkets lining the cabinets and shelves. There was a glass globe filled with colored water, a set of crystal glassware, and a photograph of Eliza Caldwell in a small silver frame. Emeline picked it up and held it for the baby to see. Vallie grabbed it and clutched it in her hand, waving it furiously before bringing it to her mouth and sucking its edge. Emeline gently pried the frame from the child's fingers and quickly looked around for a more suitable teether. Spotting a rag doll with yarn hair propped on a blanket on the floor, she bent down and sat, situating the child on her lap.

Emeline handed Vallie the doll. The baby kicked her legs gleefully, her stubby feet banging cheerfully against Emeline's thigh. Emeline nuzzled Vallie's neck and kissed her cheeks, inhaled the fragrant smell of her. The child paid no mind at all, as her attention had wandered from the rag doll to the bonnet on her head. She'd taken a sudden disliking to it. Clutching it in her fist, she tugged it hard until it sat askew on one side of her face. Emeline laughed and gently righted the little hat, yet no sooner was it properly perched than Vallie yanked it off.

Emeline smoothed the baby's hair, kissed Vallie's right ear and then her left, pausing all at once as she took in the little notch on the inner rim, the little cutout just like Rory's. She held the baby out some, wanting a better view. Now it was Emeline who held her breath, for it seemed a vise had gripped her heart.

July stepped into the room, Preston's open appointment book in hand. Glancing at his schedule, she said, "I think he can see you day after tomorrow," and then she paused, looking up.

Emeline held Vallie's bonnet in her hand. "Were you planning to tell me, July? Ever?"

The speech July had prepared all those weeks ago left her now, and she remembered not a word. Panic set in. "Don't tell Rory," she said, stepping quickly forward. "Promise you won't tell."

Emeline set the baby on the floor and slowly stood. "I have to, July – he's my husband. He's Vallie's father."

"He's not her father!" July cried. "He left me when I needed him and never came back."

"July –"

"No, Emeline. Preston's her daddy now, and there's nothing Rory can do about it."

Vallie's face collapsed at the ruckus. She let out a howl as raspy as an old hound's. July scooped her into her arms and walked over to the window. "I couldn't bear the thought of Rory knowing," she said, her body trembling. "I couldn't bear the feelings it would dredge up, the hurt it would cause." She turned toward Emeline. "If Rory finds out Vallie is his, he'll show up here tomorrow and demand to see her – and let me tell you, it will kill Preston. He loves Vallie, accepts her as his own, coddles her like no other." Her voice wound tighter as she walked a circle around the room. "You and Rory," she went on, "you'll have your own baby someday –"

"And what if we don't?"

"I don't know," July shrilled. "All I know is you can't tell him."

Emeline walked toward the door then and paused, her hand lingering on the knob. She turned toward July. "I knew Rory loved you when I married him, but I pretended I didn't. All this time I've been pretending. I thought I could make him love me, maybe forget about you."

"Oh, Emeline." Tears flooded July's eyes and spilled down her cheeks. "He *does* love you, I know he does, or he wouldn't have married you."

"Well, I guess we'll see then, won't we?"

Chapter Twenty-Seven

July imagined Rory arriving at her door, his fury bubbling over like lye in a cauldron. She'd not seen him since that day at her pa's, when he'd looked at her so cruelly and then ridden silently away. In her mind's eye she saw him that way now. After witnessing the sad, futile look on Emeline's face July knew her friend would shape her words honestly to Rory, no matter what it cost her. She'd tell him no, she hadn't seen Preston but she'd seen July, and July's baby too. He'd want to know all about it, and Emeline would work her mouth sweetly while forming those words, then look the other way and tell him the child was luscious as a strawberry, with eyes as big as buttons. He'd ask the baby's name, and she would quietly tell him Valentine. And that's when he would begin to put it together.

"Valentine? Why would July name her that?"

Emeline would look away, and then her tears would come.

He'd get it out of her, the truth, flare at her like he'd once flared at July. And when she told it all, he'd stare at her in astonishment, then fill with silent anger. He'd storm July's door, tears hot in his eyes, demanding to be let in.

And all she imagined came to pass.

Footsteps thundered on the porch, yet when he burst through the door, saw her standing pale and small against the wall, his anger quickly melted. He leaned against the door and sagged, as if the bones had left his body. "I should of seen you were carrying my child – a flush to your cheeks or some glimmer in your eye. Isn't that what they always say? 'I knew you when you was no more than a twinkle in your mama's eye'? Yet I didn't see it. It never crossed my mind, July." He exhaled, as if all this time he'd held the world's troubles.

"How could you know what I didn't yet know myself?" she said, her own breath coming in bits and pieces. It seemed she'd suffocate for wanting him, and now that she'd seen him – now that he was here at last – she couldn't imagine life without him. She reached slowly toward him, her fingers stirring the air. He pushed away from the door, his eyes red and watery, and went to her, drawing her in with the crook of one arm. She clung to him, cherishing the feel of him, the strength of his back and swell of his shoulders. She kissed him hard. He hung on as tight as she did, smothered her with kisses and lingered on her mouth.

"How have I lived without you?" she cried, her voice an anguished whisper.

He gripped her tight, and it was this embrace that told her he'd never let her go.

She lay her head against his shoulder, told how she'd ridden to his house well over a year ago to tell him of the baby. "But your mother didn't know where you were, or if you were coming back. And then you sent your ring and –"

"Had I known, I swear I'd never left you." He held July's face in his hands, told her he'd been a fool. He kissed her, and she took his hand, led him to her bedroom, pulled him onto the bed and lay next to him. Tugging his shirt from his pants, she fumbled at the buttons, then unable to move quickly enough, shoved his shirt up his chest, and tenderly kissed his belly. He pulled her up to him, gazed into her eyes as though it were the first he'd seen her. "I love you July," he said, drawing in his breath. And then he hesitated. She kissed him lightly, kept her eyes on his, began again to slowly work the buttons. He took her hands in his, stopping her, and she pulled back slightly, not understanding.

"The damage I've done," he said. "How can I right my wrongs? If I leave Emeline, that's one more person wrecked by my doings. How many people have to suffer because of me?"

July sat up then. "Emeline knows you don't love her. She told me so, herself."

"She's not you, July. She'll never be you. If I break off with her, she's liable to do something crazy. But you – you got a stubborn streak as thick as an old man's toenail, and whether I go or stay, you'll survive. More than anything, that's what I know about you. That's why I love you so."

July pushed off the bed and stood before him, her hair and dress a-tangle. "I won't survive – I barely made it the first time."

He too climbed from the bed, and stood in front of her. "I'm not yours," he told her gently, "and you're not mine – there's nothin we can do to change that."

"We can too change it. I'll never love Preston the way I love you, and you'll never love Emeline the way she wants you to. We can leave them both right now."

Rory shook his head. "I can't do that, July, and neither can you." July opened her mouth to protest, and Rory said, "I will love you until the day I day, and that's God's honest truth. And I'll love our baby too." He glanced toward a room at the other end of the house. "Will you show her to me now?"

"Rory –"

"Please, July."

Eyes welling, July tilted her head to one side, studying him. He would not change his mind, she saw that now. She took his hand then, and led him to Vallie's room. The child lay sleeping in her crib, her soft milky mouth working quietly as she dreamed. Rory watched her a long time, and when he turned toward July, his eyes too were damp. "Vallie will keep us forever tied. You see that, don't you? Through her, we'll have a love that lasts a lifetime, that only we can share."

"I won't give up on you. Not now, not ever, Rory."

He smiled his aching smile. "You don't got to give up, July. But you got to keep on livin."

*   *   *

As was his habit, Preston scooped up Vallie from the floor and smothered her with kisses the moment he walked through the door. He looked a sight, with his crumpled shirt and disheveled hair. He hadn't slept more than a few hours in the three days he'd been gone, and the bags beneath his eyes hung gray and puffy.

July didn't waste a minute, just told him how it was – how Emeline had come to see him, how she'd seen the little notch when Vallie pulled her hat off, and how Emeline had put it all together.

"Rory came, too," she said, holding nothing back. "He said he wouldn't interfere in my life if I promised to share Vallie." He hadn't couched it that way at all, of course, but by putting it so to Preston, July knew he would at least consider the arrangement. And she desperately wanted him to accept the plan, for it would keep her close to Rory.

"Share my child with Rory Morrow and the entire Houston clan?" Preston flared. "Is that what you're asking me to do?"

July nodded, asked what choice they had.

"And if we *share* our child," he spat disdainfully, "Rory will stay with Emeline and let it go at that? He won't press you to leave me and hand the baby over?"

"That's what he said," July told him, for it was closer to the truth than a lie.

"But what will people think? How am I to explain it – Valentine off to the Houston's – or God forbid, the Morrow's – while you and I sit here in Morning Tree?"

"What do you care what people think?"

"I have a business to maintain, a reputation –"

"You have more business than you can handle now," July put in. "As for your reputation, it's me they'll look down on. I'm the black sheep, not you. They'll think you're a saint for putting up with me."

"Or a cuckold, more likely."

In the end, he agreed to the arrangement because he had to. He and July shared Vallie with Emeline and Rory, turning a deaf ear to the murmuring from townsfolk. An unexpected complaint came from Abigail Kilker, the woman who had nursed July after Vallie's birth.

"Why Abigail," July said when she saw her. She grasped the woman's arm lightly, kept her voice low. "I haven't seen you in the longest while – I thought maybe you'd gone underground."

Abigail pursed her lips and poised her chin just so. "And why would you think that?"

July blinked. "I don't know. I guess I thought you wouldn't…well…leave the other women – that you'd go into hiding with them."

"If anyone were to go underground, July, I would think it would be you. I heard about your arrangement, the agreement you made with Rory Morrow to share Preston's child."

"And this affects you how?"

"I just find it peculiar is all."

"No more peculiar than sharing a husband, I would think."

That stopped Abigail short – and plenty others like her – but it didn't allay all the whispers. Preston agonized over each new rumor, and sulked every time Vallie left for the Houston's. July though, focused on Solomon's gleeful chuckle and immediate acceptance of the child. The man wanted a grandchild so desperately he would have embraced an elf hiding in the woods at Brundage if it meant a babe to bounce on his knee. His gratitude got July to thinking about her pa, wondering if he too longed to hold a child. And so she took Vallie to see him shortly after the baby's first birthday.

To be sure, Preston would have wrapped his arms around the opportunity to inform Isaac he'd known full well July was with child when he proposed – that he married her of his own volition – but his appointment book was full that day and he couldn't get away. That Preston hadn't said something to Isaac the day of their wedding was to his credit, for he had good manners, even if he longed for vindication.

Just as well he was too busy, July thought. If she had any hope of whittling away at her pa's armor she had to do her carving when Preston wasn't around. On the way out to her father's place, she wondered what it would look like once she got there. Without her mother's touch the yard and garden were sure to have gone to seed. Her worries were interrupted by the sight of two new homesteads along the way, one of which had sprung up on the left side of the road and sported a barbed-wire fence; the other, a small and shabby place, was situated not more than a quarter mile from the boundary of her father's ranch.

She could see him now, grousing and kicking at the ground, a sour look on his face. "Not so long ago you could shoot a gun and a neighbor wouldn't hear," he'd complain. "Now, they're looking right down at you."

Farmers, no doubt, eking out a living on their truck farms with water they'd stolen from the Weiser. July wondered too how far the newcomers would go. Would they hack down the trees all the way to Brundage, making a cemetery of the forest? Or clear the valley of its aspens and cottonwoods, creating a vast prairie of stumps? If each of these settlers erected fences, what would it do to her pa's ability to move his sheep? To make his own living? And not that Rory's pa had earned her sympathy – far from it – but what would become of Rory's family if Silas had to sell his cattle? July aimed to put these questions to Tom.

When she trotted up in Preston's buggy her mind was put to rest, for she saw Tom had taken good care of the place in the time she'd been gone. The newly cut alfalfa fields stood stubby as shorn rams, and the ditches ran cool and clear. She parked the buggy in her pa's barn, saw

Richard had harvested a fine crop of string beans from the garden and was now drying herbs he'd ordered as seeds from the catalogue. "Pun says they'll make tea as sweet as folks drink in the South," he said when she sat beside him on a log. He perched Vallie on his knee, and to his delight she giggled. She poked a chubby finger inside his mouth and he gummed it, greedily. She gurgled her baby song.

July glanced up at the house. Richard followed her gaze, saw through her hopefulness. "Pa ain't home," he told her. "He's hired two new herders – one to replace me, because he won't send me up again, and one to replace Pun."

"Pun?"

"He's going back to China, July. All the events here at home took the starch out of him, just like they did the rest of us. It set him thinking about his own family, how if he was ever going back, it might as well be now."

"I can't believe it."

"Me either – and truth told, I don't want to."

"Was he going to leave without saying goodbye?"

"You can ask him yourself, I guess. Him and Pa are due back in a hour or two."

"Pun gone," July repeated, shaking her head. She glanced toward the house a second time. "What'll Pa do without him?"

"He'll be okay. He let the place go after you left – tried to get Brother Kilker's second wife to come out and clean up some. She told him off and sent him on his way. When he got home he told us how she'd put him to shame and we all felt so bad that we set to cooking and cleaning like you wouldn't believe. Place looks pretty good now though, don't it?"

"Real good," July agreed.

It was quiet a while. Richard asked what brought her out this way.

"I came to see you," she said brightly, for it was true enough. "And I wanted you to meet Vallie."

Richard kissed the baby's head. "She's a jewel, July. You done real good." July smiled, told him it lifted her spirits to see him looking so well. The conversation was the slightest bit stiff, seeing as how they hadn't had a heart-to-heart for over a year now. He told her he was happier than he'd been in a long time. "I spend most my days indoors, doing things Ma once done – all except the laundry," he said. "I'm slow on that." His voice took on a wistful quality. "It riled Pa to see me building biscuits and rolling out pie dough, but with no one else around to do the cooking he learned to live with it. Now he says my poverty cake is near as good as Ma's – not that I need to hear it. I gave up needing anything from Pa a long time ago."

"I see that," she said. It passed through her head that Richard now occupied an unusual position in the Caldwell household, that of housekeeper and cook, and seamstress too. He'd stitched himself a pair of Chinese trousers, with a hem as tidy as anything Lilly ever composed. And somewhere he'd found himself a pair of open-heeled slippers, like Pun sometimes wore in the garden. The only thing he lacked was a pointed hat and pigtail, though since the raid at Brundage Pun had sported an American haircut.

Richard hadn't yet set Vallie down, nor asked anything about her. It was as though he'd known the child all his life, the way he jiggled her on his knee. It was as though he accepted her as easily as he accepted July. And when Tom came up, sweaty and dirt-covered and smelling of hay, he did too. "Well, hello there," he said, squatting in front of the baby. "This can't be Valentine, can it?" he asked, though he knew full well it was.

"She looks like Rory, don't she?" said Richard, beaming.

Tom snorted. "Rory ain't never looked so good – that baby's July, through and through."

"Speaking of Rory," said July, "I best bring you up to date on what's happened." She told of Emeline's visit and Rory's too – though she left out the parts that were private – and of Preston allowing Vallie to visit the Houston's. "They love her as much as we do – it's a wonder her little arms aren't three feet long with all the tugging they do on her."

"You suppose your pa knows Vallie is Rory's?" Tom asked.

"He knows – he whispered as much in my ear the day I got married."

"Bet anything he told Brother Kilker the one you popped out in seven months was a miracle."

"More like a freak of nature," Richard put in. "He already takes me for an odd duck – now he can tell the Elders about July sharing Vallie and how he's got two mallards in the family – me *and* July." He stood up and shuffled around in his quirky little shoes, Vallie on his hip. July watched him, told herself yes they were odd, but instead of a drake and a hen it seemed their father had himself two hens – three, if he counted Lilly, who was up to New York City, acting and singing songs.

"How is Pa?" July asked.

It was quiet a moment. Richard suggested they go inside, sit around the table with a cool drink before they went into all that. And so they filed in and gathered around the kitchen. Tom pulled up a chair and sat down too. "Times is hard, July," he told her, taking off his hat and resting it on his lap. "Not a whole lot has changed since you left. Man named Littlefield brought a band of sheep into Lumpkin Valley not long ago, but cattlemen run him off. Other sheepmen followed and their sheds was burned. Seems everyone's fightin everyone now, and the law still ain't doin nothin about it." He shook his head. "Countryside's growin too. You seen those two new homesteads outside your pa's place? They got no critters to speak of, but next you know it'll be fisticuffs over water. Isaac's got first rights, but who's going to set there noon and night, watch what them squatters are stealing?"

"Morning Tree's about to explode too," July told them. "Hardly seems possible that woman to Valentine killed herself over the lonelies – here it is, not twenty years past and now there's people everywhere. Preston thrives on it, though. 'Course, he likes to complain and tells me every chance he gets he can't keep up – that's why he didn't come along today – he's hiring an apprentice, a boy, practically – but he loves his doctoring. Says he wants to add on to the house, make a bigger office in the back." She caught the look between Richard and Tom, and when she called them on it Richard spoke for both of them.

"We knew you'd come home sooner or later to show off Vallie, but we'll admit we hoped it'd be Rory with you when you did."

"Rory's got Emeline to mind and I've got Preston," she told them. "Anyway, I can't be crying over spilt milk. I got to get on with my life, just like the two of you got on with yours."

The silence was sad and humble now, for it was plain she'd never get on – not really – without Rory Morrow. They were meant to be together, though neither Tom nor Richard pushed the matter. It was up to July to jostle it on her own.

Tom asked if it would be all right if he took Vallie down to the ditch, let her splash at the water's edge while he washed himself. July said Vallie would like that, showed him how to hold her by situating her on his hip and clutching her with his right arm, since his left now hung shorter at his side. It didn't come as natural to him as it had to Richard, but he soon got the hang of it.

"Watch her close, you hear?" she told him. "Hang onto her with your good arm while she's in the water." She watched them from the door as they strolled toward the creek, not doubting for a minute Tom would never take his eye from her. He held her tight in that one strong arm, and already she could see his attachment to her. Why, he'd never toted a lamb so lovingly, and she thought it sad he might never be a father.

"You got to get Tom to town once in a while," she chided Richard. "Otherwise he'll never meet a girl."

"He don't want no girl," Richard scoffed. "He'd sooner marry a shovel." He set a slice of apricot pie on the table, told July to taste it.

She slipped a little into her mouth. "How do you know he doesn't want a girl?"

"I asked him, and he said, 'I'd sooner marry a shovel.'"

"And you? When will you marry?"

"Oh, I won't marry, either. Tom and me, we'll probably live the rest of our lives here with Pa – the three of us ain't fit for marrying."

July speared a second bite of pie and then a third. When she finished, Richard cut her a chunk of bread and slathered it with butter. It went down smooth as settled pudding. She licked her fingers and watched him watching her, hardly able to believe it was her brother and not her mother standing before her. He looked so much like her, with his curly hair and dark eyes. Yet he was different too. His own person. It had taken a long time for the real Richard to emerge, but now that he had July could see his skin fit him well.

Strange as it seemed, their pa's arrival didn't spoil Richard's mood, either. That was different too. When Isaac walked through the door, rifle slung over his shoulder, Richard didn't sneak off to the barn to avoid him, but paid no notice at all.

Isaac stopped short at the sight of July. He blinked as if he couldn't quite place her.

"It's July, Pa," Richard told him.

"I know who it is." He clapped his mouth shut, turned to hang his gun on a rack on the wall. July's breath caught at how much he'd aged – as much or more than Lydia Morrow. His hair rested shaggy below his ears, more gray than brown now, and two new sets of wrinkles had set up stakes around his mouth. His shirt hung from his shoulders, and there was a slight stoop to his walk. He looked around the room. Not seeing a baby, he said, "Heard you had that young 'un – a girl. Where is she?"

"To the creek, with Tom," July said, quietly. It smarted that her pa hadn't reached out to her – he'd barely even looked at her, beyond seizing up those first few moments after he'd walked through the door. She glanced at Richard, caught the pity in his eyes. Yes, her brother knew what it was to seek their father's acceptance, yet Richard had somehow managed to let that all go. It was a true turn of tables that their pa now needed Richard more than Richard needed him.

Isaac took up a slice of bread. With his back toward July, he said, "Think I'll wander down and introduce myself." But he didn't invite her to come along, and when he'd gone out the door she stared after him a long while before wiping the crumbs from her mouth.

The day ended on a sad note, for not long afterwards Pun came in to say his goodbyes. He made a pot of tea, asked Richard if he'd join them. Richard said no, he'd leave them alone so they could chatter some in private. After he'd gone, Pun splashed a little of the brown, watery brew into two porcelain cups and handed one to July. "Always taste best in mudda's special cup," he said, slurping at the edges.

"Richard tells me you're leaving," she said when the Chinaman sat down.

"Time," he said. "If don't go now, nevah will." He'd always been a slight man, but now he looked downright tiny. He held his cup in his slender hands, crossed his narrow ankles. She wondered if he'd truly shrunk, or whether she'd simply grown up. She supposed it was the latter, for even the ranch seemed smaller now.

"I wish you'd stay, Pun. Pa needs you."

He sighed. "Heart hurt, miss family. China too."

July set her cup down, walked over and kneeled in front of him. Tears stung her eyes as she took his warm hands into her own and brought them to her cheek. "You've been like a pa to me, keeping me on the straight and narrow—"

"You fly crooked as drunk crow," he snorted, but his eyes glistened.

"You know what I mean."

He nodded, brought her hands to his chest and bowed.

"I love you, Pun."

"Ho, Pun love Jew-rye, too," he said, quickly looking away.

They stayed like that a long time, each understanding there was no need to say more. And while the great burly hills of Idle Valley glowed like marmalade in the setting sun, July and Pun sipped tea.

Chapter Twenty-Eight

The world was full of surprises, and nothing astonished July more than to see Silas Morrow reach out where her own pa would not. Rory's father stood on the porch, his hair combed slick and his shirt tucked proper, while Lydia stood alongside, hands in the pockets of her apron. Though it was now four years since she'd last seen Lydia, and more than five since she'd seen Silas, they stood sprite on that summer afternoon, that day in 1895, when Rory was twenty-one, July and Emeline nineteen, and little Valentine one month older than three.

At long last, Silas Morrow got out of the cattle business. "More money can be made by an acre sown than an acre grazed," he boasted, although he seemed to have forgotten it was Rory, all those years ago, who'd told him so in the first place. The notion that his land might well support a fruit orchard had taken a year to germinate, and another year to sprout, but once it had Silas sold his cattle to buy trees, conveniently forgetting he'd hated fruit growers only slightly less than sod busters. Rory discovered all this when he rode into Badger one day, not long after learning of Vallie's existence, to tell his mother she not only had a daughter, Emeline, but a grand-daughter too. He didn't care whether his pa knew it or not. While Rory sat at the kitchen table, talking of the bond he and July and Emeline had formed – how they'd become something of a family of their own – his father walked in from outside, as though he'd accidentally come upon them, despite having hidden in the dark all along. "You mean to tell me the three a you share that child, like she was a toy?"

"At least we ain't wreckin her life just so we can feel good about our own," Rory told him.

"What's that supposed to mean?"

"It means there's nothin good come out of our situation *except* Valentine," Rory said. "July up and married Preston 'cause she had to, and I married Emeline to get even."

"That's just the sort of thing people do," Lydia put in. "Hurt one another 'cause they're hurting so themselves." When she looked across at Silas, he shifted some. No one expected he'd take responsibility for all but thrashing Rory himself that day so long ago, and he did not. But the decision had cost him. Lydia took off for two months after Rory's beating, and when she returned she denied Silas access to his own bed, made him sleep on the floor. Didn't speak to him or cook for him, either, or commit to a single wifely duty. Silas had plenty of time to think on the error of his ways, and when Rory finally appeared to tell Lydia of Emeline and his baby girl, Silas was humbled some. But if he couldn't yet make amends he at least listened when Rory brought up the topic of selling out and starting up an orchard.

It wasn't long after Silas sold his cattle that Rory brought Emeline, Vallie, and July around to greet his parents. Lydia had been pestering him to fetch them out, and while his pa wouldn't admit it, he stood eager too. His face was drenched in anticipation and his armpits in sweat, when Rory and his girls came wobbling up in the wagon. They'd made it just in time too, for they'd hit a sizeable rut on the way in and it had jarred a wheel loose. Rory told Emeline he'd fix it while his pa was busy haranguing him, but to his surprise, the haranguing hadn't come.

Lydia captured little Vallie in one arm and hugged each of the women with the other. Silas shook Emeline's hand in the clumsy manner of an old cowboy, said he was glad to meet her at last. He turned toward July, his upper body stiff. His stance was cool but his face was warm, and in that moment July understood he'd never meant to harm her.

Lydia took the women inside while Rory and his pa unloaded the bags from the back of the wagon. They dropped them in Rory's old bedroom, and then the men joined the women in the kitchen. Silas walked up to Lydia, the heels of his boots clicking against the floor, and told her it was his turn to hold Vallie. When he held his hands out to the child, she froze. With a nod from July, she leaned forward and let Silas scoop her up. Vallie didn't speak, but drew her fingers to her mouth and kept one eye firmly on her mother.

July walked over and rubbed Vallie's back. "This is your grandpa," she told her, her voice reassuring. "You can call him Papa Morrow."

"I never had a child call me Papa before," Silas blurted, his delight as surprising as the apples of his smile.

July glanced at Rory, expecting to see hurt there, for surely he'd never received anything so tender from his father. Emeline must have sensed it too, for she grasped Rory's hand and squeezed it. He brought her fingers to his mouth and kissed them. July knew the gesture wasn't calculated to hurt her, but even so it tore her heart in two. She excused herself, saying she needed to wash up before supper, then strode toward a basin on the counter.

After the meal, which Lydia served just before sundown – owing to her company's late arrival – July put Vallie to bed in an alcove made up to serve as a third bedroom. The little room held two small beds and a nightstand, which was situated under a window facing the west. A lamp burned softly in one corner. When July was sure Vallie was asleep, she turned the light down low and kissed her daughter's cheek.

Emeline and Rory had gone to bed too but July didn't care to lie in the dark, listening to the sounds of her old love settling in with his wife. Emeline was as kind as she'd ever been to July, and a loving caretaker to Vallie. But it pained July to see her old schoolmate brush her lips against Rory's forehead, or her breast against his chest as she leaned in to hug him. July got up and walked out to the porch to sit a while. A warm breeze brushed the hair from her face and cooled her prickly skin.

Despite the things she'd told Richard and Tom after Vallie's birth, July still ached for Rory, and she knew he knew it too.

One day, after she'd dropped Vallie off at the Houston's, she walked into his shop and asked if he'd consider taking a portrait of Preston. She went to great lengths to describe exactly what she wanted and how Rory might go about getting Preston to pose, but Rory saw through her. He told her outright Preston would never allow it. "I know," she admitted, tears filling her eyes. "I don't care about a portrait. I came to see you." The acute sting of his silence prompted a quick apology. "I'm sorry," she blurted. "I shouldn't have come." But as she turned to leave, he told her to wait.

"I got something to show you." From the pocket of a jacket hanging on a coat tree he pulled a small leather pouch, and from that, a photograph. "Look at this." She walked over, took the picture from his hand; it was the one he'd taken of her at Valentine all those years ago. He'd never shown it to her, he said, because he'd forgotten to bring it that day he met her at school, in Morning Tree. "But I kept it all this time, and every day I wear it right here in my wallet, next to my heart." He took her hand and placed it on his chest. "I may never have you as my wife, July, but no matter what, I'll never stop loving you."

So on days like this, when Emeline clasped Rory's hand and he kissed her in return, July reminded herself it was she he truly loved.

"Heavens, it's a beautiful evening," Lydia clucked as she walked onto the porch. She carried a tray and set it on a table next to a rocker. Handing July a cup of tea, she sat in the chair across from her. Neither said anything for a long while, but sat listening to crickets singing their evening songs.

Lydia spoke first, saying it was a glorious thing when someone turned his life around. She was talking about Silas, she said, how pleased he was to have them all there.

"My pa's still sitting on his ranch, stubborn as always," July responded. "Any more, he's only got my brother and Tom to keep him company."

"Doesn't he want to know his grandchild?"

"He met her once, but never called on us to come out again. Never asked after her, either, that I know of."

Lydia sipped her tea. After a while she came out with what she was most curious about. "How does your man take all this?" she wanted to know. Then, so as not to confuse the issue, for even she could see July still loved Rory, Lydia clarified by adding, "Preston, I mean."

"He doesn't like it," July said, "but he knows I'll leave if he fights me over Vallie. For the most part, he lets me come and go as I please, so long as Rory doesn't come near the house or interfere with me and the baby."

Lydia nodded. "Still, you've got to admit it's strange."

"As long as Vallie is loved, I don't see it matters what people think about it."

"I admire you for that. Admire you too, for stepping aside for Emeline's sake. I'm sure it wasn't an easy thing to do."

"Don't admire me, Lydia," July said, her tone hotter than she'd intended. "That's Rory's doing, not mine. Were up to me, I'd have left Preston a long time ago."

Lydia's rocking slowed, and then came to a stop. She held her cup in her lap. "Don't let that angry heart eat at you, July. A bitter heart is what ate Silas, and what eats your father, still."

July remembered Pun had said the same thing about Lilly once, and it hurt to hear the same criticism made of her. Without a word she set down her cup, walked into the house, and sat at the edge of the bed. Undressing, she stepped from her petticoat and drawers, then donned a nightgown and crawled into bed. With a cool pillow beneath her head, she thought about what Lydia had said, believing the woman had it wrong. July wasn't bitter but sick with longing – longing she'd held her in heart since that day at Valentine when she and Rory had first kissed. If her true feelings were coming across as bitterness she'd work to change them, for she never wanted resentment to color Vallie's future. Never wanted her daughter to have to choose between the people she loved, to have to pick one over the other.

The clock in the parlor chimed twice before July finally closed her eyes. No sooner had she drifted off than she awoke to the call of a night bird. She lay still as a corpse, ears straining, just as she had that night at her pa's when she'd heard the hooting of a great horned owl. And like that night she got up to look for it, compelled to respond to its call. Parting the curtain and peeking out the window, she spied the figure on the roof of the barn. The moon shone on its face, illuminating its half-dollar eyes and the iridescent feathers of its neck. It rotated its head slowly to one side in search of a mouse or a vole, and finding none twisted toward July. In a violent display it flapped its wings and jumped into the air. Up it went, its wings beating furiously, its body hovering, and then down it came, crashing to the roof. It repeated its jerky dance time and again, as if a cruel master had tethered its legs to a rope. Then just like that, it bounded into the air one last time before dropping low and disappearing.

Since the death of Raymond and her mother, July had learned owls weren't bearers of good tidings but bad news, and so she crawled back into bed and shut her eyes, willing the scene from her mind.

When she awoke in the morning – saw Emeline and Rory sitting side by side at the kitchen table, little Vallie perched on Rory's knee – July understood the significance of the owl's appearance: *she* was the cruel master, the old lover jerking Rory's tether, forbidding him to fly. And as long as she used Vallie as an excuse to stay close to him, he would never be free to love Emeline. The knowledge shamed her, and she made a promise to herself to make things right again.

After breakfast, as she and Emeline walked among the apple trees behind the house, July told her friend she knew she'd hung on too tight, and it was time to let Rory go. "I hope you don't think I'm hateful for putting it so bluntly, since you're the one that's married to him, but I see now he'll never be happy until I let him go." The relief on Emeline's face tormented July, for it only confirmed how much harm she'd done them.

"I won't be stopping by your house, or the shop, either," she went on, "and I won't join the three of you here at the ranch. You and Rory can see Valentine whenever you like, but you'll have to come get her – you, Emeline, not Rory – and drop her off too. Don't send Rory, ever, for I'll tell you now my heart can't take it."

Emeline tenderly embraced July. "I've waited so long to hear you say that."

July let herself be held. "I know there's no point in my asking you not to tell him – but please, Emeline, wait until we're back to Morning Tree. I'm not so strong I won't cry once Rory knows, and I don't want Vallie to see it."

Emeline rocked July in her arms. "I love you, July," she whispered. "Truly, I do."

They stood a long time on a path dappled by the shade. Some of the trees – not in the ground two years yet – were already as tall as Silas. Earlier that year little green baubles the size of marbles had bobbed from their branches, and as the women walked by, arm in arm, one of the lower lying limbs snagged the pocket of Emeline's skirt. She paused to dislodge it, and when she'd got herself free, they strolled around the corner toward the front of the house. They stopped short at the sight of Lydia bursting through the door, Silas at her heels. The twosome careened across the yard toward the pond, a low, agonizing cry escaping Lydia's lips. July gripped Emeline's arm and together they stood, paralyzed, while their minds put together Lydia's awful keening.

July teetered as the understanding set in. She took two small steps forward, her eyes fixed on the figures hurtling into the distance. When they crashed through the cattails at the edge of the pond, Emeline too must have understood, but it was July who jerked free, and took off at a run.

Chapter Twenty-Nine

W e'll be heading out soon," Rory told his father after the women had left for their walk, "soon as I get that wheel fixed." Silas said he'd help, and with Vallie propped high in one arm, he followed Rory out to the shed. Vallie rested her own arm atop Silas's shoulder, and absentmindedly fingered the hairs at the back of his neck. He liked the feel of it, the tickle of her small hand against his skin, and was reluctant to put her down. He gave her a peck on the cheek, told her he had to help Rory fix his wagon, then set her on a toolbox. Looking around for something to occupy the child, he whistled for Dunkel to come sit beside her. The little dog, grown gimpy over the years, tottered around the corner and jumped, with some difficulty, onto the box. He nuzzled Vallie's ear with his wet, gray snout. She giggled, gently clutched the dog's nose with both hands and kissed it.

"Papa," she said, looking over at Silas with her eyes just like her father's. "I wish I could take Dunkel home with me." She traced a pudgy finger over Dunkel's grizzled eyebrow, then drew a circle atop his head. Dunkel's eyes grew droopy as he leaned against Vallie, savoring the attention.

"I wish you could too," said Silas. "But Dunkel's a country dog and if he lived in town he wouldn't have any ducks to chase out of the pond."

"We don't got a pond," she said wistfully.

"Don't got no ducks, either," Rory put in. He gave her a smile as he wrenched the wheel from the wagon, hoisted it across the expanse of two sawhorses. He whacked out its spoke with a hammer. "Tell you what, though. I seen a mouse in the corner over there, and if you can catch him, you can put him in a box and tote him home."

Vallie hopped from her seat and scurried to the other side of the shed, bending low to search for the little gray rodent. Dunkel trotted up alongside her. She squatted on her haunches and pointed at the corner. "Git em, Dunkel!" she coaxed in her small, earnest voice. "Git him so I can tote him home!"

Dunkel buried his nose in a cluster of straw, his tail quivering with excitement. While Vallie and the dog hunted for their mouse, Silas pounded the spoke from a wheel he'd junked some two years ago. Rory readied his own wheel to accept the old spoke, said he needed some grease to help slide it in. Silas reached for his tar pot but found it empty. "Think I got me another bucket in the barn," he said. "If not there, then to the house, on the back porch. I'll go up and get it."

Hunched over his wheel, Rory looked up to see his father walk through the door. The man's silhouette startled him, for he hadn't realized until that moment how much Silas had begun to wear out. Though not yet fifty, his shoulders had taken on the hunch of an older man, and his fingers curled with arthritis. Rory stood up and stared after him, compassion flaring in his heart where before not even a flame of kindness had flickered.

It seemed so clear to him now. The trouble between them had come not from their heads but their hearts – his father's love of cattle and the land, his wanting so desperately for his son to be part of it. July's troubles with her own father had come the same way: Isaac wanting her to marry a Mormon, her wanting to marry a boy with nothing more to offer than a stone house and a camera. It didn't matter how much thinking they did – what was right, what was wrong, and what they'd do to fix it. In the end, it was their hearts that mattered.

Rory set his hammer down and gazed toward the house. He'd leave Emeline, he knew that now. He'd not spent one minute loving her the way he ought to, and she deserved better. She'd argue she couldn't live without him, but there she'd be thinking with her head. She didn't love him the way she should, either, not really. She loved the *idea* of him: a husband, a house, a baby. She fussed over Valentine to be sure, but behind those tender touches was the longing for her own child, a child she'd made with the man she loved. It really didn't have to be him at all.

He turned to gaze at Vallie, but she had disappeared from the corner where she'd been playing with Dunkel, seeking her little mouse. He turned a full circle as he searched the shop, calling her name twice, then again when she didn't answer. Fear vibrated down his spine and at the back of his throat, as he strode toward the door. Looking hard across the landscape, he spotted her. She stood at the end of the dock, having made her way past the hole in the middle, and with the awkward clumsiness of a three-year-old, hurled stones into the water.

"Vallie!" he flared, his fear mixed with anger. "Get off that dock right now!" He forgot completely the curiosity he himself had felt as a child, the pull of the pond and the creatures in it, the desire to know what dwelled beneath its murky water. He was thinking as his own father had, imagining not his whipping but Vallie's, if only for the lesson she'd learn. But the sound of his voice so rattled the child that she looked up with a startled jerk, lost her footing and toppled onto her bottom, her feet in the air, before spilling sideways into the water.

Rory shot from the doorway like a bull from a chute. He charged the pond, willing Vallie to stay afloat even as he pictured her dipping below the surface. He hit the dock full force, halting hard at its edge, the memory of his own near-drowning strangling his heart and brain. He searched the water for some sign of her, some apparition of a child drifting on her stomach, arms splayed like an injured bird.

"Christ in heaven," he cried, "where are you?"

Two bubbles popped at the surface. He hesitated only one moment more, then gulped the air and flung himself into the pond. Holding his breath in the pockets of his cheeks, he searched with wide eyes for the swirl of her dress. The sun gleamed in sharp, silver stripes, illuminating the stirring grass and decaying leaves, the teeming throng of insects. Seeing nothing, he spun, and then there she was, a ghostly shadow ten feet from the dock, her body slumped in a V. He slogged toward her, the soles of his shoes skidding against the mud-slicked bottom, his lungs screaming for air. White stars roiled behind his eyes, and he leaned in, snatched her collar, then pushed hard from the bottom. Hurtling wildly upward, he burst through the surface, gasped, and clawed at a knot on the dock's slick piling, gripping it will all he had.

He held Vallie in one arm, shook her hard to get her breathing. She threw her head back, and sputtered. In that moment, he rested his mouth against her shoulder and closed his eyes, his relief so profound he began to cry, even as his legs burned and his body shook and his face stung with tears. His grip on the little knot began to slip then, and he dug his fingers in, clinging to the slimy knob, repositioning himself. He stretched one leg carefully to test the bottom, which he couldn't feel at all. And then Vallie, too, began to slip, and he threw his own head back and cried for help, but the air stood still and silent. He leaned back somewhat and looked up, straining to gauge the distance between himself and the ledge of the dock, a distance of four feet or so. But it might well have been four hundred feet, for releasing the knot to grab the edge meant sliding down with Vallie. He took a second look, thinking maybe he could do it.

He laid his face in the crook of his arm, gathering himself. Clutching Vallie, he grunted softly, inhaled, let go of the knot. Slipping under, he closed his eyes, willing himself not to panic. With his heart pounding in his ears, he counted to three, hit bottom. He bent his knees slightly for extra leverage, pushed hard, then sailed upward and exploded from the water. In one motion, he grabbed the dock's edge with his free hand, and with the other, thrust Vallie onto its surface. The action drove him outward somewhat, but he held on, then slowly drifted back. Exhausted but exhilarated, he propped one arm atop the dock, coaxed Vallie with ragged breaths toward its opposite end, past the jagged hole in the middle, toward dry and sturdy ground. Seeing she'd made it, he leaned his forehead against the dock's spongy edge, taking a moment to catch his breath, to let it sink in it was nothing now to safely pull himself out. But as he straightened his arms and heaved himself upward, the rotten wood gave way to the weight of his body, and he fell deeply into the water. He was not prepared, had taken no breaths, and when he hit bottom he began to flail, kicking desperately. His pant leg caught on a bent nail, a rusty thing sticking out from the piling. The harder he fought, the harder it held. Seized by panic he reflexively gulped for air. His lungs filled with water and his body began to spasm. A searing suffocating pain slowly gave way to a strange tranquility. Then he noticed a light in the distance moving toward him. He slowly reached for it, followed it with half-open eyes as it shifted and slid, then drifted toward the surface. Looking up, he saw a photograph – the sun and the sky and a thousand bright stars – and wondered where his camera was, and if July might bring it to him.

*   *   *

The house sat quiet for ninety seconds, and then Lydia spotted Vallie, drenched and crying, not fifteen feet from the pond. Instantly, she put together the meaning of the soaking child and absent father, and burst through the door, screaming. Silas followed, hard on her heels. July ran up from the orchard, Emeline behind her.

Lydia scooped up Vallie while Silas ran down the dock, nimbly picking his way along the soft, rotten wood, arms out for balance. He dove, fully clothed, into the water. July all but slammed into Lydia, clutching Vallie and hugging her tight, then ran toward the pond. She too dove in while Emeline stood, a stiff and pale observer.

It took six full minutes to find him. Silas rose and plunged so many times that July could no longer stand it. She began to sob as she treaded water in the middle of the pond, knowing Rory was gone. When Silas at last spotted him under the dock, he scooped his boy into his arms and lugged him to the shore. Lydia reached out for Rory and dragged him to her, falling backward, his head settling in her lap. She held him then, cried into his wet hair and plied him with desperate kisses.

July staggered forward. Fell on Rory and Lydia, and wrapped her arms around them.

Emeline watched from where she stood. Stepping back, she told herself Rory could just as easily be asleep, really, he lay so calm and quiet. She longed to wipe the mud from his face, and so turned and walked toward the house, to find his handkerchief.

Chapter Thirty

Preston took to caring for Emeline those first few months after Rory died. When Solomon couldn't persuade her to rise from bed almost three weeks after the accident, he paid a call to Preston, pleading for his help. Preston agreed to do what he could, despite his own despair, for July had already begun to pull away from him.

Though he carried his black bag over to the Houston's, he chose to console Emeline with conversation as opposed to medication. Unlike July, she was a listener. As he sat at Emeline's side, he spoke timidly at first of his own anguish, and then with greater abandon as she slowly began to respond. It was on his fifth visit that she rolled to her side, hands clasped beneath her cheek, and emerged from her anguished silence.

"I longed to make Rory mine," she confessed, "though it was as futile as asking the sun to shine at midnight."

"So it was with me," Preston confided. "July's kept me at arm's length since the day I first met her."

Likely it was this shared torment that brought them together.

Preston would never have imagined his news would cause July additional heartache and was perplexed to see her sag at the announcement he'd fallen in love with Emeline. "I thought you'd be happy to be rid of me," he told her, though nothing in his face said it was anything he'd hoped for.

"I'm sorry I haven't been a better wife to you, Preston, for you've been so good to me." When he started to object, she added, "You didn't have to marry me, but you did. And you treated Vallie like she was your own. I truly love you for that." She told him too she wished him nothing but happiness, and hoped his life with Emeline would be both blessed and beautiful.

"In all the years I've known you, July, you've chosen an unpredictable path. Is it possible you'll share Vallie with me now, as you once shared her with Rory?"

"You're her daddy, aren't you?"

His eyes grew damp. He told her he'd support her and the baby, always. But she wouldn't hear it. "No Preston. It's up to me to make my own life now."

She took up residence in Rory's old shop and taught herself photography. She hadn't his eye for detail, despite those things he'd told her, but given all she'd lost, there was an edge to her photos that his did not possess. Some said she would go far in her endeavor; others scoffed because she tried. Men sitting around the pot-bellied stove in the hardware store dissected her actions at every turn. "It don't seem right for a woman to take over a man's business," one man groused. "If she's got a yen to set up shop, why don't she be a dressmaker?"

"Or a madam at the hotel?" suggested another. He arched an eyebrow and jostled his neighbor, and they all shared a laugh.

One afternoon, when the light in the shop was a mix of rose and aquamarine, the bell above the door tinkled. Emeline walked in. The glow in the room lent an almost angelic aura to her complexion, and it seemed she'd wrapped herself in a shawl of true contentment. She wore a wide-brimmed hat and a checkered skirt. July saw at once that Emeline was with child, for the curve of her belly swelled like a melon. Yet to July's surprise, Emeline didn't mention it. "I've brought you this," was all she said, handing July a photograph. The picture was a crisscross of creases, its edges crinkled and brown. While it had faded over the years, July at once recognized it as the photo Rory had taken of her at Valentine; the one he'd shown her in his shop that day. "I found it in his jacket," Emeline said. "He would have wanted you to have it."

July held the photo in both hands and looked at it a long while, recollecting how Rory had coerced a smile from her that day. Turning it over, she saw he'd written *Portrait of Julia* on the back. Nothing else. "I'll treasure it always, Emeline. Thank you."

Emeline stood straight, her eyes fixed on July. She swallowed before she spoke. "I'm finally going to get my baby," she said, and then she smiled. "I don't know why it took so long."

July walked around the counter and embraced Emeline, told her she'd make a fine mother. "You were always so good to Vallie. I believe she loves you as much as she loves me."

Emeline held July a long time. "Preston sends his love," she whispered, and then she pulled away and walked quietly out the door.

July stared at the empty space before her. She looked at the photograph, then all around the shop, and then back at the picture. Something in the wrinkled little square spoke to her, told her to take up where Rory left off. Not in the shop, where she felt no true kinship to him, but on horseback, traveling the country and chronicling the history of Idaho. It's what he'd want for her; for himself too, had he lived.

She plucked a key from the pocket of her apron, walked outside the door and locked it. She headed for Mrs. Abrams' dress shop, told the woman she was taking a trip and needed a skirt split up the middle and stitched like men's trousers.

"A divided skirt?" scoffed the woman. "Why, they'll arrest you before you get to Badger!"

"I won't have a skirt catching on my pommel and dragging me down – besides, I don't aim to stay in one place long enough for anyone to notice."

July got her divided skirt, and a horse and mule too. For Vallie she purchased a pair of overalls, like she had worn as a girl. Tucking the child inside, she said, "You look just like me when I was your age." Vallie responded with a peek into her breast pocket. "A mouse would fit in here just right, Mama, except I haven't got one."

"Maybe we can do something about that. What do you say? Should we try?"

Vallie's face lit up, and then just as quickly folded. "We don't got Dunkel to help us."

July scooped her daughter into her arms. "I happen to know where there are some mice easy as pie to catch – up to Papa Caldwell's. Should we pay him a visit and see if he'll help us find one?"

It was the first thing Vallie blurted to Preston when she saw him. "Mama says we can catch a mouse up to Papa Caldwell's – I'm gonna stick it in my pocket."

Though July might have chosen another way to let Preston know they were leaving, she sat him down and told him again it was time she made her own way in the world. "There's too much here to remind me of Rory," she said, "and if I go, we'll both get the chance to start afresh. Emeline needs it as much as I do."

Preston sat quietly as he took in the news. In the old days he would have flared fierce as dry tinder, told July it was inappropriate and dangerous for a woman to travel with a child. But the one thing he'd learned about July was she could take care of herself. Take care of their daughter too.

He called Vallie over, and she climbed into his lap. When he told her he loved her and would miss her very much, she held his face in her hands. "Don't be sad, Papa. Mama says you can come see us anytime you want."

He hugged her hard, then stood and embraced July. "Write when you're settled, let me know where you've landed."

"I'll do better than that," she promised. "I'll send a photograph."

Six days later, she loaded up the animals with Rory's camera, tripod, and all the supplies they needed to take them to the hills. She hoisted Vallie onto the horse, climbed on behind her. "I'll introduce you to Papa Caldwell's new herders," July told her, "take their pictures if they let me, standing alongside their sea of sheep. After that, we'll head north to the mountains, sniff those ponderosas, see if they really do smell of vanilla, like Uncle Richard said. Before that, we'll be sure to catch your mouse."

*   *   *

"I always took you for peculiar," Isaac said when she told him of her plan. "You and Richard, both."

She'd sent Vallie out to the barn, so father and daughter could speak openly. "Is that all you can say, after all I've been through?"

Isaac thought on it a while, told her to wait while he brought her something he'd been saving. He got up and shuffled into the dark. When he came back, he was holding her bowler. He handed her the hat, said he'd found it under Raymond's bed. Said too he reckoned she ought to keep it somewhere safe, lest she lose it again.

She closed her eyes, inhaled the scent of it. It smelled of her mother, and of Richard and Raymond too. She glided her fingertips over its smooth edges, slid it onto her head. "How does it look?" she said.

He eyed her differently than he had before, and July let herself believe he approved. "You'll be back one day," he told her, "and when you come, we'll have ourselves a picnic like we had that day on the Weiser. Remember?"

She smiled. "I caught more fish than you did."

A moment passed before he said he'd written Lilly to tell her they had a baby in the family. "She sent a letter back, said she hoped you'd bring Vallie to New York City one day, for she got herself a job play-actin, just like she said she would. She wanted you to see her in her *element* she called it." He screwed up his face at some far-flung memory. "You reckon that girl will change?"

Julie shook her head. "I don't suppose so, no."

"Best get on," Isaac told her, staring at his shoe tops. "You got a ways to go, yet."

July stood and kissed his forehead. "I love you, Pa."

Isaac nodded, his face and ears red. He walked her outside just as Vallie came running from the barn with a mouse in a small wooden box. "Richard helped me catch it!" she squealed. "Can I put it in my pocket?"

"Not till we get to where we're going," July told her. "Keep it in the box for now." She walked over to Richard, gave him a hug. "I'll miss you," she said. "Give Tom my love when he gets back, will you?"

Richard sighed in that hard way he had, said he wished she wasn't going.

Isaac propped Vallie on Birdy's back, took hold of the child's hand. "Be careful, you hear? There's wolves and cougars out there, and any one of em will snatch your ankle and knock you down."

"Don't be scaring her, Pa," July chided.

"I ain't scarin her, July." He told her to give him the hat, and when she handed it over, he propped it on Vallie's head. "There's magic in that bowler," he claimed, "and as long as you wear it, nothin bad will happen."

July hopped onto the horse, and just like that they were off. She followed the trail to Valentine where a solitary cloud, anchored just above the horizon, built itself up and then leisurely split in two. The air, dry as summer kindling, was awash with the buzz of bees.

She came upon the old house she knew so well, with its pink stone windows, its cobwebs in the corners. She paused, thinking for a moment she saw a man on the rooftop, and then the apparition came fully into view, and she saw it was Rory. He reached up and waved.

"I miss you, Rory Morrow," July whispered, waving back. When the shadowy figure disappeared, she nudged Birdy forward. Pausing at the bridge, the horse dipped her head and nickered. The structure had been repaired some six months now, and looked as good as new. July gazed at it a moment, thinking back on the day when one of its cables broke and sent her whole world reeling. So much had happened since then, some good, some bad. Yet she had come to understand it didn't do to dwell on the past, and so she urged Birdy onward, never once holding her breath or stopping to look back. And when she got to the opposite side, she veered left, as she was meant to do, all those years ago.

The End

About the author

Renée Thompson was born in Washington and raised in Japan, Georgia, Kansas and California. She has worked as a newspaper columnist and reporter, an executive assistant, and as a volunteer at various national wildlife refuges. An avid birdwatcher and conservationist, Renée lives in northern California with her husband Steve. Her short stories have appeared in *Narrative Magazine* and *Chiron Review*, and she has placed in writing competitions sponsored by *Glimmer Train* and *Writer's Digest*. THE BRIDGE AT VALENTINE is her first novel.

Acknowledgments

There are many people who helped bring this novel to life, and to whom I'm deeply indebted. My readers and loyal friends: Linda Bishop, Lynn Straus and Shannon Delaney. My muse and inspiration: Larry McMurtry (whose steadfast encouragement and reliable correspondence truly kept me going). My cheerful and ever-optimistic editor and publisher: Jim Brumfield. The cattle rancher most willing to chat on the phone at five-thirty in the morning: Mike Byrne. Experts who provided advice, direction, and occasional office space: Margaret Soulen-Hinson, Phil and Erlene Soulen, Terry Mendenhall, Leon Sparrow, Dr. Larry Coates (Professor of History at Brigham Young University, Rexburg, ID), Stan Boyd (Executive Director, Idaho Wool Growers Association, Boise, ID), Lesa Carlton (Executive Director, California Wool Growers Association, Sacramento, CA). Most enlightening historical texts: Edward N. Wentworth's *America's Sheep Trails*, and Clel Georgetta's *Golden Fleece in Nevada*. My erstwhile and talented book-cover designer: Alex Rose. My beautiful and consistently forthright daughters: Jena Meredith and Maya Kepner. My patient and forgiving parents and in-laws: Iris and Woody Hunton, Norm and Lil Moffett, and Leal and Paul Thompson. And finally my husband: Steve Thompson, who never wavered but steadfastly believed, and who always shared his best outdoor secrets.

Misfits Country

by

Arthur Winfield Knight

In the summer of 1960 a legendary director took a cast of movie icons into the blistering Nevada desert to make a movie from a screenplay by a famed playwright. For some this would be a last chance at creating art. The Misfits was one of the most anticipated films of the 20th century, but difficult shooting locations, an unstable leading lady, an aging leading man, a crumbling marriage, and an undisciplined director all conspired to make behind-the-scene events as dramatic as the movie itself.

MISFITS COUNTRY explores the often turbulent relationships between the players and the fine line that often exists between art and life. Marilyn Monroe is the central character and is portrayed in a more complex manner than in the numerous biographies of her life. As Norman Mailer observed, a novelist tells a lie to tell the truth, whereas a journalist tells the truth to tell a lie. Though a work of fiction, this may be the most honest depiction of Marilyn ever produced.

Visit www.trespicospress.com for more information.

Copies of this book may be ordered online at

www.trespicospress.com

Postal orders: Tres Picos Press

PO Box 932

Freedom, CA 95019

Send payment of $14.95 for each copy of *Misfits Country, A Tourist in the Yucatan, Across the High Lonesome* and/or *The Bridge at Valentine* ordered. Please add 8% sales tax for books shipped within California. Shipping is free!

The Bridge at Valentine   ____ (number of copies)

Misfits Country   ____ (number of copies)

Across the High Lonesome   ____ (number of copies)

A Tourist in the Yucatan   ____ (number of copies)

Name: _____

Address: _____

City: _____ State: ____ Zip: _____

Telephone: ( ) _____

Email address: _____